RAVEN

Book 5 in the Georgina Garrett Series

Sam Michaels

An Aries Book

First published in the UK in 2021 by Head of Zeus Ltd
This paperback edition first published in the UK in 2022 by Head of Zeus Ltd,
part of Bloomsbury Publishing Plc

A CIP catalogue record for this book is available from
the British Library.

ISBN (PB): 9781800246300
ISBN (E): 9781789542219

Cover design © Jessie Price

Typeset by Siliconchips Services Ltd UK

Printed and bound in Great Britain by
CPI Group (UK) Ltd, Croydon CR0 4YY

MIX
Paper from
responsible sources
FSC® C171272

Head of Zeus
5–8 Hardwick Street
London EC1R 4RG

www.headofzeus.com

To my very funny and very wise sister-in-law, Stephanie Reynolds, who also makes the best Sunday roast dinner! Hope to see you soon for your home-made stuffing xxx

June 1949. Kent.

Georgina Garrett pushed herself up in her large bed, turned and punched her feather pillow before huffing and picking up the alarm clock from the bedside table. She checked the time. Half past three in the morning. She never slept soundly in her country house in Kent when her husband, David Maynard, was away working in London. Thank goodness he didn't go as often these days. Just twice a week to check on the business and give out his orders.

She lay back down. The gentle ticking of the clock beside her seemed to become louder and louder, driving her mad. Impatiently, she reached out for it and stuffed the clock under the pillow on David's side of the bed. At last, peace and quiet. But it was *too* quiet. Georgina had lived in the countryside for over three years but she still hadn't become accustomed to the silence, a far cry from the sounds that filled the night air in London.

Count sheep, she thought. *One, two, three, four...* Her ears pricked when she heard a noise from downstairs. Footsteps and urgent whispers. *What the hell?* She quietly threw the blankets back and swung her legs over the edge of the bed.

Georgina tiptoed across the bedroom and opened the door just a crack. She peered through and gasped when she saw the flash of a torch light from the bottom of the stairs. Someone was in the house! Her pulse quickened as she dashed back across the room and pulled open her bedside drawer. There, on top of a box of diamond necklaces, her gun sat. It hadn't been used in years. She checked the barrel, pleased to find that it was fully loaded. Of course it would be: David would have made sure of that. But David had also left one of his blokes downstairs to protect her and the children. So what had happened to Chunks? Was her bodyguard dead?

With the gun in hand, Georgina crept back across the room and peeped through the door again. Whoever was in her house was still downstairs. She ran to Alfie's bedroom first, relieved to find her son sound asleep. She shook him gently to wake him. 'Shush,' she warned. 'Don't say a word or make a sound.'

Her twelve-year-old son looked alarmed. 'What's going on?' he asked and sat bolt upright.

'I think there's someone in the house.'

Alfie's dark eyes widened in fear.

'It's all right. Come on, let's get your sister. You *must* look after her. Do you understand?'

Her son fervently nodded.

He climbed out of his bed and Georgina pushed him behind her as they sneaked from his room to Selina's at the far end of the hallway. Georgina tensed, knowing that when she pushed open Selina's door, it would creak. And it did. She silently prayed that the intruders hadn't heard.

Her seven-year-old daughter woke easily and followed

Georgina's instructions. Selina never muttered a word but Georgina could see that her girl was frightened. Alfie must have noticed too. He placed his arm protectively across his sister's shoulders. 'Don't worry. It'll be all right,' he whispered bravely, filling Georgina with pride.

She couldn't risk taking her children downstairs. She had no idea how many people were in the house or where they were. Instead, Georgina led her children through a half-width door situated adjacent to Selina's bedroom, which opened up to a narrow, enclosed staircase. The dark stairs went up to the attic, which once would have been used as the servants' quarters. Now it was just a storeroom for the family junk and memories.

As they went inside the unlit attic, Selina whimpered, 'I don't like it in here, Mummy. There's spiders.'

Alfie knelt in front of Selina and held both her hands. 'It's all right, sis. I won't let any spiders or nothing come near you.'

Selina, with tears falling from her violet eyes, nodded and allowed her brother to lead her into the room.

Georgina ushered her children behind an old trunk. She spoke clearly and firmly. 'Sit down. I want you both to stay here and don't move. Don't come out for anyone. No one at all and no sound. Is that clear?'

Her children whispered, 'Yes,' in unison.

She swiftly kissed the tops of their heads, and though only slightly chilly, she threw a dust sheet over them, more for concealment than warmth. 'Stay still. Don't move. And don't make any noise,' she gently ordered.

Georgina pushed her back against the wall and carefully descended the stairs. She glanced along the hallway, horrified to see a hooded figure emerge from her bedroom. Quickly stepping back into the darkness, she saw the uninvited guest run from her room and into Alfie's. He must have realised that she was hiding somewhere. He then pounded along the hallway towards Selina's room. Georgina pressed herself against the wall as much as she could, desperately hoping that her black silk pyjamas helped to keep her unseen in the shadows.

The man stood in the doorway of Selina's bedroom and looked at the child's empty bed. He was just feet away from Georgina, so close that she could smell the faint whiff of stale beer and tobacco emitting from him. She held her breath as she cocked her gun, ready to fire, and then lifted her arm. The man must have heard the weapon engage and was about to turn, but Georgina acted quickly and fired a single shot into his back. The sound of the gunshot echoed through the house and rang in Georgina's ears. He instantly fell forward and landed face down just inside Selina's bedroom.

Georgina couldn't see the blood that oozed from his back, but she trusted her aim and knew that he was dead. As she walked towards his body she heard another sound and froze, hardly daring to breathe. But the only sound that she could hear now was the thump of her own heart hammering loud and fast in her chest. But she hadn't been mistaken – there was at least one more unwanted person in her house and it had sounded like he was in her bedroom.

Georgina stepped back into the shadows. The half-width door was the only access to where her children were hiding. She wouldn't allow anyone to pass. If need be, she'd defend this spot with her life.

She waited. And waited. No one came out of her bedroom but she was sure that someone was in there. Still, she waited. Her mind turned. Who was the dead man on Selina's bedroom floor? Were these men just opportunist burglars or had they come to kill her? Or were they after David? After all, in their line of business, they'd made plenty of enemies and rivals.

Georgina heard movement. She knew all the sounds that the house made at night. Each creaky floorboard, every squeaky door and all the strange noises that the pipework made. But it wasn't her house making noises, it was someone shuffling through her bedroom. She strained her eyes in the dark and saw the shadowy outline of a largely built man making a run from her bedroom towards the staircase. Georgina fired at him. Two shots. But the man kept running and was soon out of sight. She was tempted to chase after him but she refused to leave the door to the attic unguarded.

An hour must have passed. It had been a very long hour and Georgina's hand was aching from fiercely gripping her gun. She wanted to go to her children and knew that they'd be petrified, but there could still be someone in her home. At least her heart rate had calmed somewhat. She drew in a long, deep breath and tried to think clearly. The sun would be rising in another hour or two and would illuminate the house. She'd wait until then before searching the place.

More time passed. The house remained silent. The birds outside began to sing and at last, the sun came up and streamed through the windows. The shadow in the corner by the narrow door where Georgina had concealed herself had gone now.

She carefully edged towards Selina's bedroom. The

lifeless body of the hooded man had bled out and soaked the cream carpet. She crouched beside the corpse and pulled down his hood to look closer at his face. He was young, probably about twenty or so. But she didn't recognise him. His clothes were unremarkable but he wore a gold band on his middle finger. And, lying just in front of his hand, Georgina saw a gun. It was clear that whoever he was, he had meant business.

She inched away from Selina's bedroom and quickly checked her own. The open wardrobe doors and a box pulled from under her bed showed that someone had been searching for her. Once she was sure that no one was hiding in the room, she checked Alfie's. Again, the wardrobe had been rummaged.

As Georgina crept downstairs, she glanced at the two bullets from her gun that were embedded in the wall. She leaned over the bannisters and looked down into the large passageway. Craning her neck, she could see that the front door was closed. She dashed down the rest of the stairs and ran to the telephone table. But when she picked up the receiver, it came as no surprise to find that the line was dead. But where was her security? Had Chunks been in on the job or had he bricked it and done a runner?

Georgina checked the rooms downstairs. Everything appeared as it should be. There'd been no attempt to steal anything. Even a wad of notes on the coffee table remained where she'd left them the day before. It was becoming obvious that whoever had been in her house had come for her or David. And they could come back at any time. With this in mind, Georgina hastily collected their shoes, coats, her handbag and the money on the table.

Back upstairs, she dragged the dead man's body further into Selina's room and then after taking some of her daughter's clothes, she closed the door. She didn't want Selina to see the horrific sight. Georgina then quickly gathered some clothes for Alfie and herself before she hurried to the attic and lifted the dust sheet off her children. 'You're safe now,' she soothed.

Alfie looked up at her and smiled. He looked so much like his father, Lash. The sight melted her heart. He had Selina huddled in his arms. The girl was sound asleep though she seemed fretful. 'Shall I wake her up?' he asked.

'Yes. We need to get out of here. Get dressed and then put your shoes and coats on. Be as quick as you can.'

Georgina hurried her children and then led them out of the attic. But as they reached the half-width door downstairs, Selina pulled away from Alfie and ran back up the steps to hide behind the trunk again. Georgina tried to talk her out but the girl looked to her brother for reassurance. It didn't go unnoticed to Georgina that her daughter trusted her brother more than her. Though it wasn't any wonder. After all, Selina had been raised by her gypsy grandparents for the first four years of her life. At the time, war had raged in London and Georgina had been in prison. But even now, after having her children home for almost four years, Selina was still wary of her mother. It hurt Georgina but now wasn't the time to be worrying about it.

At last, after some persuasion, Selina allowed Alfie to lead her downstairs, where Georgina pulled open the front door and looked from left to right before shepherding her children outside. 'Get in the car,' she said, and ran to the driver's side.

As she opened the car door, Selina screamed. A high-pitched, long scream that made Georgina's blood run cold. She dashed around to the other side of the car and that's when she saw her bodyguard. Peter Crowther, or Chunks as he was known on account of his size, lying behind the car in a puddle of his own blood. His throat had been cut from ear to ear, leaving a gaping wound in his neck. His deathly expression was strangely contorted and he was staring blankly skyward.

Alfie gazed ashen-faced at the dead man while Selina had spun around to bury her head into his chest. Georgina removed her coat and threw it over Chunks, covering his face and his hideously sliced neck.

'Get in the car,' she said firmly.

Alfie sat in the back seat with his sister who was quietly crying. 'Where are we going?' he asked, sounding concerned.

'To Molly's.'

'But... Mum... you can't drive.'

'Yes, I know. This might be a bumpy ride.'

As Georgina tried to start the car, she heard the back door open and twisted her neck to look over her shoulder. She saw Alfie climbing out of the car. 'What are you doing?' she asked frantically.

Her son walked around to her door and opened it. 'I'll drive,' he said.

'You can't drive either and you're too young.'

'I'm not supposed to tell you but Johnny Dymond lets me drive his car up and down the lane all the time. And David lets me park his car for him. Mum, I can drive better than you.'

Georgina smiled tenderly at her son. He seemed so grown-up and she realised that he probably could drive better than her. As it was, she doubted she could even get the bloody engine to turn.

They had a few hair-raising moments en route to Molly's farm. She lived there with her husband, Oppo – his real name Thomas. Oppo had gained the nickname as a child because of his limp. It had started out as Hop-along, after the cowboy, but this was soon shortened to Oppo. There were two children, Edward and Stephen, with Molly, once a Battersea girl, now adapted to life as a farmer's wife.

Alfie took a corner a bit too wide, waking Georgina from her thoughts as they nearly ended up in a hedge, but despite that, she was proud of how accomplished her son was and how mature he seemed for his age. Once again she saw that the more Alfie grew, the more he looked the spit of his dead father, and every time she looked at him, his swarthy beauty reminded her of Lash.

When they reached the farm, Molly rushed out to meet them. 'Well, this is a lovely surprise. Couldn't you sleep?' she asked, with a wide, welcoming smile.

'Men broke into our house,' Alfie announced. 'They killed Chunks.'

Molly's smile turned into a frown.

'They sliced Chunks' throat,' Georgina whispered.

'Go inside,' Molly urged. 'Georgina, do you want me to call the police?'

'No. But I need to call David. My telephone line was cut.'

Inside, Georgina called David's office while Molly fussed over the children. The line rang but no one answered. She replaced the receiver and tried again. Still nothing.

Molly, her plain-looking, mousy brown-haired, lifelong best friend, came to stand beside her. 'Anything?' she asked.

Georgina's stomach twisted and knotted as she shook her head. 'I'm really worried.'

'It's early. He's probably sleeping,' Molly placated.

'No. Something's wrong,' she answered gravely and tried calling again. There was still no answer.

'Look, come and have a cuppa and then give it another go, eh?'

Georgina swallowed hard. 'I'll give Johnny Dymond a ring first. I think I'm gonna need him.'

She made the call, relieved at Johnny's immediate response. Her right-hand man said that he'd be with her as soon as possible.

As Georgina replaced the telephone receiver, her stomach heaved. 'Excuse me,' she gasped to Molly and dashed to the toilet. Vomit had risen, burning her throat and she only just managed to close the door behind her before violently spewing into the toilet bowl. Georgina threw up until her stomach was empty. Gasping to catch her breath, she splashed cold water onto her face but couldn't stop the tears from falling. She turned from the sink and sat on the tiled floor, hugging her knees to her chest as long, juddering sobs caused her shoulders to jerk up and down.

Georgina had thought that she'd left this life of guns and death behind. She'd moved her family to the Kent countryside to raise her children in fresh air and away from a life of crime. Yet the dirtiness and bloodshed of her past had followed her. She'd feared for her life last night and had been terrified for her children. Now she'd have to send them away again to live in safety with their gypsy grandparents. Her heart broke at the thought of it, but she had no choice. She wiped away her tears and gritted her teeth in determination, vowing to avenge herself against the men who'd had the audacity to break into her home and scare her children.

She rose to her feet and smoothed down her dress. Georgina Garrett and her gun were coming out of retirement.

Johnny Dymond put his foot to the floor and drove at top speed to Molly's farm. It was just before midday when he pulled up outside. Molly's husband, Oppo, came out to greet him.

'Is she all right?' Johnny asked with urgency.

Oppo, his face serious, answered, 'Yeah, yeah, she's fine. Spitting feathers and worried sick about David but she's all right. Do me a favour, mate, don't let her do anything reckless.'

'I'll try me best, but you know what she's like. If she gets an idea in her head, there ain't much I can do to stop her. Try not to worry. You know I'd lay down my life to protect her.'

'I know you would, Johnny. Let's hope it don't come to that though, eh.'

In the farmhouse, Georgina was in the hallway and looked ready to leave, but Molly urged, 'At least let the man have a cuppa before you set off.'

'I need to get to David,' Georgina retorted.

'You will. But Johnny has had a long drive here and he's got a long drive back.'

Johnny could see the annoyance on Miss Garrett's face. 'Its fine, Molly, thanks. The sooner we get off, the better.'

'If you're sure?'

'Yes, Molly, he's sure,' Georgina snapped.

Molly looked hurt and contritely Georgina apologised. 'I'm sorry. I'm just worried sick about David.'

'I know. Go on then, get going. Keep me updated, won't you?'

'Yes, of course. And thanks, Molly. I'll arrange for Lash's parents to collect the kids as soon as possible.'

'Don't worry about that. They'll be all right with me and Oppo. My two are glad they're here. Stephen loves having Selina to play with and Edward, well, I'm sure he'll be pleased to take Alfie out on the farm to help him. With Oppo too, of course. But don't worry, I wouldn't leave Alfie with Edward unattended.'

Johnny thought it was a strange thing for Molly to say but he didn't give it any more thought as Miss Garrett hadn't seem bothered.

As Molly bustled off to her kitchen, Georgina bent down to talk to her children. 'You'll be all right here for a while,' she said softly, 'and once I've had a word with your grandparents, they'll come to pick you up.'

Thankfully, there were no protests, and after giving them a swift hug, she climbed into the passenger seat of Johnny's car.

Molly came running from the house with a package in her hand. 'I've made you some sandwiches for the journey. 'Ere, Johnny, make sure she eats something.'

Johnny smiled and gave Molly a nod, yet knew he

wouldn't be able to *make* Miss Garrett eat. The woman never did anything that she didn't want to do.

They set off and Johnny listened intently as his boss informed him of what had happened at her home. He'd been gutted to hear about Chunks. The giant bloke had been a mate of his. 'Well, I'm bloody glad that you shot one of the bastards.'

'Yeah, but there's still at least one who got away and I don't like the fact that I can't get through to David.'

That concerned Johnny too. There was always someone available to answer the phone at Mr Maynard's office and London residence. 'I should have gone to his place before I came to pick you up,' he said, his lips set in a grim line.

'No. I told you to come straight here because I didn't want you going to the office alone. You could have been walking into an ambush. What if they'd got you an' all? Where would I be without you?'

Johnny glanced sideways at Miss Garrett. She was smiling warmly at him, a beautiful dark-haired woman, but he could see the fear behind her violet eyes. 'Try not to worry. We'll get to the bottom of this and I'll fucking kill the wankers behind it.'

Miss Garrett spent the next hour picking his brain. She fired question after question at him. *Did he know anyone who wanted David dead? Had David upset anyone recently? Had he heard any whispers about a takeover? Was there anyone vying for her blood?* Johnny shook his head to answer. But the truth was, yes, there were plenty of people who wanted Mr Maynard dead. And yes, Mr Maynard had upset loads of folk. There were also men who'd like to see Miss Garrett's blood spilt too. But in all honesty, Johnny couldn't think of one person who'd have the guts or the resources to do anything against Mr Maynard and his firm, or to Miss Garrett.

The following hour of the journey was spent in silence. Johnny recognised the pensive look on Georgina's face. She was deep in thought and he knew to keep quiet. He noticed her rubbing her finger, a tell-tale habit that meant she was worried. It startled him when she suddenly shouted, 'SHIT!'

'What? What's wrong?' he asked.

'Charlotte!'

'What about her?'

'I haven't checked on her. What if they've got to Charlotte too?'

'I doubt it, Miss Garrett. She's had nothing to do with the business for years now.'

'But she still runs my café on Lavender Hill.'

'Yeah, but that's all above board.'

'I've got a feeling that someone is after *me*, Johnny. If they know enough about me then they'll know that Charlotte works for me.'

'What do you want me to do?'

'Stop at the nearest telephone box. I'll call the café.'

Twenty minutes later, in Richmond, just outside of London, Johnny spotted a telephone box and pulled in to the kerb. Georgina leapt out of the car and ran inside. Despite being keyed up with worry, Johnny's stomach rumbled with hunger. He grabbed the package Molly had given them, and pulled out a slab of apple pie. Molly was a good cook and he devoured it hungrily.

Soon after Miss Garrett climbed back into the car, and

Johnny could tell from her expression that the news was grave.

'No answer at the café either or at Charlotte's home in Alexander Avenue. Something is *very* wrong, Johnny. I don't like this. I don't like this one little bit.'

'Nor do I,' Johnny said, breathing in a deep and worried breath. Christ, he hoped nothing untoward had happened to Charlotte. And what about Charlotte's husband, Tim Batten? The bloke was an ex-copper but Johnny didn't hold it against him. After all, Tim had resigned from his job to be with Charlotte and now he worked in the offices of Garton's Glucose factory. 'Did you try ringing Tim's work?' Johnny asked.

'Yes, but he wasn't there. This is bad, Johnny, ain't it? *Really* bad.'

'It don't sound good, but let's not jump to any conclusions. We'll soon find out what's going on,' he soothed, yet in truth he was worried that their luck had run out. Things had been good since the war had ended, maybe too good. The business had been running smoothly and they'd all been raking it in. There'd been little trouble and few fights. Everyone had been playing ball and rival gangs had kept to their own turfs. In fact, with many goods still rationed, the black market was doing a roaring trade. And once the men had returned from war, the gambling and loans side of things had picked up too.

What with that and Mr Maynard expanding the drug trafficking, they were all rolling in it, like pigs in shit. And best of all, four years earlier when peace had been declared in Europe, there had been a plentiful supply of guns and bullets. So, Mr Maynard, being a smart bloke and on the ball, had started buying and selling firearms abroad.

Johnny worried that it was a foreign fucker who was starting this trouble now. It had to be. It was the only thing that made any sense. Gawd, if it was, it could be one of them evil German bastards. Johnny wasn't too proud to admit to himself that he was more than a little scared. Whatever was going down appeared to be well thought out and organised. Someone clever, maybe as clever as Miss Garrett, had to be the brains behind the outfit. And Johnny wondered how big the outfit was. Men had been in Miss Garrett's house, probably Mr Maynard's and Charlotte's too.

Fuck, Johnny thought, if only he knew who they were dealing with. But he was scratching in the dark, and glancing over at Miss Garrett again, he could see that she was afraid too.

Georgina scanned the street. From the outside, everything appeared to be normal. David's car was parked outside the house as were several others that belonged to the men who worked for her husband. The house, at the end of an affluent street next to a park, had been David's office for years, and for a while, her home too. She remembered when she'd once visited the premises with murder on her mind. It had been before she'd married David and she'd believed him to be dead at the time, gunned down by a gangster known as The Top who had taken over David's business.

Georgina had vowed revenge on The Top and had managed to sneak her gun into his office. Unfortunately, she'd shot Slugs to get to The Top. But when she'd held her gun at The Top's head, she'd been astonished to discover that he was actually David, his face badly scarred, but still the man she loved. Eventually, they'd married, and now, here she was again, outside the house with Johnny, her gun in her hand, but this time she was ready to shoot anyone who would threaten to hurt her husband.

'What are you thinking?' Johnny asked, breaking into her thoughts.

'Actually, I was thinking about the last time that we were here together before I married David.'

Johnny smiled. 'When I brought you here to kill The Top.'

'Yeah, that's right. Blimey, that all feels like a lifetime ago now.'

'It was. But the last time I brought you here, you made me wait in the car and you went in alone. Like it or not, Miss Garrett, it ain't gonna be the same this time. I know you're me guv an' all that, but I don't care what you say, you ain't going in alone.'

'I had no intention of doing that, Johnny. But this could be dangerous and I won't make you do anything that you don't want to do. If you come with me, you might be risking your life.'

'With respect, Miss Garrett – shut up.'

Georgina smiled at Johnny, recalling what they'd told each other the last time that they were here. 'I think the world of you,' she said, just as she had said before all those years ago.

'Yeah, I do you an' all. You're like a sister to me, Miss Garrett. Now, come on, enough of this soppy shit. Let's see what the fuck is going on in there.'

Georgina knew that many women would be attracted to

Johnny with his snazzy way of dressing, brown hair and blue eyes, but she'd never looked at him in *that* way. He was one of her dearest friends and she knew that he'd willingly die to save her life. She drew in a long breath and looked at the gun in her hand. 'Ready,' she said flatly.

As she ran towards the large, wooden, double doors, she licked her dry lips. Her heart was pumping so fast that it was making her feel quite dizzy. Outside the house, Georgina nodded to Johnny. He pushed the key into the lock and tried to turn it as quietly as possible. When the door unlocked, he gingerly pushed it open and slowly walked inside.

Georgina held her gun in front of her as she followed Johnny and then gasped at the horrors that greeted them.

'Fuck! Fucking hell!' Johnny spat, spinning left and right as he took in the nightmare scene.

Three of David's men lay dead on the white marble floor in the grand entrance. Their blood was splattered up the walls and over the polished tiles. Another lay askew on the sweeping staircase, his blood too was splashed up the wall behind him and had dripped down several of the shiny steps.

'It's a fucking bloodbath!' Johnny exclaimed.

'This is fresh. Their blood ain't dry,' Georgina said, appalled.

She looked at Johnny. He was running his hand through his hair and cursing under his breath.

As the shock of the sight began to wear off and reality sunk in, Georgina mumbled, 'David.' She felt sick to her stomach and fear gripped her heart like a vice. She wasn't afraid of any enemies in the house, but she was terrified of finding David's slain corpse upstairs.

Georgina flew across the hall and up the stairs. She was

mindful of not treading in the blood and carefully stepped over the slaughtered man. She looked down and saw that he had at least a dozen bullet holes in his torso. David's men hadn't stood a chance against automatic weapons. Bile burned her throat. Her head felt hot enough to explode. *Please. Please let David be alive*, she inwardly prayed, but she knew the odds of finding her husband breathing were very slim.

At the top of the stairs, three more men had been killed. One of them was slumped across a leather chesterfield. He still had his gun in his hand. Another blocked the doorway to David's office. Georgina stood motionless for a moment and stared at him in disbelief. It was Victor, she knew it was, but her mind wouldn't or couldn't comprehend what she was seeing. Most of Victor's face was missing and part of his skull was gone. His brain and blood sprayed the doorframe. There was nothing recognisable left of his head. No identifiable features. Just a mangled, fleshy, blackened mess, his nose, mouth, eyes and the flesh of his cheeks and chin, all shot away.

'Fucking cunts,' Johnny seethed. 'Fucking dirty, fucking wankers. Cunts. Cunts. Cunts,' he hissed through gritted teeth. He turned away from what was left of his best friend and punched the wall three times.

Georgina swallowed hard and fought back the puke that was tight in her chest. 'We'll have to move him so that we can get into the office,' she croaked, and sniffed back the urge to burst out crying.

Victor had been a big and heavy man. Georgina took one arm and Johnny the other, but she had to look away as they dragged him away from the doorway. 'I'm so sorry, Victor,' she said softly.

Once they'd shifted his body, Johnny took off his hat and held it against his chest. He looked down at Victor and growled, 'We'll get the bastards that did this to you. I promise, my friend, I'll fucking kill 'em.' After putting his hat back on his head, he looked at Georgina. 'He said he'd rather die than see Wolverhampton Wanderers win the FA Cup. He got his wish, poor bloke.'

Georgina barely took in his words as she stood outside the door, frightened of what she'd find on the other side. Johnny gently moved her to one side.

'I'll do this,' he said.

Georgina didn't protest. She knew that if David was in there, he wouldn't be alive.

Minutes later, what felt like hours, Johnny came back out. Georgina searched his face for any sign of hope.

'He's not there. I looked everywhere but he ain't in there.'

Georgina pushed past Johnny and burst into the room. She ran around like a headless chicken, combing every corner and then in the adjacent snug room. But Johnny had been right – there was no sign of David. 'Search the rest of the house,' she ordered.

While Johnny went from room to room, Georgina picked up the telephone. The line was dead. She looked on David's desk for any clue to what had happened. Nothing.

Johnny returned, shaking his head. 'He's not here.'

'They've taken him. If he'd escaped, he would have let me know. They must have him. Whoever the murdering gits are, they've got my husband.' Georgina felt her legs weaken. She stumbled over to the sofa and almost collapsed onto it.

'They must want him alive, Miss Garrett, or else they would have gunned him down in here.'

'Why, though, Johnny? What do they want with him?'

Johnny shrugged. He, like her, was at a loss.

Georgina struggled to get her thoughts into coherent order and ran a hand over her forehead. 'We need to check on Charlotte and get some of the blokes together,' she said, though she wasn't convinced that her old gang would want anything to do with this. In fact, if they'd already got wind of it, she wouldn't be surprised if they'd scarpered and run for their lives.

Johnny went to give her a hand to get up from the sofa but Georgina dismissed his help. She needed to pull herself together. She had to be strong. Her cosy and delightful life in the country, being a wife and mother, had changed overnight.

Standing straight, her lips set in determination. Georgina Garrett was back and she was determined that no man would stand in the way of her finding her husband.

2

As David Maynard slowly woke, he became aware of agony racking his body. His head throbbed. It felt as though there was a bloke inside his skull hammering at his brain. A sharp pain stabbed at his eye socket and he realised he couldn't fully open his eyelid. His arms ached and his wrists and hands felt painfully numb. That's when he remembered that he was bound to a chair.

'You're still alive then.'

It took a lot of effort but David lifted his head to look at the man who'd spoken. The man who'd ordered the killing of his men, kidnapped him, held him prisoner and battered him. 'I'll have you for this,' he mumbled.

'Yeah, so you've said. Oooo, I'm scared,' the man mocked.

A metallic taste filled David's mouth. He spat his blood to the side but most of it dribbled down his chin. When the man had pistol-whipped his face, David's cheek had split inside his mouth and talking had opened the wound again.

David glanced around at his surroundings. He'd had a potato sack over his head when he'd been dragged in. Now he could see that he was in some sort of abandoned small warehouse. Glass littered the floor from the smashed windows and the place was filthy with pigeon shit. There was another man standing in the far corner of the room. He looked like a thug, and obviously he wasn't in charge, as the main man circled David, deliberately and menacingly.

'Are you ready to talk?' he asked.

'Fuck you,' David answered brazenly. He knew his reply would earn him another bone-crunching blow and he braced himself.

As expected, the man punched David straight in the face. He felt his nose break as the force of the blow snapped his head back. He stayed there for a moment and tried to gather some strength. Then he slowly straightened his head but, weak, it lolled forward. Blood poured from his nose and trickled over his swollen lips, down his chin and soaked into his white shirt.

The man looked at his own bruised knuckles and shook his hand in front of him. 'I've gotta stop hitting you like that. It's damaging my health.' He grinned.

David watched through one eye as the man picked up a large spanner.

'This will do instead,' he said, as he looked at his tool with a wicked smile. 'Now, I'll give you another chance to speak before I start smashing your teeth out.'

'Do your worst. You won't get anything out of me,' David answered.

He could see that his response had angered the man but he didn't care. He was prepared to be tortured, even slowly hacked to death. This bloke and his cronies could do whatever they wanted to him but David was adamant that he'd *never* tell them anything about Georgina.

The man leaned closer to David. It was then that he realised how young the bloke was. Maybe not much older than twenty. He wondered how the hell a bit of a kid could command a bunch of hardened criminals and killers to do his bidding. And his accent… David was sure that the bloke spoke with a Liverpudlian twang though there seemed to be a bit of West Country there too. Who was he? If he were any sort of a name, surely David would know him or at least have heard of him?

'Your fucking missus shot one of my lads last night. He's dead. The poor sod was only sixteen years old. Now I've got to tell his mam that her son has been killed and I can't even give her his body to bury.'

David's heart pounded and his fury mounted. This bloke's crew had been in *his* house. His house where his stepchildren slept. With the bloke's face just inches from his own, David spat. His bloodied saliva landed on the man's cheek and slowly oozed down his face.

The man stepped away from David and wiped his face. He looked at the mess in his hand, his lips curling in disgust as he snarled, 'You filthy git.'

'You'd better not have touched my kids,' David threatened.

'Tell me where your wife is and then it'll all be over. I don't want your kids. I just want her. That *bitch*.'

David, tight-lipped and with only the one eye open, stared hard at the man.

'Fine. Have it your way. Let's see if bits of you can entice her to me. Understand this… I will do whatever I need to do to get to your wife. And once I've destroyed her, I'll have your business too. So, save us all a load of aggro and just tell me where to find her.'

David remained silent.

The man signalled the huge, ugly thug. As the bloke came towards him, David saw the cloth in his hand and knew that he was about to be gagged. He looked back at the boss – the one giving out the orders – and asked, 'Who the fuck are you?'

The man's eyes narrowed. He looked as if he were debating with himself. 'I could tell you, but I'll keep you guessing for a while,' he answered, again grinning disturbingly.

David winced in pain as the strong thug forced his sore mouth open and crammed a rolled-up piece of rag inside. He felt he was choking when the cloth was tied across his face, pulled tight and knotted at the back of his head. *Don't panic*, he told himself and tried to breathe steadily through his nose though it felt clogged with blood.

The big bloke moved back while the *boss* stood in front of David and held his hand in the air. '*Eeny, meeny, miny, mo*,' he sang, reciting the children's rhyme, pointing to each of his fingers in turn. Then, his voice grave, he said to the big bloke, 'His ring finger first.'

The thug was coming towards David with a pair of bolt cutters. He began screeching behind his gag, knowing that he was about to lose his ring finger and there was nothing he could do to stop it. Though terrified of the pain that he knew was coming, he ceased trying to scream. He wouldn't give them the satisfaction of knowing how scared he was.

The big bloke walked behind the seat and David could feel him tugging at his hand. He instinctively wriggled his fingers.

'Can't I take his little finger instead? He won't hold still. It'd be a lot easier.'

'Take whatever fucking finger you like. I don't give a shit.

Chop the fucking lot off for all I care. Just give me a piece of him,' the boss answered shortly.

David bit down into the rag in his mouth as an overwhelming searing agony shot through his hand and then right through his whole body. He could feel himself shaking as the bolt croppers crunched through his bone. Sweat dripped from his temples and tears unashamedly fell from his eyes.

'This do ya?' the big bloke asked as he walked towards his boss holding aloft one of David's unattached fingers.

David didn't hear the boss's response. He'd blacked out, unconscious and now oblivious to the pain.

Tears fell from Charlotte's eyes as she looked across to Tim, her husband. He hadn't moved or spoken since he'd been battered to the floor by a couple of men who'd broken in hours earlier. She couldn't tell if he was still breathing or not. She knew she wasn't much to look at, plain with mousy brown hair, but Tim loved her and she couldn't face the thought of life without him.

She wrung her hands, trying desperately to free them from the bindings that tied her arms to the back of the kitchen chair. If only she could scream out for help. Miss Gray upstairs might hear her. But it was impossible with a gag around her mouth.

Charlotte looked down at her swollen stomach and hoped her unborn child had survived. She'd pleaded with the men, told them that she was pregnant, and had begged them not to hit her belly. Yet it hadn't stopped them punching her three times. One of them had laughed too.

She rocked the chair back and forth, hoping that she could shuffle to the kitchen and get a knife to cut through the ropes around her wrists. But the chair fell sideways and her own weight crunched the arm that she landed on. Behind her gag she groaned with pain. She felt so helpless, tied to a chair, gagged and beaten, just feet away from her badly injured or dead husband.

Charlotte wanted to admit defeat. She wanted to give in, but then she thought of Georgina and tried to imagine what the woman would do in this situation. It gave her strength and she tried to remove her gag by using her shoulder.

The room was stifling and perspiration ran down her face as, frustrated, she struggled. Charlotte heard a sound and froze. Someone had entered the shared front door to the large house and was now knocking on the door of her flat. She frantically wriggled and tried to kick out, moving the chair around, hoping to bump into something that would make a noise. *Help me*, she screamed in her head. Relief flooded through her body at the sound of the front door being kicked in, and then moments later, Charlotte was grateful to see Georgina and Johnny burst into the room.

'It's all right, we're here,' Georgina cried as she ran towards her.

Johnny lifted the chair, and upright again, Georgina removed the gag.

'Thank God,' Charlotte cried and sucked large gulps of air into her aching lungs. Then, as Georgina began to untie her hands, she begged with urgency, 'Please check on Tim.'

'He's all right, he's alive,' Johnny called as he rolled Tim over and onto his back.

It was only then that Charlotte got a glimpse of her

husband's injuries. A sob caught in her throat at the horrendous sight. His face looked a bloodied mess. She had no doubt that he had at least a broken nose, eye socket and cheek too. She prayed his brain hadn't been damaged. When the bloke had stamped his booted foot down onto Tim's face, Charlotte had heard a nauseating crunch and had assumed that Tim's skull had been smashed. Now she hoped it was just his face.

Once free from the ropes, the blood rushed back into Charlotte's fingers, making them tingle painfully. She found herself shaking and intuitively rested her hand on her stomach.

'Are you all right?' Georgina asked gently.

Charlotte nodded. She couldn't speak for fear of throwing up.

'Do you know who did this to you and Tim?'

Charlotte shook her head. A sharp, cramping pain ripped through her womb.

'They've killed David's men and taken him. They came to my house too last night. Did they say *anything*? *Anything* at all?'

Charlotte was about to speak, but another cramp painfully squeezed her womb. She leaned forward and gripped her stomach. She felt a warm sensation between her legs and knew that it was blood. 'I'm losing my baby,' she cried.

Georgina looked shocked, her jaw hanging wide. 'Oh, darling, I'm so sorry. I didn't know that you… Come on, I'll help you to the bathroom.'

Georgina eased her arm around Charlotte's waist and led her towards the door. But Charlotte paused to look down at her unconscious husband. 'Will he survive?' she asked Johnny.

'I think so, sweetheart. We'll get him to the hospital. Don't you worry about Tim. You just look after yourself for now.'

Johnny's words were said so softly and with such care that it brought more tears to Charlotte's eyes.

In the bathroom, Georgina sat her on a stool and then she ran a flannel under the cold tap. She gently dabbed at Charlotte's bruised face.

'They were after you,' Charlotte said. 'They wanted to know where they could find you. I kept insisting that I didn't know so they tried to punch it out of Tim, and then me.'

Georgina stepped back and cast her eyes downward. 'I'm so sorry, Charlotte. You should have told them. You didn't have to go through this for me.'

'They said they'd been to your house and that you'd escaped. I guessed you was at Molly's.'

'You guessed right,' Georgina said. 'Thank you. Thank you for not saying anything.'

'They'd already kicked Tim half to death. I thought they was going to kill me whether I told them anything or not.'

'And you've no idea who they are?'

'No,' Charlotte answered and winced again. 'Christ, this hurts.'

'What do you want me to do, darling? Do I need to get you to hospital or call a doctor?'

'No, it's too late. There's nothing anyone can do. I'm losing this baby, but I'm only four months gone so just let me get on with it. See to Tim. Make sure he gets to the hospital. And find David.'

'I can't leave you alone like this.'

'Yes, Georgina, you can. I'd rather do this by myself. I've seen me muvver do it and I can do it too,' she said, but could see that Georgina was reluctant to leave. 'Please, just leave me be,' she insisted.

Georgina nodded. 'All right. I'll get Tim into the Bolingbroke. I don't want you staying here though. I'll send Ned for you. I'll get the old gang back together. I'm sure that Ned will step up. And I'll work out somewhere safe for us to stay.'

Charlotte felt the urge to bear down and quickly shooed Georgina away with her hand. 'Fine. Please, go now.'

Georgina, still looking reluctant to leave, finally closed the bathroom door behind her.

Charlotte removed her knickers and squatted down, steadying herself with one hand on the stool. The baby she had longed for, that she and Tim had tried for so long to have, slithered from her womb and onto the cold tiles beneath.

She wept uncontrollably as she peered down between her legs to look at the perfectly formed tiny baby that was so small it would easily fit in the palm of her hand. She took little consolation in thinking that her baby would never know the cruelties of the world.

Charlotte flopped to the side and sat beside her premature child. 'I'm sorry that I couldn't protect you,' she cried, her heart breaking. Those men had done this. They'd murdered her unborn child and she'd been powerless to stop them.

She carefully gathered the baby from the floor and wrapped him in a towel before holding the precious bundle close to her chest. 'I'll *never* have another baby,' she sobbed.

'I'm your mother and I failed you. I couldn't look after you. I don't deserve children.'

As Charlotte's heart ripped in half, she knew that Georgina wouldn't rest until the men who were responsible for this were dead and buried. But Charlotte wanted revenge of her own. She wanted to gut the man who'd so cruelly laughed as he'd brutally punched the life out of her unborn baby. 'I'll make him pay, little one. I'll make him pay for hurting you,' she vowed.

Charlotte knew what she wanted to do. She wanted to stretch out his intestines and she wanted him to see her do it. His fear and pain wouldn't bring her baby back, but it would at least give her some sense of retribution.

David regained consciousness but he kept his eyes closed and his head down. His hand throbbed worse than his head but he supressed the urge to groan by biting down into the rag stuffed in his mouth. The smell of burning twitched his nostrils. It flashed through his mind that the building had been set alight and he tensed, fearing he was going to burn to death. Yet the boss was still in the room. He could hear him talking.

David discreetly opened one eye and saw a small bonfire burning in the corner. The sight was a relief and he quickly closed his eye again. He knew too well about the pain of flames searing his flesh, his scarred face a constant reminder of being caught by a bomb blast during the war.

The man, whoever he was, had made it clear that he wanted Georgina. David racked his brains, trying to fathom what his wife could have done to elicit such violence. It was a mystery, after all, Georgina hadn't been involved in the business for years. This must be something from her past. But what? David had thought that she'd destroyed all her enemies. Nancy Austin was dead after Georgina had rigged a safe to blow up in the woman's face. Elsie Jacobs had been killed after *accidentally* falling down the stairs in prison. The Maltese gang who'd run West London had been destroyed – David had made sure of that. Anyone who'd ever been a threat to his wife had been got rid of. But clearly, some enemies still lurked.

He listened carefully. The man's voice was coming from the far side of the room.

'What if she won't meet you?' the big bloke asked.

'Then I'll send her more bits of her husband until she does. I don't think she'll follow my instructions, not this time. But eventually she will.'

'What if she *never* does?'

'Shut up and stop asking stupid fucking questions. Just get that package dropped off to the jewellery shop in Battersea.'

'Righto, Guv. Shall I bring us back something to eat? Some sausages to put on the fire?'

'We're not on a fucking day trip, shit for brains! FUCK OFF!'

David heard a seat scrape back and heavy footsteps pound across the room. The sound of the footsteps faded as they got further away and then he heard what sounded like a door slam. From what he could gather, it seemed that he was now alone with the maniac boss. If David had any chance of escape, now would be the time to try. But with his arms, hands and feet firmly secured, he knew that freedom was out of his reach.

He slowly lifted his head and scanned the room with his one seeing eye. The boss was sat at a rickety-looking wooden table, rubbing his chin, and seeing that David was awake, he walked across the room towards him.

David tensed. When the gag was removed, he hissed, 'Tell me who you are.'

The man arched his back and smirked. 'Nah. It's more fun watching you trying to work it out.'

'It doesn't take much working out to suss that you're going to kill me. I don't know if I'm going to die a long and slow, painful death or if you'll show me mercy and put a bullet between my eyes. But either way, I'd like to know who the fuck it is that's going to send me up to meet my maker.'

'If you tell me where to find your wife, I might let you live.'

'We both know that me getting out of here alive was never part of the plan. The only reason you're only keeping me alive now is to use me for body parts.'

The man scratched the top of his head, then lunged towards him. David flinched.

The man laughed. 'Ha, fooled ya.'

'Yeah, you did. Very funny. So, you're a clown as well as a fucking nutter.'

'Oi, less of the lip. You've got a gob on you bigger than the Mersey Tunnel. Maybe I should cut your tongue out next.'

'Do your fucking worst.'

'You're a hard bastard, David Maynard, and a rich one too. Is that what Georgina saw in you? Was she with you for your money? I mean, let's face it, she wasn't with you for your devastatingly handsome looks.'

David wasn't bothered by the man goading him about his scarred face. Yes, he'd been badly burned during the war but his horrific injuries hadn't stopped Georgina from loving him. And he fervently loved her back. The thought of this man finding her and hurting her was eating away at him, gnawing in his stomach and grinding in his chest.

'I can see I'm getting to you. You're dying to know who I am.'

'Are you going to tell me?'

'How badly do you want to know?'

'Bad enough.'

'Bad enough to play a game?'

'What game?'

'I'll give you three clues. With each clue, you give me an answer. But if you give me a wrong answer, I'll burn you.'

David watched the man walk across to the fire. He wrapped a cloth around his hand and pulled a metal rod from the flames. The end was glowing bright orange. 'I'm bored. Humour me. Say you'll play?' he said as he approached David.

'Do I have a choice?'

'No, not really.'

David looked at the red-hot poker. His heart thumped hard at the thought of being branded. He was well aware of how much pain the burns would cause.

'Clue number one...' the man announced. He began circling David as he spoke. 'You, and your slag of a wife, both knew my father. Think hard, David… What's my name?'

David's mind turned. The man talked about his father as if he were dead.

'Come on, David, give me a name…'

David racked his brain. The man was standing behind him. It unnerved him and he could feel his panic rising.

'A name, David, NOW…'

He was just about to answer but felt an excruciating, searing agony on the back of his neck. He could hear the sound of his skin hissing under the hot tip of the metal rod. He wanted to pull away from the suffering but he was trapped and couldn't move.

'I should have explained the rules more clearly. Once I've given you a clue, you have five seconds to answer. Right, let's try again. Clue number two… I was born in Liverpool.'

David didn't need any more time to think. Everything slotted into place as he realised who the man was. And now he could see how much this young man looked like his father. There was no doubt in his mind. And now, it was all beginning to make sense.

3

November 1939. Liverpool.

Thomas Kelly sauntered in through the front door with his stomach grumbling. He found his mother sitting at the kitchen table, twiddling her thumbs, and was disappointed that no pots were bubbling on the stove. At thirteen years old, he was a big lad for his age and needed food to keep him growing, especially if he was going to bash up Eugene Hawkins. The boy already towered over him by a foot and a half, yet that wouldn't deter Thomas from giving him a clump. After all, Eugene had asked for it. And beating up Eugene would make Thomas's father proud of him.

'I'm starving, Mam. What's for tea?'

His mother's head shot up and Thomas could see the anger in her amber eyes. 'Duck, under the table, and out again.'

'Aw, Mam, seriously. What's for tea?'

'There's nothing for tea, Thomas, and if your father

doesn't pay me your keep, then there won't be anything for breakfast either,' she spat.

'What are you on about? Hasn't one of dad's lads dropped any money off?'

'No, Thomas, no one's been for two weeks. I've no pennies and the cupboards are bare. Our baby is hungry too but I can't feed you both if your father is going to start playing silly games.'

'That's not like him. He always pays up.'

'Yes, he *did*. But I bet that new silly red-headed tart he's married to is behind this. Mabel has always been jealous of me because I've got you and your sister. She doesn't like it that I gave your dad children and she can't.'

Thomas pulled out a seat at the table and sat opposite his mother. Her anger seemed to be subsiding to give way to her pain. The unshed tears in her eyes that glistened reminded him that she still loved his dad. And probably always would. Yet Kevin Kelly, the big gangster, the head of the Portland Pounders, had discarded his mother like an old fag butt.

'Don't worry, Mam, I'll go and see him to get this sorted out.'

'I'd rather you didn't, son. Mabel won't make you feel welcome.'

'I'm not bothered about her.'

Ida sighed and then scraped back her chair. 'All right, I suppose we don't have any choice but I'm coming with you. Your father needs to know that he can't muck us about like this. You and Beth are *his* responsibility and it isn't fair that you're going hungry, not when he's sat in his big house with his fancy cars and the rest.'

As they walked down the passageway, Ida called up the stairs, 'Beth, me and Tom are off out for a bit. We won't be long.'

Beth came to the top of the stairs and looked down. Her long, chestnut hair fell over her face, covering her amber eyes that were just like her mother's.

'Did you hear me, our baby? We're going out. We won't be long. Stay in and be a good girl.'

Beth nodded and skipped back to her bedroom, probably to play with her dolls, Thomas assumed. Their mother had told Beth that at eleven years old she was too old for her dollies but Beth had kicked up such a fuss that she'd been allowed to keep them. Her dolls were her only friends. A quiet girl, she never played out on the street with the rest of the kids. In fact, she rarely spoke. Thomas thought that Beth lived in her own little world, but his sister seemed happy there, oblivious to the war and the gas masks and the Anderson bomb shelter in the back garden.

His mother had quite a pace on and marched determinedly down the street. She was clearly a woman on a mission. 'When we get there, you let me do all the talking, all right, lad.'

Thomas nodded. He wouldn't go against her, not when she was in one of these moods. He'd dared to give her some backchat once and she'd given him the cane across his backside. He'd been sore for days and had never given her any lip again.

As they made their way through the Liverpool docks, some of the dockers loading and unloading the big ships stopped momentarily to glance at his mother. A few made lewd remarks. Thomas wanted to turn back and knock their lights out but his mother caught his sleeve and dragged him on.

'Just ignore them,' she hissed and pulled her shawl around her.

It was a bitterly cold day, yet and there were several women hanging around. Thomas knew that they were prostitutes who sold their bodies for sex. And he knew all about sex too, not that he'd had it yet. Oliver Maxwell in his class had dragged Cora Hind behind the old science block in school and they'd had sex. Oliver had told him all about it. He'd said that Cora would let Thomas fuck her too for a couple of bob or suck his dick for half the price. But Thomas wasn't interested. His father ran brothels and Thomas had always been warned to stay away from the whores. His dad said that they were dirty and he'd catch all sorts of diseases. It sounded to him like Cora Hind was a whore and he wouldn't go near her with a bargepole.

As they came to the end of the docks, Thomas saw his father's grand house looming and was pleased to see his car outside. At least they hadn't had a wasted journey. The sight of the house seemed to spur his mother on and she walked even faster.

'Remember what I said. You leave the talking to me, lad.'

Again, Thomas nodded in agreement. He hadn't seen his dad for at least three weeks and would rather like to tell him about his plans to beat up Eugene Hawkins. That would impress his dad. Especially when he'd explain that he was giving Eugene a pasting because the boy had taken two of Beth's dolls and ripped their heads off in front of her. His dad would expect him to stick up for his sister. It showed family loyalty, something his father had harped on about for as far back as Thomas could remember.

When they arrived outside the impressive building, Thomas thought it was odd that none of his father's men were standing outside. Kevin Kelly, the guvnor and most feared man in Liverpool, *always* had protection on his house.

His mother, if she'd noticed, didn't mention anything and rapped heavily on the large front door. It was the old housekeeper in her black maid's dress and white apron who opened it. After her initial look of surprise, she cast her eyes downward and pulled the door open wider.

Ida barged through and stamped into the massive front room. Thomas, in her wake, smirked at the two, gold throne-like chairs at the end of the room that sat under a huge painting of his father. The house had never looked like this when he'd lived in it with his mam and sister. But once they'd been thrown out, his second wife redecorated. And then after her, this other new wife of his, Mabel, who had ostentatious tastes, had changed everything again. The only familiar thing was the large fire burning in the hearth, something that was now sorely lacking in theirs.

Finding the room empty, Ida spun on her heel to be faced with the nervous-looking elderly housekeeper. 'Where is he?' she demanded.

'I'll fetch Mrs Kelly, err, Mrs Kelly,' the housekeeper mumbled and fled from the room.

Ida paced the room impatiently as Thomas studied the painting. The man it portrayed, his father, had an air of authority that came across well in the brushstrokes. Thomas thought that he resembled his dad, except that he was already the same height and still sprouting upwards.

He had his father's steely blue eyes, not his mother's warm amber. He had his build too, stocky, with a neck that almost disappeared into his broad shoulders. And he wanted to be just like his father: feared and respected.

The large double doors opened again and the slim figure of Mabel Kelly stumbled in with as much grace as a drunken ballerina. The woman crabbed her way across the room to the cocktail cabinet. She poured herself a large brandy but didn't offer one to Ida. 'I'm going to need this,' she said, holding her glass aloft. 'I knew you'd show your sour face eventually.'

It was obvious that the woman had already been drinking but she knocked the brandy back and poured herself another.

'Where's Kevin? I want to see him,' Ida asserted.

'Ha, you'll be lucky.'

'What's that supposed to mean?' Ida asked.

'Haven't you heard?'

Thomas's hackles rose as Mabel, bleary-eyed, glanced at him. Her lip curled as if Thomas was a bad smell under her nose.

'He's dead,' she blurted and swayed sideways.

'Dead?' Ida parroted.

Thomas didn't believe the woman. She had a cruel streak and this was probably her idea of a laugh.

'Yes, that's what I said, didn't I? He's dead. Shot down... right out there,' Mabel pointed out of the window to the sweeping gravel drive outside.

'Dead?' Ida repeated again. 'Are you sure?'

'Of course, I'm bloody sure! Unless we buried his doppelganger in a grave.'

The colour drained from Ida's face and she stumbled backwards, falling onto a gilt-edged sofa. There she sat silent, shaking her head in disbelief.

'Make yourself at home, why don't you?' Mabel sniped sneeringly.

Thomas found himself once again staring at the huge portrait of his father. He couldn't believe that the man was dead. Not Kevin Kelly, the larger-than-life character who commanded the most revered gang in Liverpool. Surely no one would have the balls to kill him. Feeling numb, he pulled his eyes away from the painting to look at Mabel and asked flatly, 'Who did it?'

Mabel had gulped down yet another drink and was putting ice into her empty glass. 'Jack Garrett. He's dead too,' she answered in a nonchalant manner.

'Who's Jack Garrett? Why did he shoot my father?'

'I don't bloody know. What do you think I am, an encyclopaedia?'

'You must know something!' Thomas pushed.

'Only that his daughter, Georgina Garrett, is some sort of face in London. I've no idea why the man wanted my husband dead and I couldn't give a monkey's.'

Ida rose to her feet. 'You ruthless bitch,' she spat. 'You never loved Kevin. You only ever wanted him for his money.'

'And now I've got it all,' Mabel replied with a sickly grin. She began to chuckle and then her chuckle turned into a high-pitched, hysterical laugh. 'Poor me… I'm the merry widow… A very *rich* merry widow.'

Thomas's stomach knotted and anger burned in his chest. 'SHUT UP!' he growled. 'SHUT THE FUCK UP!'

Ida's eyes widened. 'Thomas,' she exclaimed, sounding surprised that he'd used bad language.

Mabel stopped her wicked laughter and glared disdainfully at him. 'You sound just like your father when he was angry. But I won't be spoken to like that anymore, not in my own house. So go on, get out, the pair of you.'

Ida threw Thomas a look that he knew was a warning to keep his gob closed.

'Thomas didn't mean anything by his outburst, Mabel. He's just found out that his father is dead and he's upset, naturally.'

'Well, you know now so you can both bugger off.'

'But there's things that need discussing.'

'No, I don't think so. I can't think of anything that I want to discuss with you.'

'Yes, Mabel, there is. Money for one. You know that Kevin and I had an arrangement. I've not received any cash for two weeks now and I've rent to pay and I need food in my larder.'

'What's that got to do with me?'

'Well… surely you can organise my payments?'

'Why would I want to do that?'

'Kevin is dead but he still has two children who need feeding.'

'They're not my kids. They're yours. And you'd better make plans to support them because you won't be getting a penny out of me.'

'But it's Kevin's money. His children are entitled.'

Mabel grinned wickedly. 'They're not. Kevin left *everything* to me, and seeing how he made his living, you can't contest anything. Nothing that the man did was legal.

He also never paid a bean in tax, so as far as the courts will be concerned, he had nothing. Which means… you and his little brats get nought. Ta ra.' Mabel waved drunkenly as she pushed her nose into the air and tried to walk haughtily across the room. Her ankle, in her high-heeled slippers, went to one side but she managed to stay on her feet.

Thomas watched in stunned silence. It still hadn't sunk in that the man he looked up to and idolised had been mercilessly gunned down outside his own front door. And who was Jack Garrett? As his mind turned, he saw his mother fly after Mabel.

Ida grabbed the back of Mabel's immaculately waved hair and yanked her backwards. 'You evil tart. You'd see my kids go hungry! Kevin would kill you if he knew!'

Ida released her grip and Mabel spun around, almost toppling over with the effects of the alcohol. The woman had a look of venom in her eyes but it didn't stop his mother from whacking her. She swung her arm and slapped Mabel hard across her face. Already unsteady on her feet, the blow knocked Mabel sideways and she landed in an undignified heap on the floor.

Mabel, looking quite shocked, held her hand over her red, inflamed cheek. 'Get out of my house before I have you thrown out,' she screeched.

Ida glanced over her shoulder at Thomas. 'Come on, we're going.' Then she looked down at Mabel. 'But you haven't seen the last of me, Mabel Kelly. I promise you, my kids will get what they deserve.'

Thomas stomped across the room to stand beside Mabel. He glared down at her, his heart filled with hatred and fury simmering. 'Slag,' he growled and spat in her face.

Mabel wiped off the phlegm with her cuff, her look one of disgust as she glared at him. 'See, just like your father. A nasty piece of work. I hated your precious dad but who's laughing now, eh?'

Thomas had the urge to pull back his booted foot and kick the woman in her overly made-up face but he felt his mother tugging on his coat as she said urged, 'Come on, son. Leave her be. She'll get her comeuppance soon enough.'

He reluctantly stepped away from Mabel and marched out of his father's house. Standing momentarily on the top stair that led down to the driveway, he wondered where his father had lain, dying, bullets in his body, shot by Jack Garrett. He'd always remember that name and that of Georgina Garrett. She must've had something to do with the murder too, he thought bitterly. He'd never forgive them. Never!

Ida Kelly closed the front door, and though the house was no warmer inside than out, she was relieved to be away from her ex-husband's house and back in the familiarity of her own home. Only this home wasn't owned, it was rented. How the hell was she going to keep up the payments? It angered her that she wasn't going to get any of Kevin's money. He should have made provision, at least for the children.

She put the kettle on the stove to boil and then turned to look at her son. He was sitting at the table with his shoulders slumped. A pang of guilt stabbed at her heart. She hadn't considered how hurt Thomas must be feeling. After all, he loved his father, looked up to the man and did everything he could to please him. To discover about Kevin's death in such a cruel fashion must have been painful for the boy.

'Are you all right, our Thomas?' she asked gently, her eyes full of concern.

He shrugged.

'At times like this, you don't have to be the man of the house, you know. You can cry if you want to.'

'Leave off, Mam. I'm not going to cry. I'm too flamin' angry to cry.'

Ida nodded and turned back to the stove. Of course Thomas wouldn't cry. The boy hadn't shed a tear since he'd been three years old and had fallen over and grazed his knee. He'd cried then, until Kevin had warned him to stop or he'd get a good hiding. *Real men don't cry, son*, Kevin had said. And from that day, Thomas never had again.

'Call our baby down for me, love. I suppose we should tell her that her dad is dead.' Ida wasn't worried about breaking the news to Beth. She doubted that there would be much reaction. Beth rarely showed any emotions. She seemed content in her own world.

At Thomas's bidding, Beth came to sit at the table stroking the woollen hair of her rag doll. She smiled at the doll, her head cocked to one side. Ida wished that her daughter would sometimes gaze at her in the same way, but Beth reserved her smiles for her dolls.

'Darling, look at me. I have to tell you something. Something not very nice,' Ida said softly, choosing her words carefully. She crouched beside her daughter and took her small and delicate hand in her own. Beth didn't like to be touched and pulled it away. Ida carried on regardless and, looking deeply into Beth's eyes, she blinked back tears as she said, 'Your father has died. He's gone to heaven to be with the angels so that means you won't be able to see him ever again.'

Beth looked across to Thomas and then back at her mother. She nodded and then jumped down from the chair.

'Do you understand what I'm saying, Beth?'

Again, the girl nodded but remained pan-faced as she asked, 'Can I go back to my room now, please?'

'Yes, our baby, of course you can,' Ida answered, followed by a long and deep sigh.

The kettle on the stove whistled and she heard Beth's door click shut. 'I don't know, Tom. You sister didn't seem upset, but surely she must be. Maybe I didn't get through to her.'

'Nothing touches her, Mam. She's not all there, is she?' Thomas answered and pointed to his head.

'No, she's not. But it's not like she's backward or anything like that. Beth is bright enough. Look how she is with numbers. She can do her sums so quickly, like one of them adding-up machines, and always gets them right.'

'Yeah, she can, and she can read better than me.'

Ida poured boiling water onto twice-used tea leaves in the pot and carried it over to the table. She brought across two cups and saucers and sat opposite her son. As she poured the weak tea, she studied his face. The tautness in his jaw made him look more like a man than a boy and his eyes held a festering anger. She bit down on her bottom lip, worried about how and when her son's temper would manifest itself. He had many of his father's traits, including

Kevin's explosive character, and one day, Ida knew that it would land her boy in deep trouble.

For now, with more pressing worries on her mind, she gratefully sipped her hot tea, nursing the warm cup in her cold hands. There was no milk or sugar to add to the tea and very soon, the tea leaves would be gone too. Her mind raced. The kids still hadn't had anything to eat, and the rent was due on Monday. She was penniless. Kevin had left her without a pot to piss in. Yet she was silently grieving the death of the only man that she'd ever loved. *Her rescuer*, she'd called him, the day they'd met. He'd been her hero. A punter had been roughing her up and Kevin Kelly had swooped in. He'd dragged the lad off her before giving him a good beating.

Ida had stood against the alley wall and watched as Kevin had kicked the lad half to death. Then he'd taken her by the hand and pulled her out the alley and into a nearby club. There, he'd cleaned her wounds and she'd drunk his whisky. As she'd looked over the edge of her glass at her tough and brave hero, she'd instantly fallen in love. She hadn't known that he'd owned the club and several more besides. Or that the punter he'd kicked the shit out of owed him money. And neither had she known that he was Liverpool's biggest gangster who would turn out to be a right nasty bastard. Yet, no matter how many women he took to his bed, or how many times he'd given her a slap, she had never stopped loving the man.

The pent-up sorrow that she'd held in began to spill out. A tear slipped from her eye and then another.

'Don't cry, Mam,' Thomas said. 'I'll look after us, I promise.'

Ida dabbed at her wet cheeks. 'I know you will, darling,' she sniffed. But deep down, she already knew what she'd have to do. In order to keep a roof over their heads and food in her children's bellies, Ida Kelly would have to go back on the game.

4

A week later, his first day back at school since his father's death, Thomas sat behind a wooden desk at the back of the class. His eyes bored into the rear of Eugene's head. He could feel his cheek twitching with anger at the thought of Eugene Hawkins terrorising his little sister. It had been just before his dad had been killed. Thomas had seen Beth in the schoolyard, standing forlornly and trying desperately to put the head back on one of her dolls. The other was on the ground and by the look of the dirty shoe print on the doll's face, someone had stood on it. Beth never spoke or even looked up at him but he could tell that she was deeply distressed.

Thomas had demanded to know who had done this to her dolls and she'd pointed at Eugene. He would have gone over right there and then and smashed in Eugene's face but he had to look after his sister and get her home.

The bell rang, signifying lunchtime, snapping Thomas from his recollections of that day. He watched as Eugene packed away his books and then ambled out of the room. Thomas followed.

In the school corridor, kids were piling out from other classrooms. Teachers were yelling, ordering them to stop running. Thomas kept his narrowed eyes on Eugene.

Outside, in the schoolyard, Eugene met up with his mates. Thomas thought they were a right bunch of posh nancy boys. Eugene's father was a local councillor and good friends with the headmaster. But Thomas knew that Eugene's father had been on his dad's payroll. Most of the Old Bill had been too.

Eugene sauntered towards the school gate, laughing and joking with his prissy pals. Thomas seethed. His fingers curled around the handle of the knife in his coat pocket.

Yards away from the gate, as if sensing that someone was watching him, Eugene turned around and stopped when his eyes fell on Thomas. His mates stopped walking too and checked to see who or what Eugene was looking at. When they saw it was Thomas, they nudged each other and mumbled amongst themselves. The tension felt thick. Everyone seemed to sense that there was going to be a confrontation.

Eugene stuffed his hands into his trouser pockets and stood with his hip poked out to one side. His relaxed shoulders and easy manner irked Thomas. Eugene showed no fear of him, or any remorse for what he'd done to Beth. That was about to change. His father wasn't around anymore so it was down to him to show the likes of Eugene Hawkins that they couldn't mess with his family.

'Shouldn't you be babysitting your dunce sister?' Eugene asked spitefully. 'Or is she busy playing with her dolls?'

Thomas saw red. His feet pounded across the yard towards Eugene, his fists flaying as rage engulfed him. He wasn't sure if Eugene had hit him back or not. If he had, Thomas felt no pain. But somehow Eugene managed to get his arms around Thomas's torso and the pair wrestled until he felt himself falling to the ground. The weight of Eugene landing on top of him winded Thomas, and then he felt a sharp pain in his ribs as Eugene punched him.

'I'll have you,' he seethed, and reaching into his coat pocket, he felt the handle of his knife.

As he went to pull it out, Eugene suddenly jumped off and Thomas peered up to see the headmaster standing over him. The man was tall and thin, his long, pale face reflecting his annoyance.

'Get up!' Mr Graves barked.

Thomas, thankful that the knife was still in his pocket, pushed himself to his feet. Mr Graves grabbed him by the top of his ear and twisted it sadistically, which caused Thomas to wince in pain.

'Fighting again, Thomas Kelly. You'll be expelled from school this time, especially now that you haven't got your father to fight your battles.'

'Get off me,' Thomas yelled.

When Mr Graves attempted to drag Thomas by the ear back towards the school building, Thomas swung his arm round and his swift fist landed in Mr Graves's groin. The blow caused the man to release his grip of Thomas's ear and double over in pain.

Thomas's ear throbbed. He swung out again, this time catching the side of Mr Graves's head. The headmaster remained on his feet but was still bent forward with his hands protectively clutching his man parts. 'You are expelled from this school indefinitely!' he barked.

'Good,' Thomas spat. 'I'm never coming back to this shithole again. You were all scared of my father, the lot of you. And I'll make sure that you'll all be scared of me too.'

He glanced around. A crowd had gathered. Stunned faces stared back at him. He spotted Eugene.

'I'll be coming for you first,' he warned and wagged his finger at him. 'Watch your back 'cos I swear I'm going to rip your head off and shove it up your posh backside.'

Thomas walked out of the school with his shoulders pushed back and his chin jutting forward. He was no longer a schoolboy. He was a man now. And he'd do whatever it took to look after his mother and little sister, just as his father would have expected from him.

Half an hour later, the gravel on his father's drive crunched under his feet as Thomas marched up to the front door. Full of confidence, he hammered on it until the nervous-looking elderly housekeeper answered. Without saying a word, he walked past her and into the big front room where the throne chairs were and the oversized portrait of his dad. Thomas immediately noticed that the painting was gone. He heard the doors bang close behind him and turned to see Morris Palmer standing there with Mabel beside him.

'What are you doing here?' Morris asked, his voice gravelly.

The giant of a man had worked for Thomas's dad. He'd been Kevin Kelly's right-hand man. He guessed that Morris had probably taken over the business and was now the guvnor of the Portland Pounders. Thomas cleared his throat. His bravado had vanished and he suddenly felt very small in the presence of the massive man. 'I've come for a job.'

Morris laughed as he walked towards him. He took a

puff on his cigar and blew the smoke directly into Thomas's face. Thomas leaned back and turned his head away. Meanwhile, out of the corner of his eye, he saw Mabel was at the cocktail cabinet and pouring two glasses of brandy.

'You've come for a job. What sort of job? My shoe shiner? Or perhaps you'd prefer to be on the docks, a bum boy for the perves?'

Thomas felt disgusted at the suggestions and spat, 'No way. I'm Kevin Kelly's son. I know how the business works and I want a part of it.' He pushed his chest out, trying to regain his bravado, but inside he was shaking.

'Fuck off, you silly cunt. You're only just out of short trousers. *A part of the business*,' Morris guffawed. 'Did you hear that, Mabel? The lad wants to be a part of the business.'

'Yes, I heard. I suppose your mother sent you here to beg?'

'No, she didn't, and I'm not begging. I just want what's rightfully mine.'

Morris jabbed Thomas firmly in the chest with his fat sausage finger and his bushy eyebrows knitted together. 'You listen to me, *boy*, good and hard. Your father's dead so I'm the boss now. You've got his name but you're getting fuck all else. Is that clear?'

Thomas wasn't ready to give up and said, 'I'm not asking for money for nought. I'm prepared to work hard. I'll graft.'

Morris poked him in the chest again, harder this time. 'Piss off out of my house and don't show your ugly mug round here again or you'll end up buried in the same grave as your sicko father. Now, is that fucking clearer for you?'

Thomas could see that Morris wasn't talking in jest. He

meant every word. The man's threat was real and he had no doubt that Morris would carry it through. Thomas felt his throat constricting with fear. Unable to utter a word, he nodded.

'Right, you little prick. Now you know the score so FUCK OFF,' Morris growled.

Thomas didn't wait to be told twice and dashed past the mountain of a man. After anxiously fumbling with the doorknob, he hurried out. But not before hearing Morris spit, 'What a piss-taking prick. I bet he ends up taking after his depraved father.'

Any dreams that Thomas had of working in his dad's business were dashed, but away from Morris now, his anger mounted. He was Kevin Kelly's son, but he'd been made to look weak, a fool. He scowled, determined that one day he'd make Morris Palmer eat his words. His dad would never have stood for this. And if his dad was watching over him from beyond the grave, then Thomas was hell-bent on making him proud.

His father's words rang in his head. *The bigger they are, the harder they fall.* That's what his dad had always said. And once he'd shown Morris Palmer who the *real* boss was, he'd get his revenge on that Georgina Garrett bitch too.

Ida peered at her reflection in the mirror. At thirty-two, she wasn't too old to pull in the punters and she'd kept a tidy figure after birthing two kids. But the shame of it! She lived in a respectable street with neighbours who had decent jobs. The thought of going back to work in the labyrinth of Liverpool's run-down slum areas left her feeling sick inside.

She dreaded the notion of rotten, stinking men pawing at her body, yet she had no other option. She'd managed to avoid the rent man thus far and Thomas had pinched a loaf of bread and some veg, but they couldn't continue to live hand to mouth like this. A second visit to Mabel had proved fruitless so now Ida resigned herself to selling herself for sex.

She heard the front door slam shut and went to the top of the stairs, calling down, 'Is that you, our Thomas?'

'Yes, Mam.'

Ida dashed down the stairs and found her son in the kitchen, peering at the empty larder. 'What are you doing home? You should be at school.'

'I'm not going back there.'

'But you must, son. An education is important if you want to get on in life.'

'My father wasn't educated and he did all right.'

'Your father's work wasn't legit – you know that. You're not going to follow in his footsteps. I won't have it. Don't you want better for yourself?'

Thomas turned from the larder and Ida was shocked to see his face twisted in anger. She'd seen that same look on Kevin's face many times.

'You never complained about what my dad did for a living all the while you were getting his money,' Thomas growled accusingly. 'And don't you ever bad-mouth my father again.'

Ida didn't like her son's tone, and began to fear her hold over him. Nevertheless, her voice hard, she said, 'Don't you dare talk to me like that, Thomas Kelly. You're getting a bit too big for your boots lately.'

'I'll talk as I see fit, Mam. Let's face it, you're not going to earn any money; it's going to be down to me. So, that's it. I'm not going back to school. I'll go out and graft or else we'll all flippin' starve to death.'

Before Ida could say anything, Thomas marched out of the kitchen and into the front room. She quickly followed, determined to talk him round and persuade him to finish his education. But as she went to voice her argument, they heard a heavy knocking on the front door. 'Oh no, that'll be the rent man. Quick, duck behind the sofa,' she whispered urgently.

Ida crouched behind the sofa and ushered her son towards her. But Thomas remained stood where he was, peering out through the net curtains that covered the bay window.

'Thomas… come here… he'll see you.'

She heard the rent man's voice on the other side of the front door. 'I know you're in there, Mrs Kelly. Open up.'

'I'm not having this. I'll tell him to sling his hook,' Thomas seethed.

To Ida's horror, she saw her son walk into the passageway and then heard him opening the front door.

Ida stood up and sloped into the passageway, her mind racing as she tried to come up with an excuse for not paying the rent and arrears.

'Ah, young Thomas. Where's your mother?'

'Get lost.'

'I don't think so,' the collector said. 'Step aside.'

'I told you to get lost.'

'Let him in, Thomas,' Ida ordered sharply.

The man stepped over the doorstep with Thomas glaring ominously at him. He walked into the small passageway and came face to face with Ida. The weedy-looking rent collector with greasy, lank black hair and beady eyes, ran his tongue over his thin lips and leered at her. As his eyes roamed over her from head to toe, Ida's stomach turned.

'Mrs Kelly, always a pleasure to see you,' Mr Raynor drooled.

'Come back at the end of the week and I'll have the money I owe you. Now, if you don't mind, I'm rather busy. Good day to you.' Ida spun on her heel and went to walk away from the man but he called after her.

'I'm afraid the end of the week will be too late. You'll be evicted by then if you don't pay your arrears.'

Ida turned briskly back to face him. 'We've lived in this house for years and never once been late with the rent. Doesn't that count for anything?'

'But circumstances have changed, Mrs Kelly. I know it was your late ex-husband who paid the rent and now it's apparent that you can't afford it without him. So, tell me, how are you going to find the means to meet the payments?'

'I'll pay it. That's all you need to know.'

The rent man peered over his shoulder at Thomas and then stepped closer to Ida. His voice was barely more than a whisper when he leaned towards her and said, 'We could come to another arrangement. You could pay off some of your debt to me in *another* way. Get rid of the boy. What do you say?'

Ida's immediate thought was to tell the horrid man to *sod off*, in no uncertain terms! She felt insulted that he'd even suggested such a thing. But then the reality of her situation hit her like a steam train. She had no means to pay the debt and she'd already decided that she'd have to whore herself to support her family. Opening her legs to this weasel would be no different than selling her body on the streets. She hated herself for doing it but said to Thomas, 'Go and meet our baby from school.'

'But school isn't finished for hours yet,' Thomas protested.

'Well hang about until it is,' she ordered, tight-lipped and glaring at him. 'I have things to discuss with Mr Raynor.'

Thomas huffed. 'I'm not a kid, Mam. I should be included in any discussions.'

'Just do as you're told, Thomas,' Ida barked.

Thankfully, her son didn't defy her and slammed the front door as he left.

Mr Raynor stepped towards her. 'Now then,' he said, 'we can clear a week's rent in half an hour.'

Ida's stomach turned in disgust. She wanted to cry but she knew what she had to do. 'Put the bolt across the door,' she instructed, but determined not to have the man in her pristine front room on her sofas, or in her bed, she walked through to the kitchen.

Once there, Ida turned to face Mr Raynor. She lifted her skirt up to her thighs and over her stockings.

Mr Raynor, with his eyes fixed firmly on the tops of her legs, quickly undid his trousers and let them slide to around his ankles. 'Suck it,' he ordered.

Ida lowered herself to her knees to take his flaccid penis in her mouth. A foul body odour emanated from between his legs and she had to fight back the bile that rose in her throat. As her lips moved back and forward over his manhood, Mr Raynor groaned in pleasure. Ida felt sick to her stomach and silently cursed Kevin for leaving them nothing and making her sink so low. She could only hope that Mr Raynor would finish quickly and her vile ordeal would be over soon.

Thomas steamed down the street with his arms swinging. He hated that his mother treated him like a child. He was the man of the house and it was about time that he was shown some respect instead of being dismissed to babysit his sister.

He considered how his father would expect him to behave, soon coming to the conclusion that his dad would want him to take charge. *I'm not having this*, he thought, and turned back towards the house. When he got to the front door and tried to push it open, he realised it was locked. Thomas couldn't fathom why his mother would bolt the door in the middle of the day. He hurried down a narrow alley by the side of the house, through the garden gate, past the privy and straight up to the back door. Flinging it open, he gasped at the sight that met him.

His mother was leaning over the kitchen table with her skirt hitched up to her waist and Mr Raynor was behind her. His spotty, white bum was moving back and forth rapidly as he pumped himself in and out of Thomas's mother. Neither of them had appeared to notice that he had walked in and was gaping at the scene with disgust.

Thomas reached inside his coat pocket and pulled out the knife that he'd intended to use on Eugene. In four swift steps, he was standing directly behind Mr Raynor. He raised his arm, then promptly brought the knife down, thrusting it hard into Mr Raynor's back. As Thomas pulled it out, blood spluttered across his face. Mr Raynor cried out and slumped forward on top of his mother. Thomas plunged the knife into the man again, noticing the squelching noise it made as it sliced through his flesh.

Mr Raynor tried to stand up and turn around but instead he fell face first to the floor with the knife protruding from his slain body.

His mother stood up and spun round. Her hands flew to her mouth as she took in the sight of Mr Raynor lying dead on the floor and Thomas covered in the man's blood.

'He won't touch you again, Mam,' Thomas said, his chest puffed out with pride.

'Oh, son… What have you done?'

'Stopped the filthy bastard, that's what.'

'But, Thomas, they'll hang you for this!'

Thomas swallowed hard. He hadn't thought about the consequences.

'We've got to get rid of him,' his mother said with urgency.

Blood was seeping from the knife wound and dripping onto the floor, pooling around the rent man's chest.

'I'll dump him in the canal.'

'No, Thomas, you could be seen. You can't take his body out of this house. Christ, you stupid boy!' his mother cried, panic in her voice.

'It's all right, Mam, I'll work something out.'

'How? How exactly are you going to do that? There's a dead man lying on my kitchen floor with a knife in his back. The police will have the bloody pair of us for this. We'll both be swinging on the end of a rope. And then what will happen to our Beth?'

Thomas's mind raced but he had no answers, and instead of pride, he was now full of fear.

'Go and get your sister from school. Don't stop and talk to anyone. Straight there and back, do you hear me?'

'No, Mam. We've got to clean this up first. Beth can't come home to see this!'

'Bring her home and take her up to her room. I'll pack bags for us while you're gone. We'll have to go, Thomas. We'll have to run away. We can't stay here.'

'But—'

'Now, Thomas. Go. We've got to get away before anyone starts looking for him. The sooner we're out of Liverpool, the better.'

'Where are we going?'

'I don't know yet. But there's no time to waste. I'm not having your neck breaking as you swing from the gallows. Get your sister. We'll work it out as we go along.'

Thomas could see the seriousness in his mother's eyes and knew that they had no other choice. After all, he'd killed a man in cold blood. A man who was an upstanding member of the community. Yet as Thomas watched Mr Raynor's blood ooze from his lifeless body, he felt no remorse for his act of murder. He didn't feel bad about taking Mr Raynor's life. In fact, he couldn't feel anything except for the fear of getting caught.

As he headed towards the front door, his mother called after him.

'Thomas. Wait. What's wrong with me, I'm not thinking straight. You can't go out looking like that. Wash your face and leave your coat off.'

Thomas stopped and held his hands in front of him. It was then that he realised he was covered in blood. He went back to the kitchen and stepped over Mr Raynor's body to get to the sink. As he washed his hands and wiped his face, the cold water in the bowl turned pink.

While he dried his hands, his mother went upstairs to pack their clothes. For a moment, he gazed at Mr Raynor's body and an idea came to him. The man would have money on him, money that they needed. He gave the bloke a light kick and then rolled his body over. As he rifled through the man's pockets, his dad's words came into his mind: *You should never take the life of a man lightly, son. But if anyone ever hurts you or yours, kill 'em. Kill 'em and never regret it.*

5

They had been living in Bristol for four weeks now. Ida was feeling more confident that the police wouldn't catch up with them, but she still kept an eye over her shoulder. She had initially been horrified that her son had killed Mr Raynor, yet had come to realise that he'd acted instinctively to protect her. Kevin Kelly would have killed the man too and Thomas was becoming more and more like his father.

She was grateful that Thomas had taken the initiative to steal Mr Raynor's money before they'd fled. Ida wouldn't have thought to do that and was glad of her son's ability to think on his feet. The cash had set them up in a couple of rooms in a large, shared house. Ida and Beth bedded down in one room, Thomas in the other. The kitchen was used by all the tenants and the outside privy was shared between two houses. It was a big step down from the substantial house that Kevin had rented for them, and the area wasn't nearly as affluent as their old neighbourhood. In fact, Ida thought that the streets weren't much better than the slums. But it would have to do for now.

'I'm going out for a while, pet,' she told Beth, knowing

her daughter would never attempt to leave the room. 'Sit tight, our baby. I'll be back soon.'

Beth didn't raise her head from a game with her dolls. Ida worried about her daughter. The move from Liverpool to Bristol had unsettled the girl. Beth didn't like change and smiled even less these days. Ida had considered putting her into school but Thomas had talked her out of the idea. He'd said that it would be too much for Beth, especially as he wouldn't be there to watch over her. Her son had grown up quickly and had a wise head on his young shoulders. He talked a lot of sense so Ida had agreed with him. Anyway, what good would schooling do for Beth? The girl could already read, write and count in a way that was well beyond her years. So, Ida kept Beth at home with her, but the situation wasn't ideal. It meant that Ida had to take her customers into Thomas's room but, thankfully, her son was out all day and oblivious to what she was doing. The last thing that she needed was a repeat of what had happened with Mr Raynor!

Ida pulled her coat around her thin frame. The biting December wind chilled her down to her bones. She wasn't looking forward to being out on the streets in this weather to tout for business. With a heavy heart and cold feet, Ida hoped she'd find a customer soon. She could probably earn more touting during the hours of darkness, but there was no way she'd be able to hide what she was doing from Thomas, and she dreaded to think how he'd react if he found out.

Stopping outside a pub, Ida looked up and down the street. This seemed to be as good a place as any and she couldn't see any competition nearby. She'd soon learned the places to avoid, where whores and pimps had threatened her.

Ida stamped her frozen feet in a bid to get some feeling back into her numb toes. *Come on*, she thought, her teeth chattering as she hoped for custom soon. The door of the pub opened and two men came out. They ignored Ida's offer of a good time. So did the third man and then the fourth man gobbed on the ground in front of her feet. Ida was becoming weary and disheartened. But she wouldn't give up yet. She couldn't. She needed the money. Granted, Thomas was bringing in a few bob and pinching grub for them, but he didn't earn enough to cover all the rent and bills. She knew her son was up to no good and earned his money through illicit means, but Ida didn't ask him any questions. They needed his earnings and she'd readily accept cash from wherever it came.

The door opened again and Ida jumped forward to stand in front of the middle-aged fella. She fluttered her eyelashes and cocked her head to one side. 'Fancy a bit of fun, mate?' she purred.

Expecting to be declined, she was thrilled when the bloke said yes. He wasn't much to look at, but at least he looked clean. He had a good build on him without a big beer gut. She'd picked up a lot worse in the past few weeks!

'Yeah, all right, but not in the open,' the man said.

'Come back to mine then. It'll cost you ten shillings, but I promise you, my darling, it'll be the best ten shillings you've ever spent.'

The man shrugged. He didn't look impressed. Ida grabbed his hand and pulled him along the street before he had a chance to change his mind.

'Here we are,' she said, opening the front door. 'In here.' Ida led him through to Thomas's bedroom and gently closed the door behind them.

The man smirked and walked towards her. He shoved her hard and she fell backwards onto the bed. Ida's heart sunk. She could tell that this fella liked it rough. She knew his sort. He'd slap her about, rough her up, and he'd get a kick out of hurting her.

'I want payment in advance,' she stated.

The man fished in his trouser pocket and threw some coins onto the windowsill. 'There's an extra couple of bob there but I'll expect you to make it worth my while.'

Ida smiled at the man but was cringing inside. 'You won't be disappointed,' she husked and pulled her dress up to her waist.

As the man lurched forward, his dark eyes veiled with menace, the bedroom door opened and Ida leapt to her feet. Oh God, she thought, Thomas! She jumped in front of the man, sure that her son would attack her customer. To her great relief, she saw Beth standing in the doorway and holding her favourite doll close to her chest.

'Go back to your room, our baby. Mammy will be in soon.'

Beth nodded and ambled away. Ida closed the door behind her and leaned against it for a minute to calm her racing heart. Thank goodness it hadn't been Thomas come home early!

The man stepped closer and shoved his hand up her dress, grabbing her roughly between the legs as he husked in her ear, 'I'll give you a guinea for half an hour with the girl.'

Ida was mortified and furiously shook her head. 'She's not for sale.'

'Two guineas, and that's paying well over the odds.'

'No, sir, I've told you, she is *not* for sale,' Ida repeated firmly. She could feel her heart pounding hard in her chest and her mouth felt so dry that her teeth stuck to her lips. She'd seen that the man was sinister but she hadn't expected this. Fear coursed through her veins. She wanted him out of the house and, trying to keep her voice steady, she said, 'I think you should leave now.'

The man took his hand from under her dress but Ida's relief was short-lived when she felt him grip her throat. He pushed his body up against hers, squashing her against the door and leaving her unable to move. His large hand around her neck got tighter until she could feel herself struggling to breathe.

'Please…' she managed to croak as she clawed at his hand.

Ida's pleas were ignored and the man squeezed tighter. She could feel her windpipe being crushed and her lungs ached for air. She stared into his eyes, terrified to see the sickening look of pleasure that he was taking in strangling her.

'Can't… breathe…' she croaked.

The man's fingernails were cutting into her skin as his hand crushed the life out of her. Ida could feel her eyes bulging. She tried to gasp in air. Her chest burned. The room was fading. Death was upon her and Ida's last thought was of Beth.

★

Thomas handed over the package wrapped in brown paper in exchange for an envelope of money. He flicked through the bank notes, quickly counting them.

'It's all there,' the pub landlord said.

Thomas ignored him and carried on counting. Once he was satisfied that the payment was correct, he loosely saluted his flat cap and headed back to town.

It hadn't taken Thomas long to find his feet in Bristol and now he was running drugs for one of the hardest gangs in the area. Thomas smiled to himself. The Slashers, as they'd named themselves, weren't the brightest of criminals and not nearly half as hard as they liked to think they were. Thomas had no respect for their small-time operations and his boss was nothing more than a jumped-up thug. The Slashers thought that they were big-time gangsters, but they were nothing compared to Kevin Kelly and the Portland Pounders. They'd chosen their gang name because of their reputation for slashing the cheeks of their adversaries. But from what Thomas had heard, only one lad had ever had his face sliced and it had been his boss, Roland, who had nicked the lad's cheek with his penknife.

It hadn't installed fear in Thomas. Far from it. In fact, he found it laughable. But for now, he needed the money for his mam so he was happy to work for Roland Harris. In the future, he planned to take over. To be the boss. Just like his father had been. And when that happened, he'd make sure the Slashers became bigger and better than the Pounders. For now though, Thomas would bide his time, but when that day came, he'd be giving Morris Palmer a run for his money. He'd see to it that the man suffered for belittling him and taking over his father's business.

'There'd better not be any money missing,' Roland warned as he snatched the envelope from Thomas.

'It's all there. I checked.'

Roland handed Thomas his small cut and then stuffed the money into his pocket. 'I've got another job for you tomorrow. A bloke owes me. I want you to do a job on his shop. Smash it up. Donny will be with you. Do you reckon you can handle it?'

Thomas knew that his boss underestimated him. Roland Harris had no idea that he had stabbed a man to death. Trashing a shop would be a walk in the park. 'Yeah, of course I can handle it,' he answered with confidence.

'Good. Come tooled up. The man's not a big bloke but his missus is the size of the fucking iceberg that sunk the *Titanic*. You ain't worried about knocking out a woman, are you?'

'I'll do whatever it takes,' Thomas replied. He didn't give a shit about hitting women. He'd have liked to have kicked in Mabel's head and would have if his mother hadn't of stopped him. He'd seen his dad knock women about. Thomas hadn't liked to see his mam get a hiding but his dad had told him that a woman needed a slap to keep her in line and be reminded of her place. Thomas supposed it made sense but he hadn't hit a woman yet. Though if this fat slag in the shop got in the way of him putting the frighteners on her husband, then Thomas wouldn't give a second thought to putting her on her flabby arse.

'Don't be late,' Roland warned as Thomas sauntered off.

When he reached home, he was surprised to find the street door wide open and frowned. But with at least three families living in the house, people were always in and out.

He went straight through to the shared kitchen and poured himself a glass of water. There were no pots simmering on the stove, so Thomas assumed that his mother was going to feed them jam sandwiches again.

He went to his room and pushed the door but it didn't open fully. Something was blocking it. Thomas's hackles rose. Someone must have been in his room, but there was nothing in there worth nicking. He wasn't stupid enough to leave behind any money, or his knife.

He gave the door a good shove and forced his way in. What Thomas found behind the door was an image that would haunt him for the rest of his life.

He fell to his knees beside his mother's lifeless body, then placed his ear to her face and listened for sounds of her breathing. There was nothing and his stomach churned as he looked at her chest to see if it would rise and fall. Though he didn't want to accept it, Thomas already knew that his mother was dead. He could tell from the grey pallor of her skin and blue tinge to her lips.

Vomit rose and burned his throat. He jumped to his feet and ran to the window where he opened it just in time to throw up his guts outside. Then, as he wiped the back of his hand across his mouth, he walked gingerly back to his mother. It was then that he noticed the bruising around her delicate neck. This had been no accident. His mother hadn't just dropped dead from something like a heart attack. Someone had slaughtered her and looking at the disarray of her skirt and underwear, Thomas thought that his mother had probably been raped too.

He thought of his sister and ran to the room next door, hoping that Beth was oblivious to the horror in his room.

He charged through the door but stopped dead when he saw his sister's half-dressed and motionless body, naked from the waist down and spread-eagled on her bed.

A sob caught in Thomas's throat. His legs felt weak and he collapsed to the floor, holding his face in his hands. An agonising ache gripped him, pain burned in his chest, his heart was breaking, but no tears fell. Thomas was a man. He wouldn't bawl like a baby. He had to be strong. It's what his father would have expected of him.

After giving himself some time to pull himself together, he then he rose to his feet, standing ramrod straight. He was alone now in this cold and wicked world. No powerful father. No dear mother. And no sweet sister. His eyes narrowed. He'd kill the man who had taken the lives of his beloved mother and innocent Beth, though he had to find him first. With no idea where to start, he feared that he'd never discover who was behind it and his teeth ground with frustrated anger. Unable to bring himself to look at his sister any longer, Thomas marched out of the house and vowed that he'd never look back. He wouldn't allow his sorrow to destroy him. If anything, it would drive to make him stronger – just like his beloved dad.

A determination engulfed him. He knew that he'd be living on his wits, but he would work hard and rise up the ranks. He'd make himself a reputation, one that would be so feared that no one would ever dare to cross him. Thomas Kelly had a plan. Things were going to change. He wouldn't allow anyone to stand in his way. Not Morris Palmer or Georgina Garrett and especially not his boss, Roland Harris.

★

Half an hour later, Thomas found Roland in an abandoned railway carriage that he used as his meeting place. As usual, Roland had Titch on one side and Walter on the other. Both men were big, but slow, and Thomas suspected that once they saw what he was going to do to Roland, they'd run for their lives.

Roland looked over the top of his hand of playing cards but didn't acknowledge Thomas, though his disdain was clear to see.

Thomas sauntered over to the upturned crate that they were playing cards on. He gripped the knife tightly that he held behind his back. Titch didn't lift his eyes. Walter looked at him blankly, while Roland threw a card on the crate and picked up another. None of them suspected what was coming.

Before Titch or Walter could react, Thomas lifted his knife and slammed into the back of Roland's neck. The man's eyes widened in shock, and then Thomas plunged the knife into him again. Titch and Walter leapt to their feet. Both appeared to think about jumping Thomas but seeing the maniacal look on his face, they stared at him for a moment, terrified, before turning to run out of the carriage.

Roland Harris was now face down on the crate with blood pumping from the back of his neck. Thomas stood over his body, breathing fast after the sudden burst of adrenaline, and triumphant at the sight of his dead boss. He thought of his mother and dear sister, abused and murdered. Anger, pain and grief consumed his soul. 'Argh,' he screamed as he stabbed the knife into Roland's back. Over and over, he plunged the knife in and out until the man's spine was exposed.

Spent, he slumped onto the seat where Titch had sat. A shadow was cast in front of him and he looked up to see Titch and Walter standing in the doorway of the carriage. 'I run this place now,' he mumbled in between inhaling large lungfuls of air. 'I'm the boss. Right?'

'Right,' the men agreed.

'And this is why we're called the Slashers.' Thomas thumbed towards Roland's maimed body. He'd proven himself and earned the fear and respect of Titch and Walter. But he wanted more. So much more. And one day, just like his father, he'd have it all.

6

Present Day

1949. London, Battersea.

'Kevin Kelly's son… You're Kevin Kelly's son,' David stated.

'That's right, I am. Well done, Maynard, I knew that you'd work it out eventually. I'm Thomas Kelly. Pleased to meet you.'

The back of David's neck felt as though it was on fire. He knew that his skin had blistered. The burn from the red-hot poker had seared deeply, the sting agonising. He tried to focus on what Thomas was saying but was finding it difficult to concentrate on anything other than the intense pain in his neck, head, nose and hand. 'But I thought that Morris Palmer headed up the Portland Pounders,' he muttered.

'He does.'

'I've always had an understanding with the Pounders. We choose to stay away from each other. So what's all this about?' David asked.

Thomas sat back at the table. He rubbed his clean-shaven

chin as he spoke. 'Things have changed. I want my rightful place. The Pounders should be mine.'

'What's that got to do with me?'

'When I take over your business, Morris Palmer won't be in a position to touch me. I'll destroy him and take from him everything that was once my father's.'

'And Georgina?'

'Her father killed mine.'

'But that wasn't her fault.'

'She must have ordered it.'

'She didn't. She had no idea that Jack Garrett had travelled to Liverpool.'

To David's surprise, Kelly picked up the spanner from the table, sprung to his feet and steamed across the room. David knew what was coming but was powerless to stop it. He closed his eyes and waited to feel the blow from the tool.

When nothing came, he slowly opened his eyes again. Thomas Kelly was standing in front of him, his face contorted in anger.

'I was going to smash your teeth out but I quite like having a conversation with you. But if you defend that slag again, I swear, I'll knock every fucking tooth out of your head and then I'll have your gob sewn up.'

David swallowed hard and could taste the blood in his saliva. He'd already been battered and mutilated but now at least he knew who he was dealing with. Kelly had shown his hand. The man wanted payback for the death of his father by killing Georgina. And he also intended to kill him and take over his business. David couldn't see a way out but he wouldn't die quietly. 'Your father *raped* Georgina,' he seethed.

'Shut up. Shut the fuck up,' Thomas Kelly yelled. 'You don't know what you're talking about!'

'Yes, I do, and I'm telling the truth whether you want to hear it or not. Your father had Georgina's husband killed. Lash was gunned down in the street for no reason, and at the time, he was holding his young son's hand. Your father then raped Georgina in the church during Lash's funeral. That's the sort of sick, twisted bastard he was.'

Thomas glared down at David with blazing eyes. His chest expanded and his hand gripped the spanner tightly. 'I said, SHUT THE FUCK UP!'

Despite the pain he was in, David smirked. He could see that he was hitting Kelly where it hurt. The man had probably idolised his father but now he was learning a few home truths. He thought that seeing Thomas Kelly's horrified shock might well be his last pleasure in life. Now he would tell him more about the bastard who had fathered him. 'Kevin Kelly was a rapist and he trafficked kids for sex. He was behind hundreds of children as young as two and three being stolen and sold to kiddie fiddlers. They were abused and passed on until they died from heinous injuries. You must be so proud to be his son.'

'You're a liar!'

'I'm a lot of things, but I ain't a fucking liar. If you don't believe me, ask Morris Palmer. He'll tell you the same. Morris never liked what your father did, and after he was killed, Morris put a stop to it. Kevin Kelly was a filthy bastard and deserved to die,' David goaded. He tensed, expecting the man's fury to be unleashed upon him and hoped that now at least, death would come quickly.

★

Georgina's heart was racing and thoughts were firing through her mind. Who were these men and where was David? She really didn't want to leave Charlotte alone but the girl had insisted. And although Georgina would have stayed with Charlotte, she was quietly pleased that she'd been asked to leave. She had to find David!

'What now?' Johnny asked as he started the car.

'They seem to be one step ahead of me and they clearly know what pies I've had my fingers in, though I shouldn't think they'll have any idea about Mary's Marvels. Drop me there, go and fetch Benjamin and then gather as many of the blokes as you can. I'll have a plan by then.'

Johnny drove round to the back of Mary's Marvels, a second-hand clothes and furniture shop in Tooting Broadway. A few years earlier, Georgina had gifted to Mary the initial set-up fees for the shop and now her old life-long next-door neighbour turned a modest profit. She lived in the flat above with her husband. Georgina knew that she could trust Mary. The woman had proven it when Georgina had escaped from Holloway prison. Mary had willingly helped her evade capture and Mary's husband had even constructed a getaway route between their houses.

'I'll come in with you and make sure that everything is all right,' Johnny offered.

'No, it'll be fine. No one knows about this place. It's Mary's, not mine. Just bring Benjamin and the blokes here as quick as you can. And get Ned to bring Charlotte here too,' Georgina urged. Placing her hand on Johnny's arm, she gently warned, 'Be careful. Make sure you're not followed.'

As Johnny sped off, Georgina knocked on the back door and when it opened, Mary looked delighted to see her. 'By Jesus Christ, Mary mother of Jesus, you're a sight for sore eyes, so you are. Aw, it's so good to see you, child. Come in, come in.'

'It's good to see you too, but close the shop,' Georgina said. 'We need to talk.'

Mary tutted. 'Lord above and all the saints in heaven, you're in trouble, gal, aren't you?'

Georgina nodded. 'Yes, Mary, of the worst kind.'

'Sit in my kitchen while I close up.'

Georgina walked through to the tiny kitchenette that adjoined the storeroom. There was no room for a table, just two sagging but comfy-looking easy chairs, a sink, a cupboard and a little stove with a kettle on top. She filled the kettle and put it on the gas to boil.

'So, what's wrong?' Mary asked as she bustled into the room.

Georgina turned to look at the kind face of the red-haired Irishwoman whom she'd known since her childhood, and had to fight to hold back tears. 'Oh, Mary,' she said, 'where do I begin?'

Mary urged her to sit on one of the chairs and handed her a handkerchief. 'At the beginning,' she said. 'Start at the beginning.'

Georgina related everything to Mary and openly cried as she told the older woman about Charlotte losing the baby and how cruel it had been. 'It's all my fault. I swear, Mary, I attract death. From as far back as I can remember, death has followed me… My mother died giving birth to me… My gran's husband, Percy, was buried in a barrel in our backyard and even Ruby, the lady who once looked after me, she threw herself into the Thames. And all that before I'd even started school.'

'Now, now, pet, don't go getting yourself all maudlin. It wasn't your fault that your mother died. And that's nonsense about Percy. The man was a drinker and went off one day and never came home.'

Georgina shook her head. 'No, me gran told me what really happened and now that she's no longer with us, it's safe to tell the truth. Percy treated her badly, and one day she just snapped. She picked up her frying pan and caved his head in. Then her and Ruby put him in a barrel and buried him in the bit of ground next to the coal bunker.'

Mary crossed her chest and smiled through her astonishment. 'Ha, Dulcie was a fierce woman, God rest her soul. I can't say I blame her for what she did. There's been many times that I've been tempted to do the same to my old man.'

Georgina's found herself smiling softly too. The memories of her gran were so precious, and being with Mary had a calming effect. Her old neighbour was her only connection to her childhood, where she'd lived in a small, terraced house, and had been raised by her gran and her dad. Mary handed Georgina a cup of sweet tea, and as she sipped the warm liquid, she wondered what her gran would tell her to do in this situation. 'I need to find David, but first and foremost I have to protect my children.'

'Where are they now?'

'With Molly, but they'll be safer with their grandparents.'

'Do you know where they are?'

'Back in Ireland. But it will take days for word to reach

them. And then they'd have to travel to Molly's. To save time, I was wondering if you would like a holiday?'

Mary chuckled. 'I can guess what you have in mind. It would be nice to see my brothers and sisters. None of us are getting any younger and I'm sure Alfie and Selina will enjoy a trip to Ireland with their aunty Mary.'

Georgina sighed with relief. 'Thank you. Thank you so much. I'll arrange for someone to drive you.'

'Let's hope the car ferry crossing will be smooth,' Mary mused, and then head cocking to one side, she added shrewdly, 'And as you'll have to lay low, I'm guessing you'll be wanting to stay in our flat with Charlotte while we're away?'

'If you wouldn't mind, Mary, that would be a great help too.'

'It's fine. Now you finish that tea while I go upstairs to pack. There's more in the pot if you want it.'

Reassured that her children were going to be safe, Georgina poured herself another drink. Once she'd sorted out a driver for Mary, she could concentrate fully on finding David. She just prayed she would find him alive.

Johnny pulled up at the back of Mary's Marvels and turned to Benjamin, his voice solemn. 'I'll come in with you. She's not going to take this well.'

Benjamin pushed his round-rimmed glasses up his nose. 'Thank you. I'd – erm – appreciate that,' he replied nervously.

Benjamin was a trusted member of Georgina's team, her accountant, and he'd once been her manager of the members-only Penthouse Club for men. He now worked out of an office in the back of his father's jewellery shop in Clapham Junction. Johnny smiled to himself. Benjamin's father, though an old fella now, was still the best and most discerning fence in Battersea. He knew that Georgina's dad, Jack, had been dealing with Benjamin's father for most of his life until he'd been untimely killed by Kevin Kelly. He supposed that Georgina had come to know Benjamin through selling her nicked gear to Benjamin's father. From what Johnny had heard, when Georgina had been a youngster, she'd been a good pickpocket and burglar. He couldn't imagine her like that now – she was such a classy bird.

'This is going to be, erm, uncomfortable,' Benjamin mumbled.

Johnny liked the man but found him to be a bit of an oddball. He had a nervous disposition, yet in the Penthouse, his personality would switch to become flamboyant and confident. It was no secret that Benjamin preferred men to women but Johnny didn't care. As far as he was concerned, who Benjamin took to his bed was none of his business. Just as long as the man could be trusted; that's all that Johnny was bothered about. Benjamin had proven his worth on many occasions, and Johnny knew that the awkward accountant would risk his life to protect Miss Garrett.

They knocked on the back door and Georgina answered it, leading them into a small kitchen. Johnny could see from her red and puffy eyes that she'd been crying and his heart went out to her.

'Hello, Benjamin,' she smiled sadly. 'Thanks, Johnny. You can fetch the blokes now.'

'Actually, Miss Garrett, there's something we need to show you first. Sit down, eh, and I'll pour you a cuppa.'

'I don't want any more tea, Johnny, just show me,' she demanded impatiently.

Johnny glanced anxiously at Benjamin who then stepped forward. Benjamin's hand shook as he held out a piece of paper towards Georgina.

'This was dropped off to the, erm, shop,' he said, tentatively.

Miss Garrett snatched the paper from Benjamin's hand. Her face drained of colour as she read the message. 'And the rest of it. Where's the rest of the message?' she asked.

The slightly built, Jewish man placed his briefcase on top of the cupboard, opened it and reached inside. He pulled out a cigar box and then turned to Miss Garrett. 'It's in here. Are you sure you want to, erm, see it?'

'I've no reason to fear my husband's finger,' she replied and snatched the small box from his trembling hand. Georgina opened it, and with what looked a supreme effort, she didn't baulk or retch at the sight of the severed digit. She cleared her throat, snapped the box closed and told Johnny, 'Right, off you go, round up the men and no dawdling.'

Johnny was surprised at how calmly she'd taken the message, but maybe he shouldn't have been. When Miss Garrett had run the businesses, she'd never shown fear, and had ruled them all with a fist of iron. He'd seen her knock out a bloke with those fists, her boxing skills as good as any man's. He'd seen her dressed as a man too, but also looking a stunner in women's clothes. Yet looking at her now, despite her trying to hide it, Johnny could just about spot her vulnerability. But she couldn't be blamed for being worried, especially after seeing the message. He knew exactly what it said. He'd read it and remembered every word.

Georgina Garrett
  Here's David's finger.
  You'll do exactly as I say if you want the rest of your husband back in one piece.
  Meet me at Clapham Common bandstand. Sunday. Midnight. Come alone.
  T

Johnny left the shop and raced from Tooting back to Battersea. As he drove, he wondered what Miss Garrett was going to do. And who was *T*? He couldn't think of anyone with that initial. Would she go alone as instructed? He hoped not. He wanted to be there to protect her but she was a determined woman and he never went against her orders. He gripped the steering wheel tightly, determined that on this occasion, if Miss Garrett told him that he couldn't go with her, he would defy her, whether she liked it or not.

7

Thomas Kelly had tied the gag back around David's mouth. He didn't want to hear another bad word about his father. Especially as he feared that the accounts were true.

He shivered with cold in the filthy, stark warehouse, and threw more wood on the fire. Then sitting at the old table, he propped his head in his hands as he thought back to when he'd been a child. He couldn't have been any older than six, maybe seven, when he'd seen two little girls taken down to his father's cellar. When he'd questioned his dad about it, he'd been told that the girls had run away from home and had been found on the docks. They were being locked in the cellar for their own safety, until their mother arrived to collect them.

Thomas hadn't questioned it further. Why would he? Anything that his father had said to him was taken as gospel. Yet now, recalling the look of terror in the little girls' eyes, he realised that he'd been lied to. He'd seen that same expression on the faces of a couple of young boys who'd been bundled into the back of one of his father's trucks. His dad had explained that the boys were caught pinching apples from trees in the back garden and were being taken

85

to the police station. Thomas could see the truth now. His father wouldn't have taken anyone to the cops, especially not young boys for nicking apples!

He ran his hand through his hair in despair. The more he thought about it, the more memories sprang to mind. The child trafficking had been going on right under his nose, in blatant sight, but he'd been too young to understand. He felt sickened at the thought of what had happened to those poor kids, some the same age as he had been, some younger.

The image of his beloved sister lying dead, semi-naked and wide-legged, flashed through his head. A man had taken her innocence and gruesomely killed her. Most likely, the same fate had been bestowed the children he'd seen at his father's house.

Thomas stood and began to pace the floor. He'd always known that his dad had been ruthless, but now he hated the thought of how low his father had stooped to make money. And a rapist too… could that be true? Thomas banged his palm hard against his head several times as he realised that, yes, unfortunately, it probably was. He'd once seen his dad drag a maid onto the dining room table but he couldn't understand what was going on. His father had growled at him, telling him to *piss off*. He could remember running from the room, but had glanced over his shoulder to see his father pinning the maid down, and hearing the young woman's cries.

His dad had done the same to the cleaner, this time on the hallway stairs, and again his father had ordered him to bugger off. Thomas had bumped into the cleaner later that day with a small suitcase in her hand. She'd had a black eye and a split lip. No doubt, he now realised, his father had given her a backhander for fighting back. She had never returned to the house, and after that, probably due to his mother, only middle-aged women had been hired in service.

The muffled sound of David groaning in pain brought Thomas from his thoughts. His eyes narrowed as he wondered how far he'd have to go to get Georgina Garrett's attention. He'd heard that she was a force to be reckoned with and even though it was David Maynard who ran the business, she was just as capable. Thomas wanted Maynard's business and nothing was going to deter him from taking it over. Despite what his father had done, Georgina Garrett had to die. He had to avenge his father's death. It was a matter of honour, but first he had to find her.

Charlotte hadn't wanted to leave Tim's bedside but the doctors had said that he was unlikely to come out of the coma any time soon, if ever. As Ned had led her from the hospital and to the car, she'd fought back tears. She'd already lost her unborn baby and now she was facing the harrowing prospect of losing her husband too.

'I should be with him,' she said in despair, hesitating before climbing into the car.

'You heard the docs, Charlotte. There's nothing that you can do for him right now. Let me take you to Miss Garrett and then I'll run you back here tomorrow, eh?'

Charlotte nodded. She supposed that it made no sense to sit at Tim's bedside when she could be helping to find the men who had done this to him. Her jaw tightened and she gritted her teeth, the thought of revenge the only thing keeping her going. Now that she was no longer by Tim's

SAM MICHAELS

side, her anger rose from the pit of her stomach, burning its way through her chest, consuming her, and she growled, 'When I find out who did this, I'll kill 'em.'

'If Miss Garrett don't get to 'em first,' Ned commented.

Charlotte didn't want that, but said nothing. Though she thought that Ned was probably right and Georgina would get to the men first.

Ned started the car, and as they drove off, he tutted. 'If I had my way, I'd be with the rest of the blokes but it looks like I'm stuck with looking after you,' he moaned but with a chortle.

Charlotte didn't find anything funny about his griping. She wasn't in the mood for any banter and she wasn't overly keen on Ned. He had been a face in the Battersea gang long before Georgina had taken over and had worked for both Norman and Billy Wilcox. Yes, he'd shown his loyalty to Georgina, but Ned always voiced his opinion whether it was asked for or not. Charlotte supposed that with him being one of the oldest and longest serving members, he felt that he had the right to say whatever he wanted. But she thought that there were times when he should learn to keep his mouth closed and his opinions to himself.

They were soon pulling up at the back of Mary's shop. Johnny let them in, and in the small kitchen he pointed to an old chair, saying kindly, 'Sit down, sweetheart.'

It wasn't lost on her that Johnny had known she'd miscarried just a few hours earlier. She knew that if she met his eyes, she'd see sympathy there and would be unable to hold back her sorrow. Instead, she brushed past him, ignoring the seat, and found Georgina just coming out of the shop, carrying a bundle of clothes.

'I've just been sorting out a few bits to wear,' she said. 'I didn't bring much with me when I left. How's Tim?' Georgina asked.

'Not good. He's in a deep coma and they're saying that he may never recover.'

'I'm so sorry, Charlotte.'

'They're wrong though. He'll get better. I *know* he will. And in the meantime, I want to kill the bastards who did this to him... and me.'

'Well, some progress has been made,' Georgina said and then she handed Charlotte the note from 'T'.

'Shit, Georgina. Do you know who sent this?'

'No, the initial means nothing to me.'

'Are you going to meet him?'

'I have to.'

'Alone?'

'Those are the instructions.'

'But he might kill you!'

'What choice do I have? If I don't go, he'll kill David.'

'I'm coming with you.'

'No, Charlotte, you've been through enough and I'm not putting you at any more risk. I've had Nobby and Eric Barker here, along with a few of David's blokes who weren't slaughtered. I've got a plan, and that plan does *not* involve you.'

Charlotte rolled her eyes. She should have known that Georgina would have a plan. The woman always did! And it was reassuring to know that the Barker twins were on board. Johnny and the twins had always worked well together and were Georgina's hardest and toughest men. 'Tell me about this plan then.'

'For now, all you need to know is that you'll be staying upstairs while Mary and her husband take my children to Lash's family in Ireland. Ned will be with you for every minute of every day and night. He'll drive you back and forth to the hospital to see Tim but you are not to go anywhere else.'

'Hang on a minute… you're telling me that I'm being kept under guard here? Like a prisoner?'

'No, Charlotte, not like a prisoner. I just don't want you hurt so it's for your own protection. Please, I've got a lot on my mind at the moment so just do as I ask.'

'*You've got a lot on your mind*,' Charlotte parroted bitterly. 'My husband is in a coma and might never wake up. I've just had my baby punched out of my belly. My home was broken into. My sister is harbouring *your* children, which puts her and the rest of my family at risk. And you're telling me that *you've* got a lot on *your* mind. That's bleedin' rich, that is!'

For a moment Georgina's eyes flared, but then what Charlotte had said must have sunk in and she said, 'I'm sorry and I deserve that. I know you've been through the mill and back too. I didn't mean to sound unsympathetic.'

Charlotte drew in a breath to contain her anger. It wasn't helping, but something inside her had snapped and she hadn't been able to stem her words. 'I'm sorry too, Georgina. I know none of this is your fault.'

Georgina's jaw tightened and her eyes gleamed with hatred. 'I need to get the bastards who've done this. Knowing that you're out of harm's way will be one less thing for me to worry about.'

'I know you want to keep me safe, but I don't want to be pushed to the sidelines. This is my fight too.'

'It's me they want, Charlotte. It's my fight and I promise I will make them pay for what they've done to you and Tim. Please, just trust me.'

Charlotte gently lowered herself into one of the saggy chairs. The tears that she'd been fighting to hold back sprung to her eyes and she couldn't stop them from falling, but along with tears her anger still burned. 'Kill them, Georgina. But make sure that they die slowly. And make sure they know that their long and painful deaths are for the life of my baby.'

8

David shivered. He couldn't get warm and yet his body felt hot and clammy. He knew that an infection had set into his hand where his finger had been crudely cut off and it was spreading now, poisoning his blood. There had been moments when he'd longed for death but Kelly seemed determined to keep him alive. Food had been roughly shoved into his mouth and water poured down his throat, almost choking him at times. It was only the thought of Georgina that gave him the strength and will to survive.

The days and nights had merged into one long arduous ordeal of pain and torment. He wouldn't have known what day it was or how long he'd been held captive if it wasn't for Thomas Kelly's excitement. His torturer seemed in good spirits, though anxious, as he taunted him.

'Sunday at long last! Tonight's the night that I finally get to meet your bitch of a wife. That's if she shows up... What do you reckon, Maynard? Do you think that she loves you enough to want to save your life?'

David kept his head bowed and his eyes closed, pretending to be unconscious. He knew that Georgina would do everything in her power to rescue him but he wouldn't give Kelly the satisfaction of knowing that. She'd be there, without a doubt, because that was the sort of brave woman that she was. Though on this occasion, David wished that his wife would abandon him and save her own life.

He felt a fistful of his hair being pulled and his head yanked back.

'Oi, wake up. You don't want to miss all the fun,' Thomas Kelly mocked.

David kept his eyes tightly closed. Kelly leaned in closer and David could smell the man's musty breath.

'I said, WAKE UP!'

David flicked his eyes open to see the man's face just inches from his own. Kelly had released the grip on his hair, so using the opportunity, and mustering all of his waning strength, David threw his head forward as hard and fast as he could. His forehead connected with the bridge of Kelly's nose, sending the man falling backwards.

David looked down and smirked at the sight of the man on his arse and holding his bleeding nose. 'I'm awake. Did I miss something?' he asked sarcastically.

Two of Kelly's men had stomped across the room and were standing each side of David, waiting for instructions. Kelly pushed himself to his feet and looked to each of the blokes with a wry smile. 'The cheeky fucker. Can you believe he nutted me? Caught me a right one on me hooter. It's all right, stand down. I'll have the pleasure of this one. Bring me the metal rod.'

One of the men walked purposely to where the small bonfire was dwindling. David watched as Kelly, a little unsteady on his feet from being headbutted, began to slowly remove his belt from his trousers. He then wrapped the belt under David's chin, pulled it up the sides of his face and then tightened it on top of David's head. He was powerless to struggle. His jaw was now clamped closed, rendering him unable to open his mouth.

The man returned from the fire with the metal rod that he'd pulled from the hot ashes. The tip wasn't glowing red this time but David knew it would still be searingly hot.

Kelly waved it in front of David's face and said menacingly, 'An eye for a broken nose? Sounds fair to me.'

Terror shot through David as the end of the hot metal rod came towards his eye. He rocked his body and twisted, trying desperately to avoid the poker.

'Hold him still,' Kelly ordered.

The man moved behind him. David's muffled yells didn't stop the thug from grabbing his head and holding him firmly.

'You'll think twice before you try and pull another stunt like that,' Kelly warned.

David squeezed his eyes closed, but he was powerless to stop what happened next. An indescribable burning pain pressed against his lid. The pressure in his eye socket built up until he felt sure that his eye would pop out. With his mouth strapped shut, his screams were gurgled, and all the while, he could hear Thomas Kelly sniggering.

The man let go of his head and the sound of the metal rod reached David's ears as it clanged on the floor. His head flopped forward until his chin rested on his chest. He didn't try to open his eye. He wasn't even convinced that he could. He could smell the sickening stench of his burnt skin. The damage inflicted had been bad but he thought his eyeball was still in place. At least, he hoped it was, but the incredible agony made it difficult to know for sure.

'I can't wait for your wife to see the fucking mess I've made of you,' Kelly said. 'And the only reason I haven't poked your eye right out is so that you can watch her scream and beg for mercy while I slice the bitch from head to toe.'

His pain was so unbearable that David could feel himself about to pass out again. Unconsciousness would be a welcome relief from his suffering and from the fever burning his ravaged body. As dizziness and darkness consumed him, he thought of Georgina. Her beautiful face. He had wanted to die quickly, but now realised that he wanted to live. He had to do whatever he could to save her from the torturous hands of Thomas fucking Kelly.

Georgina answered the door to Mary's flat and Johnny came in with Larry, one of David's trusted men.

'Have you got everything?' she asked.

'Yep. It's all here.'

She took the bundle from him and went straight into Mary's bedroom, calling over her shoulder, 'Charlotte will help you to get ready, Larry.'

In the bedroom, she laid out the bundle on the bed, pleased to see that the outfit looked as though it would be a good fit. Quickly undressing, she folded her dress before slipping into the men's trousers, shirt and pullover. She slid her feet into the clumpy boots and lastly, pulled a flat cap over her head. Standing back, she examined her reflection in the mirror on Mary's dressing table. 'Hello again, *George*,' she said aloud with a reflective smile. It wasn't the first time that Georgina had dressed as *George* but she hoped that it would be the last.

Charlotte looked up when Georgina walked into the front room. 'I've found the scissors,' she said and told Georgina to sit on the newspaper on the floor in front of her. 'Wait 'til you see Larry. But try not to laugh at him,' Charlotte whispered. 'He's a bit sensitive about it.'

Georgina heard the sound of the scissors slicing through her long, dark locks and grimaced when she saw her hair fall onto the paper around her. But losing her crowning glory was a small price to pay to save her husband.

As Georgina's hair was being chopped off, Larry came into the room, wobbling in a pair of mid-heel shoes. He was wearing a wig, and shoved back the dark hair that had fallen across his face. Then, tugging at his skirt, he announced belligerently, 'I feel like a right bloody poofter in this get-up.'

'I'll tell you what, Larry *the lady*, you ain't 'alf giving me an 'ard-on.' Ned laughed.

'Fuck off, Ned, you mouthy git.'

Georgina chipped in. She couldn't have them in-fighting. She needed them focused on the plan. 'Hey, the pair of you. That's enough,' she warned.

'Yeah, sorry, Miss Garrett,' Larry said. 'It's just that I feel like a complete idiot.'

The man was clearly uncomfortable being made to look like the image of her so she said softly, 'I really appreciate what you're doing and so will David.'

Her words didn't placate him and he growled, 'If you ask me, it's a stupid fucking plan, but you're the boss.'

'That's right, Larry, I am and I didn't ask you,' she snapped. The tense atmosphere felt explosive, but it wasn't surprising when they were embarking on something that they all knew was fraught with danger.

The tension was broken when Charlotte announced, 'Welcome back, George.'

Georgina stood up and looked at her reflection in the mirror over the mantel. The masculine hairstyle completed her disguise and she shoved her cap back on before giving them a twirl. 'Well then. Do you reckon I'll pass as a bloke?'

'Not if you spin around like that,' Johnny answered. 'It's been a long time since you've donned a fella's clothes. You gotta remember to carry yourself like a man.'

'Johnny's right, Miss Garrett, but don't go copying how he walks or you'll look like a right prat.'

Georgina smiled as she walked splay-footed across the room with her shoulders rounded and her hands in the trouser pockets. 'Is that better?'

'Yeah, you'll do,' Johnny drawled. 'Put it this way, if I bumped into you on the common, I wouldn't chat you up. I might have a go with Larry though.'

'You cheeky bastards,' Larry said, but chuckled. 'If you tried it on wiv me, I'd flatten you.'

The mood had lightened but Georgina could still feel the thick tension in the room and knew that Johnny and Charlotte could too. It was written in their furrowed brows and tight jaws. 'I know you're worried about me, but I'm not going to get myself killed tonight,' she offered, trying to reassure them.

It was Ned who spoke first. 'I hope you don't think I'm talking out of turn, Miss Garrett, and I hate to say this, but whether you turn up tonight or not, the odds aren't good for Mr Maynard.'

'I know. I've been thinking about nothing else. But I've got to try. I won't give up on him. If I don't go along tonight, I'll never know who is behind this. It's my only chance to find out.'

Charlotte was chewing nervously on her fingernails and Johnny's leg was jigging up and down. Ned twiddled his thumbs and Larry practised walking in his heels. Georgina looked at the clock. Nine-thirty. Two and a half hours to go. 'We should think about getting into place,' she said.

Charlotte leapt to her feet and ran across the room. She threw her arms around Georgina and pulled her close, saying, 'Please, please be careful.'

Georgina, never one for open displays of affection, peeled away Charlotte's arms to take her firmly by the shoulders. She looked her squarely in the eyes. 'I have no intention of dying tonight. I'm a mother and have my children to think of. Alfie and Selina have already lost Lash. They won't be losing me too. I'll be home. I swear.'

Charlotte nodded but Georgina could see that the young woman didn't look convinced. In fact, Charlotte's nerves were beginning to rub off on her. 'I'll see you later,' she said, impatient to get away before her bottle went.

Georgina climbed into the car next to Johnny with Larry in the back seat. Nothing was said between them on the journey to Clapham Common.

Johnny parked the car up a side road and well out of sight. Georgina sucked in a large lungful of air. 'Right, are you ready?' she asked.

'Yeah. Let's get this over with,' Larry answered.

She picked up a half-full bottle of whisky and got out of the car. 'I'll see you soon,' she told Johnny before closing the door.

Once on the main road, and just in case anyone was watching, Georgina swayed and swigged from the bottle. Then she staggered aimlessly, losing her footing a couple of times and stumbling up the kerb. She thought she was carrying off a believable performance of a drunken man. She'd had plenty of examples set by her father when he'd fallen through the front door three sheets to the wind.

Georgina appeared as if she was wandering aimlessly onto the common and then clumsily lay down on the grass. She stayed like that for a good hour, discreetly watching and listening for anyone within the proximity. A courting couple passed, oblivious to her lying in the darkness. A posh-looking chap came by, walking his small dog. Georgina was pleased that the animal was on a lead and hadn't drawn attention to her. No one was standing on, or close by the bandstand.

She rose to her feet again, being careful to look drunk, and swigged more of the whisky. Then she staggered towards a bench that looked directly at the meeting place. She flopped down and lay back on the wooden seat. The yellow glow from a tall gas light beside the bench highlighted her presence, but she was confident that she wouldn't raise suspicion. After all, she looked like a bloke who'd drowned his sorrows and spent his week's wage in a pub.

Several large trees stood around the bandstand, some with wide trunks the size to easily conceal a man behind. Georgina wondered if T was waiting behind one of them, ready to pounce and gun her down when she made her appearance. But it would be Larry who was turning up instead of her. *Good old Larry*, as everyone called him, and though he'd moaned a bit about wearing women's clothes, he'd still stepped up, willing to do whatever was asked of him. He'd been saved from being slaughtered in David's office the day of the attack because he'd been sent on an errand to Southampton docks. Yet even after being informed of how gruesome the killings had been, *good old Larry* had still agreed to take on a very dangerous role in tonight's plan. If they survived this, Georgina made a mental note to ensure that Larry was generously rewarded.

She heard the click of heels coming along the path towards the bandstand and knew it would be Larry. She turned her head slightly to surreptitiously watch him, impressed by how well he'd mastered the skill of walking elegantly in heels. In the dim light, wearing woman's clothes and the dark wig, Larry could easily be mistaken for her.

Larry stopped in front of the bandstand and looked around. Georgina, still lying on the bench, carefully scanned the area too. Her pulse raced as she waited for T to show himself. Larry then carefully climbed the stairs up to the bandstand. With his back to the common now, Georgina was worried that someone would jump from the shadows and shoot him. She wrapped her hand around the handle of her own weapon that was shoved into the back of her trouser waistband. It was fully loaded; she'd checked it before she'd left and then again in the car. A light breeze rustled the leaves on the trees. The sound and movement startled her, but still no one showed themselves. Larry was standing in the middle of the bandstand now. He looked small compared to the grand structure so surely his disguise would fool T.

Georgina's heart pounded hard. And then, at last, a big bloke, bigger than Victor or Knuckles had been, stomped along the path. Georgina pretended to have passed out, the whisky bottle hanging loosely from her hand, almost falling to the ground. Her eyes were closed but she sensed the man was looking at her, gauging if she was a threat or not. Relief washed over her when she heard his heavy footsteps pass. She opened her eyes to see him stomping up the steps towards Larry. Was this T?

The man reached into his jacket pocket and Georgina tensed, expecting him to pull his gun. Larry must have thought the same and raised his weapon. Georgina sat up as a tremendous BANG sounded, followed by another. Both men fell to the floor of the bandstand where Georgina couldn't see either of them. She jumped to her feet and ran towards the structure. It was a relief to see that Larry was alive and on all fours, waving his gun in front of him. The other man was still alive too. Larry pushed himself to his feet. His left arm hung beside him and blood dripped from the end of his fingers. He raised his right hand and cocked his gun.

'NO,' Georgina shouted. 'Don't kill him!'

But it was too late. Over the sound of her shouting, Larry fired his gun again. As she ran onto the bandstand, she saw that the bullet had struck the man in his chest. His body jerked and then there was no doubt that he was dead. Georgina slumped. Now she'd never know what had happened to David.

'I didn't have a choice. It was me or him,' Larry explained as he whipped off the wig.

Nobby and Eric Barker, the twins, emerged from the trees. 'He was by himself. We didn't see anyone else,' they said.

Georgina studied the dead man's face. It wasn't one that she recognised. But then she noticed that his gun was in his left hand and it had been his right hand that he'd put into his jacket pocket. 'Search him,' she ordered Nobby.

Nobby went through the man's pockets and retrieved a piece of paper that he held out to Georgina. She snatched it from him and read the note addressed to her.

> *I knew you couldn't be trusted to come alone. This was a test. You will receive new instructions shortly. Unfortunately for you, the man you have just killed could have told you who I am and led you to where I'm holding your husband. He had been instructed to bring you to me. You have one more chance to get it right or David dies. T*

On the other side of the paper, the following words were scrawled:

> *I've been told to tell you to follow me and I will take you to your husband.*

Georgina's heart sank. She realised that she would never have seen the note if the man had lived. Instead, she would have been taken to her husband. They'd messed up. This man, T, was playing games with her and their lives.

And still he was one step ahead of her. 'Get Larry's shoulder seen to,' she told the twins.

Georgina marched back to the car. Johnny was waiting for her on the edge of the common.

'I ain't seen anyone come off or on to the common, not on this side. What happened? I heard gunshots.'

'Larry was shot but he'll be all right. The man who was sent is dead. It was a set-up, Johnny, designed to test me. Look,' she said and handed him the note.

'The sly git,' Johnny seethed. 'But what has he achieved? I don't get it, Miss Garrett. If it's you he wants, why didn't he just ambush you? I mean, judging by what happened at Mr Maynard's office, I reckon he must have the manpower.'

'I'm guessing that he knew that I wouldn't have come alone. I'm surprised that he risked one of his men's lives to test me, but this way he only lost one man. If there'd been a shootout, he would have lost a lot more and he knows that. When I get the next set of instructions, he'll know I won't risk David's life and he'll assume that I'll turn up alone. Then he can easily take me down with no risk… or so he thinks.'

'So, there's gonna be another plan?' Johnny asked, looking confused.

Georgina nodded as her mind turned. She could tell that T's brain worked in the same way as hers. They thought alike. She may have lost tonight's battle but at least she now had an insight into how T operated. It gave her hope that she'd find David alive. She just had to outsmart the beast who was holding him.

9

Thomas Kelly threw his head back laughing. 'The stupid bitch. I knew she wouldn't turn up without her men. Well, she proved me right and now I've got her exactly where I want her.'

'There was nothing we could do for Nelson. We had to leave his body on the bandstand before the cops turned up.'

'Fuck him. Nelson was a waste of space and I sent him because he's dispensable. But I don't intend on losing any more of my lads. Good job, youse two. You did well tonight.' Thomas smiled. Wally and Titch had been hiding on the common and had witnessed the night's events. Thomas had always known that Georgina Garrett would turn up and had expected her to come mob-handed. He'd been surprised to hear that she'd sent a man disguised as herself and that she'd been dressed as a drunken vagrant. The woman was brighter than he'd given her credit for.

'What do you want us to do now, Boss?' Wally asked.

'Take another one of his fingers and then drop it to the jeweller's in Battersea with this note. You know how to do it,' he answered.

'Yes, Boss.'

Thomas glanced at David. The man was still unconscious

and appeared to be on his last legs. He doubted that David would last the night. That was fine. Thomas had always planned on killing him, though he would have preferred to have kept him alive for a while longer.

Titch held David's hand as Wally used the bolt croppers to remove a second finger. David flinched and groaned but didn't regain consciousness.

Thomas placed the detached finger in another cigar box and handed Wally the note in an envelope. 'Take the message first thing in the morning. For now, Titch, I want you to keep guard. I'm going to get some rest.'

As Thomas walked across the small warehouse, his boots crunched on the glass from the mostly smashed windows. Outside, several other units stood abandoned and empty, some just piles of rubble after suffering extensive bomb damage during the war. While much of Wandsworth had been undergoing extensive rebuilding, this area, close to Wandsworth Common train station had been overlooked and deserted.

Thomas climbed into his car and turned the engine, but he paused before driving away. Something was drawing him back to the warehouse and David Maynard. He wasn't sure what it was. Just a feeling that he had to be there when the man drew his last breath. Was it the pleasure that he'd feel in seeing him die? No, he didn't think so. After all, he'd witnessed plenty of men die at his hands. Yet he'd never taken down anyone as formidable as the great David Maynard, his reputation widely known. Maybe that was it. Thomas licked his lips as he realised that he was feeding on Maynard's power. And he was hungry for more. He could learn a lot from Maynard. He'd made a mistake in allowing the man to slowly die and he realised that now. He was so focused on revenge that he'd nearly let an opportunity pass him by.

He headed back to the warehouse and as Thomas pulled open the door, he strained his ears, sure that he could hear Maynard's voice. Perhaps the man was going to last longer than anticipated. This now pleased Thomas.

He found Wally pouring water into Maynard's mouth.

'Sorry, Boss,' Wally blurted and jumped away from the man, looking worried.

'It's fine. I'm in no rush to lose him.'

'He's in a bad way.'

Thomas circled the wreck of a once powerful man, noting that he seemed to have passed out again. He still wanted him alive so that Maynard could watch what he was going to do to Georgina Garrett, but now there was also another reason. 'Untie him and lay him down. He's in no state to do a runner. Make him comfortable. Get some brandy down his neck.'

'Boss?' Wally asked, sounding perplexed.

'Just do as I fucking tell you! Make sure he doesn't die. If I come back tomorrow and find him dead, I'll fucking bury you with him.'

Wally did an action similar to tugging his forelock and hurried to untie David Maynard, while Titch rushed around to make a makeshift bed near the fire. Thomas, satisfied that they'd look after the man, headed back to his car. He'd never shown anyone mercy before but David Maynard was different and Thomas had come to realise that he could learn a lot from London's most revered gangster. In a twisted way, he respected the man and wanted to glean his knowledge. In fact, David Maynard was everything that Thomas wanted to be. And if he intended to take on the man's businesses, it made sense to understand how his mind worked and what made him tick.

The only way to gain that knowledge was by keeping Maynard alive. For now.

Johnny crawled into his bed and gratefully rested his head on the pillow. He only had the chance to snatch a few hours of desperately needed sleep. He closed his eyes and felt Kathy's arm drape over him. She snuggled in behind him and nuzzled the back of his neck.

'I'm glad you're home. I've been lonely without you,' she purred.

Johnny threw her arm off. 'Leave off, sweetheart. I'm knackered and just want to get me head down.'

'Oh, Johnny, don't be like that.'

'I ain't got time for this. If you don't like it, you know where the door is. Now shut up and let me rest, woman.'

Kathy huffed, clearly annoyed at being rebuffed, turned over in the bed and took the blankets with her.

Let her sulk, thought Johnny. He couldn't care less about the tart. Johnny refused to allow himself to get involved with a woman again. He'd been burned twice and that was enough for him. First his beloved Daisy had died and then he'd been betrayed by Elsie Flowers. Both women had broken his heart so now it was *love 'em and leave 'em*. Kathy was just another in a long line of women who had passed through his bed. But she was becoming far too clingy for his liking so he'd have to kick her out soon.

It didn't take Johnny long to fall into a deep slumber, and the next thing he became aware of was his alarm clock. It was in six in the morning and he struggled to open his eyes.

'Turn that bloody thing off,' Kathy moaned.

Johnny reached out for the clock and knocked the off switch to silence the bell.

'Christ, Johnny, this is a ridiculous time to be awake. You've only been home for a few hours.'

'Yeah, well, I'm busy.'

'Too busy for me?' Kathy asked as she pushed her naked body up against him.

Johnny threw the bedclothes back. 'Yeah, too busy for you,' he answered, yet he was tempted. He sat on the edge of his bed and glanced over his shoulder to look at the woman. Kathy had a fine body, curves in all the right places and a massive pair of tits. With milky white, smooth skin and auburn, tousled hair, he quite liked the idea of getting back into bed and clambering on top of her. But then cold, stark reality hit. There was work to be done and lives at risk. 'I'll be gone all day, maybe longer.' He pulled his trousers on and then, as he buttoned his shirt, added, 'I'll leave a few quid for you on the side and I'll see you when I see you.'

He heard Kathy call his name as he went to the bathroom to splash some cold water on his face and clean his teeth. But, ignoring her, his mind was already on the duties of the day. His pulse quickened. Resting his hands on the sink, Johnny stared at his face in the small mirror above it. He looked haggard and old. His brown hair was showing signs of thinning, crow's feet creased around the corners of his blue eyes and deep furrows etched his brow. Johnny clicked his finger and pointed at his reflection. 'But you're still a handsome fucker,' he said aloud.

'Who ya talking to in there?' Kathy called.

'Meself. I like to have a chat with meself when I want an intelligent conversation.'

'You cheeky sod.'

Johnny smiled. Yep, that was him. A cheeky sod with plenty of charm to boot. But all the charm in the world wasn't going to help him today.

Kathy, obviously keen to go back to sleep, murmured a goodbye. Johnny left, climbed into his car, and twenty minutes later pulled up in Grant Road. Benjamin Harel's father's jewellery shop was a short walk away and when he arrived there, the Barker twins were already waiting outside.

'Wotcha, Johnny. You all right, mate?'

'Yeah, Nobby. I'm good. Just bleedin' knackered.'

'Us an' all. I was just saying to Eric that I hope we ain't waiting around here all day for nuffink.'

'I know what you mean. But Miss Garrett is convinced someone will turn up this morning with another message for her.'

'Do you think they will?'

'I dunno, mate. But it'll be unlucky for them if they do.' Johnny scowled.

Benjamin arrived, greeted them, opened the shop and walked inside. Before following him, Johnny told the twins where to keep watch. Eric nodded and waited nearby, while Nobby walked to stand at a tram stop on the main road, but within sight.

Johnny went into the shop where he waited impatiently. Feeling restless and fraught with nerves, he was grateful for the cup of coffee that Benjamin made him. Time passed, and at nine o'clock Clapham Junction became a hive of activity but nobody had shown up at the shop.

'If they don't come today, will you, erm, be here every day until they do?' Benjamin asked.

'If that's what Miss Garrett orders,' Johnny answered. 'It's not like there's anything else we can do.'

'Do you believe that Mr Maynard is still alive?'

'I dunno, Benjamin. I hope so. That woman has been through enough in her life. I wouldn't like to see her hurt again.'

The entry system that Benjamin's father, Ezzy, had installed years earlier, suddenly sounded. Johnny jumped to his feet and dashed from the office. He stood in the doorway that led through to the shop and peered towards the glass frontage. A young lad was standing outside and shifting from one foot to the other, looking as though he was desperate to use the toilet.

'Who is it?' Benjamin asked, standing behind Johnny.

'I dunno, a kid.'

'We don't usually have, erm, such young customers.'

'I'll deal with this. Go back to the office and lock the door.'

Once Benjamin had hurried off, Johnny pressed the button that released the door, and the lad nervously loitered on the doorstep. Johnny rushed towards him. The lad held out a familiar-looking cigar box and envelope, saying, 'These are for you, mister.'

He snatched the boy by the scruff of his neck and yanked him forward as he used his other hand to grab the box and envelope, placing them on the counter. 'Who sent you?' he growled.

The boy's face had drained of colour and he looked up at Johnny with fear-filled eyes. 'I... I dunno. There was a bloke round the corner. He gave me a crown to drop the stuff off. I ain't in trouble, am I?'

Johnny dragged the boy outside. Eric was there.

'This man who paid ya, what did he look like?' Johnny asked.

'I dunno. Big.'

'What else?'

'I dunno. I didn't take no notice.'

'Think, boy, what was he wearing?'

The lad shook his head and began to blubber. Johnny pulled him onto the main road. 'Look around. Can you see him?'

The boy's head turned from left to right and then he pointed down the hill towards Arding and Hobbs department store. 'There... that's him,' he said, excitedly, indicating a man who was walking towards a car parked half on the pavement.

'Get after him, Eric,' Johnny urged while pointing him out to Nobby, who also sprinted off.

The man looked behind and must have seen Eric running towards him. Johnny could see him fumbling with the car door handle before he began sprinting too, clearly trying to get away from Eric. Nobby, who had acted quickly, was already halfway down the hill and hot on the man's heels too.

With no idea if T or any more of T's men were around, Johnny stayed where he was to protect Benjamin. He released the boy and said, 'Good lad. Off you go.'

The boy scampered off as Johnny pulled a coin from his

pocket. ''Ere, you can have this,' he called. But the youngster didn't look back.

Johnny walked into the shop again and knocked on Benjamin's office door. 'It's all right, it's me,' he called.

Benjamin nervously opened the door and asked, 'Have you caught anyone?'

'Not yet, but Nobby and Eric are chasing a bloke.'

'If they catch him, I hope they've got the sense to hold on to him without making a scene. We could do without the police sniffing around.'

'They ain't stupid – they know what they're doing. Now we sit tight and wait to see if they bring him back here,' he told Benjamin. He moved back into the shop and sneaked a peek inside the cigar box. Though he wasn't surprised to see another of David's fingers, his guts churned at the sight and he was thankful that he hadn't had any breakfast. Johnny was no stranger to gory scenes. He'd witnessed Miss Garrett relieve Geert Neerthoff of his hands when she'd chopped them off with an axe. He was no stranger to inflicting pain either and had kneecapped many a man, along with seeing gunshot wounds of all descriptions, though none worse than those he'd seen inflicted on his pal, Victor. Yet seeing a finger like this, he found something creepy about it that left him nauseated.

After quickly closing the box, he read the accompanying note.

Last chance to get it right or Maynard dies, and next time I'll send you his heart instead of his finger.

You know the rules. ALONE. The big pond on Wandsworth Common. Wednesday at midnight.

T

It was Monday, Johnny thought, so Miss Garrett would have time to formulate a plan. Though he couldn't second-guess what she'd do this time, but knowing her, it would be well thought out and would probably involve someone's death. She was a strong, and sometimes ruthless woman, but she never inflicted violence or took a life unless it was well deserved. He just prayed that she came out of the confrontation on Wednesday alive and with some knowledge of Mr Maynard's whereabouts.

'I see. Good work, Johnny. Get over here and pick me up, as quick as you can.' Georgina replaced the telephone receiver and turned around to find Charlotte hovering behind her.

'What did he say? Have they caught someone?'

'Yes. They're holding him in the café. Johnny's on his way to collect me.'

Charlotte spun on her heel and headed to the bedroom. 'I'm coming too,' she called.

'Hold your horses, missy. There's no need for you to come. I'll deal with it.'

Charlotte turned with enraged eyes. 'But he could be one of the men who killed my baby!'

'I said, I'll deal with it. Anyway, you should be visiting Tim.'

Charlotte cast her eyes downwards and muttered, 'Yeah, I suppose I should.' Then she looked back up with her face twisted in pain and asked, 'Do me a favour?'

'Anything.'

'If he admits to being in my flat, gut the bastard. Gut him alive. Pull out his intestines and make sure he watches.'

That wasn't what Georgina had expected to hear but she didn't baulk. She could understand Charlotte's hatred and anger towards the men who'd caused her to miscarry. Though Charlotte hid her sorrow well, Georgina could see her anguish. 'It will be my pleasure,' she answered. 'Rest assured, darling, they will pay for what they've done to you and Tim.'

An hour later, as Johnny drove her to Clapham Junction, Georgina's heart raced with anticipation. At last, she might finally get some answers. 'Do you reckon this man will talk?'

'If we give him enough *persuasion*, I'm sure he'll talk like a fucking budgie.'

'Heard many talking budgies then, have you, Johnny?'

'As a matter of fact, I have. When I was a kid, my next door neighbour had one. Little blue and white thing. It was sweet 'til it opened its mouth. Then it'd say things like, *got a shitty bum* and *get me some quim.*'

'Really?'

'Yeah, dirty little fucker. The woman who owned it, her husband was a lighterman on the Thames and brought it home one day. The bird had belonged to an old sailor. No wonder it swore like one. The woman was embarrassed when she had visitors and would throw a blanket over his cage.'

'Well, let's hope that this bloke has more to say than *got a shitty bum.*'

Georgina marched into her old office at the back of the café on Lavender Hill. There she found that Nobby and Eric had handcuffed the big bloke to a pipe that ran down the wall in the corner of the room. His ankles were tied together and they'd placed a potato sack over his head.

'Great job. Has he said anything?'

'Not yet, Miss Garrett, but he will.'

She walked across the room and pulled the sack off his head. Just like the intruder she'd shot in her house, this bloke appeared young, probably no older than twenty. He had a thick mop of light brown hair, chubby cheeks and baby blue eyes. She thought he looked far too cute to be a threat to anyone but she knew that looks could be deceiving. 'Who are you?' she asked calmly.

The man glared at her but remained silent.

'Fine,' she snapped. She walked over to her desk and sat behind it. Leaning back and crossing her legs, she rubbed her finger where her mother's wedding ring had once been. 'I've been giving this situation some thought. See, you have information that I want and I intend to get that information from you. We can play it one of two ways. Either I pay you handsomely and help you on your merry way. Or, I'll have it beaten out of you. The choice is yours. So, which would you prefer?' Her eyes bored into his and she could see that he wasn't yet ready to talk. 'I'll assume that your silence means that you've opted for the second choice. It's such a shame that your pretty face is going to be ruined. Not to mention saying goodbye to your manhood.'

The man blanched as he looked down at the area between his legs.

'That's right, say goodbye to it. Your boss takes fingers. I take dicks.'

'Nah, you wouldn't... she wouldn't... would she?' the man asked, his anxious eyes flitting around the room nervously to Johnny, Nobby and Eric.

It was Johnny who answered. 'Oh yeah, without a doubt.

I've seen her do it and believe me, it ain't a pretty sight. I don't think I've ever heard grown men scream like they do when their bits are being sliced off. Cor, turns me stomach to hear something like that and gives me nightmares, it does.'

'It's not too late to change your mind,' Georgina offered. 'There's still a generous payment on offer for the right information.'

The bloke bit on his bottom lip as he considered his options. 'But if I talk to you, me boss will kill me.'

'You'll be under my protection.'

'I don't know—'

'-Give me your knife, Nobby,' Georgina interrupted abruptly. She had to find David and didn't want to spend any more time on persuasion, not when her husband's life was at stake. 'I think this bastard needs some help to make up his mind.'

'But it's a bit blunt, Miss Garrett,' Nobby replied, placing it on her desk.

'Oh well, it'll still do the job. It just might take a bit more hacking,' Georgina said, sounding unconcerned. 'Eric, pull his trousers down and, Johnny, you can help to hold him still.'

The man, wide eyes in disbelief, cried, 'No... no,' as Eric advanced towards him.

Georgina took Nobby's slightly rusted knife, then nonchalantly pushed back her chair. She stepped towards the man, his trousers now around his ankles, and said to Eric, 'Hold your hand over his mouth. We don't want anyone to hear him screaming.'

'No – no, don't. I'll talk, for fuck's sake. I'll talk.'

'Good decision,' Georgina said, and smiled with satisfaction.

'You'd better look after me 'cos my boss is a mad bastard and he'll do a lot fucking worse than chop my dick off.'

Georgina sat back down, pleased that she wouldn't have to resort to violence. 'I said I would and I don't go back on my word. Now, we'll start with your name. Who are you?'

'My name is Walter Boff, but everyone calls me Wally.'

'Right, Wally, that's a good start. Now tell me, who do you work for?'

Wally swallowed hard. It was clear that he was scared of spilling the beans but he spat, 'Thomas Kelly.'

Georgina frowned, her mind turning. *Kelly* – she hadn't heard that name in years. 'Is Thomas Kelly related to Kevin Kelly?'

'Yes. Kevin was his father.'

Georgina was grateful that she was sitting down. If she hadn't been, she knew her legs would have gone from under her. Kevin Kelly had almost ruined her life. He'd killed Lash and her dad. But that wasn't all that he'd done and her stomach churned. She could still smell the scent of his overpowering aftershave from when he'd raped her. The memories of pain and hurt that he was responsible for causing came flooding back. She'd thought that Kelly was in the past and rarely allowed thoughts of him to infiltrate her present, but now his son was in town, threatening to take away all that she loved. 'Where is he holding David Maynard?'

When the man didn't answer immediately, she yelled, 'Tell me, or I'll go ahead and cut your fucking dick off.'

'In a bombed-out warehouse area near Wandsworth

Common,' Wally blurted out quickly. 'I can draw it out on a map for you.'

Johnny had been right. Given the right *persuasion*, Wally was, indeed, talking like a budgie.

'Is David still alive?'

'Yes, but he's in a bad way.'

Oh, David, David, stay alive, Georgina cried inwardly, while on the outside she hid her angst and asked, 'What does Kelly want with us?'

'He hates you. He wants you dead, and then he'll take over Maynard's business. When he's done that, he's going to take down Morris Palmer. Mr Kelly believes that he should be rightfully heading up the Portland Pounders.'

'How many men does he have working for him?'

'Only seven, including me. Actually, no, six. Nelson was killed on Clapham Common.'

'Are all five men, including Kelly, in this warehouse?'

'No. There's only Titch and Ralegh, they take it in turns. Oh, and Mr Kelly, of course. The other two have been sent back to Bristol to run the operations down there for now.'

'How the fuck did seven bits of kids manage to organise breaking into my husband's house and annihilating most of his best men? And also break into my house and a friend's flat?'

'Mr Kelly paid some blokes to help us out.'

'What blokes?'

'I don't know, Miss Garrett. I really don't. If I did, I'd tell you.'

'You must know something about them?'

'Only that they was foreign.'

'How did Kelly get hold of foreigners? Where are they from?'

'They was off a ship on the Bristol docks, but I don't know what country they came from. They travelled down here in the back of one of our vans. They did the job, got paid and went back to their ship. I don't know when or where it was sailing.'

Georgina bit on her bottom lip, thinking for a moment, before asking, 'The guns used. Automatic weapons. How many does Kelly have?'

'None now. They belonged to the men off the ship.'

'All right, Wally. You're doing really well. Now, describe the layout of where Mr Maynard is being held.'

Georgina handed a pad and pencil to Johnny who took notes and drew pictures. Wally went into great length and soon they had a clear idea of the set-up.

'I think that's all I need from you for now. Oh, one more thing... when my friend's flat was broken into and someone punched her in the stomach, were you there?'

'No, Miss Garrett. That was Titch with a few of the blokes from the ship.'

'You're sure?'

'Yeah. I didn't go to your house either,' Wally answered and then he lowered his head as a mumbled, 'But I was at the other house, where we took your husband from.'

'Your honesty has been noted,' Georgina managed to grind out, inwardly seething.

'You are going to keep your word... you're not going to kill me now, are you?'

'No, Wally. I'm not going to kill you. But you won't be free to go until I have my husband back.'

'Go! Go where? I'll never be safe as long as Thomas Kelly is alive.'

'I said I'd pay you handsomely for information, and I will. You'll be given enough to find somewhere well away from the man.' Georgina didn't feel any sympathy for Wally. He'd helped to kidnap David and was lucky she hadn't ordered his death.

She turned away from him as Nobby asked, 'What do you want us to do with him, Miss Garrett?'

Georgina spoke quietly. You couldn't be too careful and she wouldn't give away too much in front of Wally. 'He can stay here for now, but keep him out of sight. Larry can keep an eye on him. Call him. And tell him to be nice. When he arrives, I want you and Eric to come straight up to Ezzy's shop. I've got to get out of here. I can't stand to be under the same roof as that bastard any longer. It's taking all my strength not to kill him.'

Johnny slumped into the chair on the other side of the desk. 'Fuck me,' he blurted, 'Thomas Kelly. That's a turn-up for the books.'

'Ain't it just.'

'You could have knocked me down with a feather when he came out with the Kelly name.'

'Yeah, me too.'

'What now?'

Georgina headed towards the door. With a steely determination in her eyes, she answered, 'We get my husband back. That's what.'

Charlotte had taken the call from Eric. He'd told her that Miss Garrett wanted Larry at the café to guard Wally, the bloke who they'd captured dropping off the message at Ezzy's jewellery shop.

'She said that I have to go with you,' Charlotte lied to Larry.

'What for?' he asked.

'I dunno. Maybe because I've got keys to the café. Or maybe because your arm is in a sling 'cos of your gunshot wound. Maybe she thinks this Wally bloke needs the two of us to guard him.'

'Three,' Ned chipped in. 'My orders are to stick to you, Charlotte, like shit to a blanket. If you're going, so am I.'

'Come on then. What are we hanging around for? Are you all right to drive, Larry?'

'Course I am. I've been shot in the shoulder but there's nothing wrong with my eyesight.'

'In that case we'll take both cars. You never know when they might be needed,' she said sagely.

Ned drove his car, Charlotte in the passenger seat, and Larry followed in their wake. They soon arrived at the café where Nobby and Eric were, waiting to leave on their arrival. Swift goodbyes were said.

In the back office, secured to a water pipe, Wally stared fearfully at Larry and Ned. He hardly took any notice of Charlotte. This irked her. Didn't he realise that she was the one that he should be afraid of?

She ran her eyes over the huge bloke. He didn't appear to have a mark on him. No split lips, black eyes, swollen ears of bruises. She'd expected him to be battered. There should be blood. She couldn't understand why he hadn't been hurt.

Ned must have thought the same. 'It looks like it didn't take much to get him talking,' he said.

'Wanker,' Larry added as he kicked Wally's tied legs.

'Leave me alone. I made a deal with Miss Garrett... Please, don't hurt me.'

'Yeah, I bet you fucking did. I bet you squealed like a fucking pig to save your bacon,' Larry scowled.

'It turns my stomach to even look at the cunt,' Ned snapped.

Larry stomped from the room and Charlotte went after him. 'Are you all right?' she asked.

'No. I fucking ain't. That bastard in there killed men who I've worked with for years. Friends, Charlotte. Mates I went to school with, who I grew up with. I would have been dead an' all if I'd been at Mr Maynard's house that day. Yet he's in there, alive and fucking breathing and I've gotta babysit him. It makes my blood boil. I just wanna throttle the bastard.'

'I know how you feel,' Charlotte said ruefully, 'but you need to calm down so I'll brew a pot of tea. The cure-all. We'll have a cuppa and leave him to rot in there.'

Tea made, Charlotte popped her head around the office door and told Ned to come and join them. She handed round the cups and saucers and placed a plate of biscuits on the table.

'I'm busting for the loo. Tuck in. There's loads more biscuits where they came from.' She smiled, trying her upmost to look sweet and innocent.

Ned picked up a digestive and dunked it in his tea. Charlotte's ruse was working. She slipped away but instead of going into the toilet, she crept into the office and gently closed the door behind her.

Wally peered up at her. He didn't look afraid. As Charlotte walked towards him, she reached into her dress pocket and pulled out the knife that she'd concealed when making the tea.

'What? What the fuck?' Wally blurted, his eyes popping at the silver glint of the sharp blade.

'This is for Tim and our baby,' Charlotte hissed with venom. She leant down and plunged the knife into the side of Wally's neck. The man screamed. As she pulled out the blade, blood gushed from the wound. Wally screamed louder. Charlotte struck him again, this time in his chest. He was a big bloke and she wasn't convinced that the short blade had passed through his fat to his vital organs. She stabbed again and again, three, maybe four or five times – she wasn't counting. But with every plunge of the knife, she thought about her lost baby.

As Wally quietened and the life faded in his blue eyes, Charlotte felt strong hands dragging her away. Ned and Larry had a hold of her. Ned took the knife from her blood-covered hands and Charlotte smiled. Her work was done. Wally was dead and she'd avenged her child's life.

*

When David regained consciousness, it took him a while to realise that he wasn't any longer tied to the chair. He had been laid on several empty sacks with two coats thrown over him. The warmth from the bonfire felt welcoming. Though in excruciating pain, he felt a little better than he had done throughout the night and he wondered if his fever had broken.

His ears pricked at the sound of men talking and he opened his eyes a slit to see Titch and Ralegh sitting at the rickety table. He couldn't hear Thomas Kelly, and guessed by what the two men were saying that he wasn't around.

'Fucking good, eh, Titch. He wants us to keep Maynard alive yet he was happy to let my brother die,' Ralegh moaned.

'I know. I don't get him sometimes. I was sorry about your brother, mate. Nelson was a good bloke, despite what Kelly said.'

'He was sent to that bandstand like a fucking lamb to the slaughter. Kelly knew that Nelson could be killed but he didn't give a shit.'

Titch changed the subject. 'I gotta ask… your names, Ralegh and Nelson, how the bloody hell did you get stuck with them?'

'Ha, it's thanks to my dad. He was in the navy for most of his life.'

'What's that got to do with it?'

'Admirals, Titch. Me and my brother were named after navy admirals.'

'Oh, right.'

David was pleased to learn that there seemed to be some discord amongst Kelly's men. Well, at least from Ralegh. This gave him a small amount of hope. Maybe he could work on Ralegh, offer him money and protection in exchange for turning a blind eye to his escape. It was a long shot but worth a go. But he'd have to bide his time and wait until he was alone with the man.

David's mouth felt dry. 'Water,' he croaked, hoping that one of the men would hear his weak voice.

It was Ralegh who came over with a metal canister. David held his head up as Ralegh placed the vessel to his lips. He drank slowly, coughing a few times, but weak and unable to support himself any longer, he flopped back down. He couldn't try to escape yet. He'd be lucky to even get on to his feet, but he could start building a rapport with Ralegh. 'Thank you,' he whispered. 'I'm grateful.'

Ralegh glared at him with disdain before grunting and ambling back to the table. He sat down again and said to Titch, 'Kelly's taking the piss. How are we supposed to keep him alive? You've seen the state of him. It would be kinder to put the bloke out of his misery.'

David heard every word. They believed he was dying. He was determined to prove them wrong. Yes, he was weak, but he wouldn't die. He refused to give in. He had to break out and be with Georgina. As long as Kelly didn't get to her first.

'I'll get us some grub. Take good care of him,' Titch said before mooching off.

David waited until he was sure that he was alone with Ralegh and then he croaked for water again. Ralegh traipsed back over with obvious reluctance, but this time he eased David's head up and supported it while he drank.

'Thank you. You're a good man.'

'Just following orders. Personally, if it was up to me, I'd fucking kill you,' Ralegh hissed. 'Your wife had my brother shot and now he's dead.'

'That was Kelly's fault. He sent Nelson to the common to *test the waters*. He knew he wouldn't be returning.'

'Maybe, but your wife was the one who had him killed.'

'She wouldn't have had any choice. She was protecting one of her own men... men she cares about. Unlike Kelly who didn't give a fuck about your brother.'

Ralegh looked perplexed.

'A good leader... a good boss... cares about his men. I care about mine. I would never treat my men in the way that Kelly treats you lot. You're all expendable to him.'

Ralegh said nothing but David could see that he was mulling things over.

'You don't have to work for him. I could pay you more and you'd be well looked after.'

'Piss off. You'd say anything to get yourself out of here. Do you think I'm stupid enough to fall for a line like that?'

'It's not a line, Ralegh. I'm a man of my word, you can ask anyone and they'll confirm it. I'm offering you a better life.'

'Bollocks. If I help you out of here, as soon as you're back on your feet, you'd have me *disappear*.'

'Why would I kill the bloke who helped me? You'd be valuable to me. You would have proven that I can trust you and have earned yourself a respected place in my organisation.'

While Ralegh began to pace back and forth, David hoped

that his offer was tempting the man. What little strength he'd mustered began to drain away, but somehow he pushed again, saying, 'Kelly is a nutter. He's only interested in himself and he hasn't got the brains or the manpower to take on the Portland Pounders. You'll end up dead for the sake of Kelly's ego. But help me, work for me and you'll have a better and longer life.'

'I don't know... you could be bullshitting me.'

'I'm not, Ralegh. Let's help each other, eh?'

A door creaked and David heard the now familiar footsteps of Thomas Kelly returning. When he came in, David could feel a palpable change to the atmosphere.

'Where the fuck is Wally?' Kelly screeched.

'Don't know, Boss, he hasn't come back yet,' Ralegh answered with a shrug of his wide shoulders.

'Shit. He should have been back hours ago. I knew I was taking a risk by sending him to that jeweller's again. I bet that bitch had an ambush waiting for him. Fuck!'

David inwardly smiled. Of course Georgina would have her men there. And as Wally hadn't returned, she almost certainly had him. Kelly had very much underestimated his wife. He wondered if Wally would talk. Probably. David knew that his wife would use any force necessary to get the man to blab.

Red-faced with fury, Thomas snatched the spanner from the table and threw it across the room. Then he swept his arm across the table, sending cups, cigarettes, an ashtray and a pack of playing cards flying. 'Fuck – fuck – fuck,' he growled like a rabid animal and seemed to be close to tearing out his own hair.

Ralegh stood against the wall, white-faced, as his boss

raged out of control. David caught the man's eye and ran his thumb across his throat, mouthing, 'Wally is dead.'

'I'll fucking kill that bitch when I get hold of her,' Kelly continued to rave.

'Help me,' David mouthed to Ralegh, a plea in his eyes. He wasn't too proud to beg, not when there was a chance that Kelly could finish him off at any moment. He had to stay alive. His beautiful wife would be likely to burst in at any moment, all guns blazing, and Kelly wouldn't know what the hell had hit him.

However, suddenly, as though a switch had been turned off, Thomas Kelly calmed. He stood deep in thought for a few minutes, and then asked, 'Where's Nelson?'

'He's just popped out to get some food.'

'Right, here's what we're going to do,' Thomas said, issuing Ralegh with orders.

Thomas Kelly had snapped his orders and they'd picked up Titch, who was now sitting beside him as he drove towards Richmond. Ralegh was in the back with David Maynard, whose health seemed to be deteriorating. Ralegh had near enough carried David to the car and helped him inside. The whole thing had been a bit of a fiasco. He'd noticed that Ralegh was being unusually solicitous with David, to the point where it had infuriated Thomas. He'd ended up shouting and swearing at Ralegh, screeching at him to just drag Maynard along and bundle him into the car.

'What are we going to do, Boss?' Titch asked.

'I don't know yet. Shut up and let me think,' he ground out, gripping the steering wheel as tightly as his jaw was clenched. It wasn't supposed to have worked out like this. By now, Georgina Garrett and David Maynard were supposed to be dead and he should be firmly in place running the London operations. Instead, he was two men down and on the run. But he still had Maynard and knew that Garrett wouldn't rest until she had her husband back.

Thomas screeched the car to a halt. 'If she wants her husband back, then I'm going to give him to her.'

'What?' Ralegh asked.

'You'll see,' Thomas answered. This fight wasn't over yet. And Georgina Garrett was soon to get the shock of her life!

Johnny's car raced towards Wandsworth Common but it wasn't moving fast enough for Georgina. 'Faster, Johnny, faster.'

'I'm going flat out. We should be there in about ten minutes.'

She drummed her fingers on the car door, anxious to get to her husband.

'Is there a plan, Miss Garrett?' Nobby asked from the back seat.

'Yeah, there's a plan… steam in, kill Kelly and get David out.'

'We ain't gonna sneak in then?'

'No, Nobby. We are just getting in and out as quickly as possible.'

Georgina hadn't given her plan much thought; after all, what was there to think about? Two, possibly three men at most were holding her husband captive. She felt confident that she and her gang were capable of taking them down with minimal risk to their own lives.

Johnny stopped the car up the road from the warehouse and they all piled out. Georgina led the way and, from Wally's extensive description, they soon found the abandoned building. She ignored her sweaty hands and racing pulse. Georgina was focused on one thing – David.

Outside, her hand on the door, she looked from one to the other of her trusted men. 'Ready?' she asked.

Guns poised, they each nodded.

The door creaked as Georgina pulled it open and then Nobby ran through first, closely followed by Eric, Georgina, and then Johnny. As they ran through the dilapidated building, her nostrils caught the whiff of a fire. But there were no voices. No guns firing. Just the sound of her shoes crunching on broken glass and the ruffled noise of pigeons wings as they took flight from the rafters.

'They've gone,' Nobby said, deflated.

Georgina looked around the room where her husband had been held. A table at one end, a smouldering bonfire in the corner and a hard wooden seat in the middle. She walked to the seat and saw ropes on the ground. And blood. So much blood and she guessed it was David's. 'We're too late. They've done a runner,' she said, fighting the urge to cry.

'Yeah, but Mr Maynard must still be alive. They wouldn't have bothered taking him if he was dead,' Johnny said.

'You're right,' Georgina agreed, feeling a surge of relief that quickly turned to anger. 'But how the fuck am I going to find him now?'

'Let's go back for another chat with Wally. He might have an idea.'

'Yeah, it's worth a try,' Georgina said, her lips pursed.

The mood was sombre in the car on the journey back to Clapham Junction. Georgina gazed out of the window her thoughts twisting and turning. She'd hoped to find David but now those hopes had been dashed and she was back to square one. She tried to remain positive. After all, she still had Wally and he might be able to suggest a place where Kelly could have taken her husband.

'We'll find Mr Maynard and that bastard, Kelly,' Johnny growled. 'And when we do…'

'At least we now know who we're up against,' Georgina muttered, though the mere thought of the Kelly name made her blood run cold. It felt as though her nightmares, the ones that woke her gripped in terror, were coming to life and playing out in front of her eyes. Kevin Kelly had been the one man she'd feared and he'd almost destroyed her. It now felt that he was laughing at her from beyond the grave, cruelly mocking, and as a cold feeling ran up the back of her spine, she shivered.

'Are you all right?'

Georgina drew in a deep breath. 'I'm fine,' she assured him, stiffening her resolve. She wasn't going to show any weakness. She'd kill any male in the Kelly lineage, no matter how old or young. Never again would anyone with the name Kelly breathe a threat on her, or her family.

11

'What the fucking hell has happened here?' Georgina's voice rang out.

Charlotte, Ned and Larry all turned to see her staring open-mouthed at Wally's blood-soaked body. His white shirt was now stained red and he was slumped forward, lifeless. Charlotte glanced down at her clothes and realised that she was covered in the man's blood too.

'Charlotte must have lost her mind,' Ned said. 'We heard him screaming but by the time we got to him, it was too late; she'd already killed him.'

Georgina looked at Charlotte's bloodied hands. 'You did this?' she asked, disbelievingly.

Charlotte's chin jutted forward. 'Yeah, that's right. He deserved it and he's lucky I didn't gut him,' she answered defiantly.

Georgina stamped across the room and took Charlotte by surprise when she slapped her hard across her face. The slap stung her cheek and, holding a hand over it, she recoiled at the venom in Georgina's voice.

'You stupid, stupid, stupid cow! Have you got any idea what you've done?'

'I only did what *you* should have done.'

'He,' Georgina shouted, pointing at the bloody mess in the corner, 'was the only person who might have been able to help me find David and the man responsible for all of this. But now he'll never fucking talk again. Well done. Well fucking done, Charlotte. If my husband dies because of you, I'll never forgive you.'

Georgina's words stabbed worse than the knife wounds in Wally's chest. 'I'm sorry,' she mumbled as her defiance turned to despair. Tears pricked her eyes. 'I just wanted to pay him back for what was done to Tim and—'

'-I know exactly why you did it,' Georgina interrupted, 'but you were told to stay out of this. 'And he,' she spat, pointing at the body again, 'wasn't even in your flat. He didn't touch you, or Tim.'

Charlotte felt sick, and shook her head in anguish, aware now that she'd slain an innocent man. But was he so innocent?'

'Get out of my sight,' Georgina seethed. 'Ned, take her back to Mary's flat.'

Charlotte scuttled off, but as she climbed into the car, her mind turned and her defiance rose again. Yes, she'd killed the man, but he was part of the gang that had kidnapped David Maynard. Her thoughts continued to turn. Georgina had always been her mentor and she was only following the woman's example: Georgina always protected her own. She made sure that anyone who hurt her family, paid for their actions with their lives. Revenge. As far as Charlotte was concerned, she'd taken revenge too. She just hoped that Georgina, once calm, would see that.

★

Johnny shook his head as he gaped at Wally's lifeless body. 'I'll get the cleaner in. He's getting good money from us lately with all the work we're putting his way.'

'Yeah, you do that, Johnny. Thanks. And you,' Georgina said, turning to Ned with her eyes blazing, 'how the hell did you let this happen?'

'It didn't occur to us that Charlotte would kill the bloke. She's cute, that one, Miss Garrett. Too fucking cute. We never had a clue. She acts like butter wouldn't melt but she's a bleedin' maniac. She wants sending to bedlam.'

'All right, Ned, keep your opinions to yourself. What's done is done, but Gawd knows how I'm going to find David now. Wally was my only link to Thomas Kelly. Just take Charlotte back to the flat and don't let her out of your sight again.'

Johnny was only half-listening. He was deep in thought as he tried recall Wally's words. Hadn't he said something about foreigners from a ship working for Kelly? 'Bristol. Kelly's business is in Bristol,' he blurted.

Georgina clicked her fingers. 'Yes, yes, Johnny, you're right. How did I miss that?'

'Other things on your mind.'

'Larry, get yourself down to Bristol. Dig around. Find out what you can. Relay everything back to me or Charlotte at the flat. Here's the telephone number,' Georgina instructed as she scribbled the number on a piece of paper.

'Charlotte?' Johnny questioned.

'Yes, Charlotte. She fucked up but we still have work to do.'

Johnny inadvertently raised an eyebrow, but he was pleased that Charlotte wasn't in the doghouse. He had a lot of time for the girl and had always felt protective of her. And in all fairness, he secretly admired what Charlotte had done. If he'd been in her shoes, he might have done the same. Though he wouldn't want to face the wrath of Miss Garrett.

'I'll just make a few calls before I leave,' Larry said and sat at Georgina's desk. 'Now that we know who's behind this, I'll talk to some of the men on Mr Maynard's payroll. They might be able to dig up some information on Thomas Kelly too.'

'Yeah, good idea,' Georgina agreed. She then sent Nobby and Eric to check on Benjamin at the jewellery shop and ordered them to stay with him until further notice. It didn't take Larry long to finish making his calls and then he headed off to Bristol.

'Let's have a cuppa and a bite to eat. It might help to clear our heads and think about our next move,' Johnny gently suggested.

He half expected Georgina to jump down his throat and take offence at the suggestion of eating something when Mr Maynard's life was in danger, but he was pleasantly surprised when she agreed and, after going into the café, she pulled out a seat at a table. Johnny rummaged through the cupboards. The bread and cakes were stale but he found tins of spam, some potatoes that were only just starting to sprout roots and several eggs. He smacked his lips together at the thought of egg and chips, a favourite that his mum had dished up once a week as a special treat. Eggs were rare in some homes when he'd been a kid. Many families had struggled to put food in the bellies of their children. The legacy could still be seen today in the bowed legs of men and women who had grown up with rickets due to malnutrition. But Johnny had been luckier than most. His mother had worked her fingers to the bone to feed him and his brothers. In fact, she'd worked herself into an early grave.

'You all right back there?' Georgina called, breaking into his recollections.

Johnny had rolled up his sleeves and was peeling the spuds. 'Yep. You just sit there and look pretty. Leave the woman's work to me,' he replied with a chuckle.

Half an hour later, he placed a plate of food in front of Miss Garrett. She looked at him gratefully through her dark lashes. Johnny's stomach grumbled at the smell of the vinegar soaking into his chips. It seemed surreal, tucking into his favourite dish while a dead body was slumped in the office behind them.

'I've been thinking. Kelly's last note said to meet him on Wandsworth Common tomorrow night. There's a chance he might still turn up.'

'I thought the same,' Johnny agreed as he dunked a big chip into his runny yolk.

'And Kelly doesn't know that Wally is dead. He might be willing to exchange David for him.'

'I wouldn't count on that, Miss Garrett. I think that David, sorry, I mean, Mr Maynard is worth more to Kelly than Wally is.'

'Hmm, possibly. But it still gives us an extra bargaining tool.'

'Your food all right?' Johnny asked, pointing his knife at her plate.

'Handsome, Johnny, bloody handsome. Just what I

needed. Listen, there's no point you hanging around. You may as well drop me off at Mary's and get home. I'll need you back tomorrow night to run me to the common.'

'If you think I'm leaving your side at a time like this, then think on.'

'Don't you have a fancy woman in your bed at home waiting for you?'

'There's a woman but there ain't nothing fancy about her.'

'Who's the latest one?'

'Kathy. But she won't be around for much longer. The bleedin' woman is getting on my wick.'

'They never last long with you. If you was a woman, we'd call you a right old tart.'

Johnny laughed. Yeah, he supposed he was a tart really. He'd had more women in his bed than he'd had hot dinners. But none of them could ever hold a candle to his beloved Daisy who'd been taken from him too soon. As Johnny wiped a chip across his plate, soaking up the last of the egg and vinegar, a thought crossed his mind – tomorrow night, on Wandsworth Common, the way their luck was running lately, he might well be joining his Daisy in death.

12

Georgina felt surprisingly calm as she waited on Wandsworth Common for Thomas Kelly to show his face. Her serenity was due to now knowing who the enemy was, and from learning that Thomas Kelly lacked resources and intelligence. She couldn't believe it when Wally had turned up at Ezzy's shop. She hadn't expected Kelly to be stupid enough to have sent someone to the same place. If the man had thought his plans through properly, he would have come to the conclusion that she would have set an ambush. She now believed that Thomas Kelly wasn't as astute as she'd first given him credit for.

She looked towards the main road. Johnny's car was parked under a streetlamp and he was standing outside, leaning on the bonnet. She could just about make out the glow of his cigar. She hadn't come alone as instructed. She wasn't prepared to offer herself as a sitting duck. Nobby flanked one side of her and Eric the other. Two of David's men were with her too. One in front, one behind. If Thomas Kelly wanted to negotiate, then he'd have to accept that she came with protection. Without these men shielding her, Georgina feared that Kelly would gun her down.

'Someone's coming,' Nobby whispered, 'but it looks like a woman.'

Georgina stretched her neck to look past Nobby. She could see that the figure approaching was most definitely a woman. Her heels click-clacked along the tarmac path. She wore a fur cape over her shoulders and a tightly fitting skirt. As she came closer, Georgina could see that her peroxide-blonde hair was piled high on her head and she had heavy make-up around her eyes, along with bright lipstick on her thin lips. The woman was a brass. Georgina could spot a prostitute a mile off. After all, she'd employed plenty of them.

'Hello, boys,' the woman cooed. 'A geezer on the road up there paid me a tidy sum to drop this off to Georgina Garrett.' The woman sidestepped Nobby and looked at Georgina. 'That must be you, love. 'Ere, this is yours. I hope it's something fancy.'

Nobby took the package from the woman. It was wrapped in brown paper and tied with string.

'Toodle-pip.' The woman smiled, showing her yellow teeth and then turned to walk away.

'Wait. Where is the man who sent you?'

'Just up there on the main road. He's got a right flash car. Not a bad-looking fella either.'

'What car?'

'I dunno, a black and cream one. Can't say that I've seen many of them around 'ere.'

Georgina glanced at Nobby and Eric. 'Go,' she barked. 'See if you can find him.'

Nobby handed Georgina the package and then he set off with Eric, running towards the road.

'All right if I get off? I can see that this ain't no romantic liaison. I don't wanna get caught up in no trouble,' the woman said nervously.

'Yes, go, that way,' Georgina answered and pointed in the opposite direction from where the woman had come.

The woman swung her hips in an exaggerated manner as she click-clacked away.

Georgina looked down at the package, and for the first time that night, her heart began to pound heavily. She had a terrible feeling that yet another bodily part of David was inside. She couldn't face opening it yet, and walked back Johnny's car. Nobby and Eric turned up too, both breathless.

'We saw him, Miss Garrett. The cheeky bastard waved at us.'

'Did you note the make of the car?'

'Yeah. An MG saloon. Right nice motor, black on the bottom, cream on top, just like that tart said. Cream hubs an' all. It stands out like a sore thumb. Can't miss it.'

'Did you see who was in the car?'

'The bloke who waved at us was driving. It had to be Kelly. There was someone sat next to him. We didn't get a chance to see if anyone was in the back seat 'cos the windows are blacked out.'

'What's that?' Johnny asked, pointing to the package in Georgina's hands.

'Probably a bit more of David,' she answered, stifling a sob.

'Let me take it, eh?'

'No. Thanks, Johnny. I've got this.'

Georgina thanked David's men and told them to circle the area for an hour to see if they could spot the distinctive car. She told them that she would be in touch soon before climbing into the front of Johnny's car, with Nobby and Eric in the back.

'Drive around. Look for his car,' she ordered. 'We've got to find him.'

'Kelly must be doing all right for himself to have a flash car like that,' Nobby commented.

'He probably 'alf-inched it,' said Johnny.

Georgina wasn't really listening to their chat. She had her eyes on the package on her lap. Part of her was desperate to open it but another part dreaded it. Her mind raced at the possibilities of what it might contain. *Please*, she silently prayed, *please let David be alive*.

Charlotte still didn't feel bad about killing Wally and just hoped that Georgina wouldn't remain furious with her for too long. She had taken a call from the hospital earlier and since then, she'd been desperate to share her news with Georgina. She'd heard Johnny's car pull up at the back and had run to the front door to meet them. 'Tim's awake,' she gushed as Georgina come through the door.

'That's *really* good news,' Georgina said. 'And we could all do with some of that right now.'

'The hospital called. They said he opened his eyes and asked for me.'

'You'd best get up there then.'

'They said he's sleeping now, heavily sedated, so there's no point in me rushing to his side 'cos he won't know if I'm there or not. But I can't believe it, Georgina, he's awake and he spoke!'

Georgina's smile was weak and Charlotte swallowed hard before saying, 'I'm sorry, I shouldn't have killed that bloke, but after losing my baby and nearly Tim too, I was desperate for revenge.'

'It's all right. Let's just put it behind us.'

Charlotte smiled gratefully and then noticed a package in Georgina's hands. 'What's that?' she asked.

'I don't know, and to tell you the truth, I dread to think. It's from Thomas Kelly.'

Charlotte blanched. Was it another body part? She fought for composure. 'Look, go and sit down. I'll make us a drink and then you can tell me all that's happened.'

Georgina nodded and Charlotte darted to the kitchen. She felt bad for being so euphoric about Tim in front of Georgina when David was still missing. But since talking to the ward sister, she'd found it impossible to contain her joy.

When she carried the tea tray through to the front room, Johnny was in mid-flow relaying the night's events to Ned.

'What? Kelly was sat in his car next to the common?' Ned asked, his eyes wide with astonishment.

'Yeah, the brazen bastard. If he'd been in my sights I'd have shot him.'

'He's got some front.'

'Ain't he just! I reckon he's either showing off, making out he's braver than he is, or he's just plain bleedin' stupid,' Johnny said with contempt. He went to light a cigar but then appeared to think twice about Georgina not liking the smell, and he popped it back into his holder.

Charlotte handed cups of coffee around. She noticed that Georgina was peering at the package on the coffee table in front of her and rubbing her finger.

'Ain't you got anything stronger?' Johnny asked. 'A whisky or something?'

'No, Johnny, only tea or hot chocolate,' Charlotte answered, with her eyes still on Georgina. The woman looked sick with worry so Charlotte offered, 'Would you like me to open it?'

Georgina shook her head. 'No,' she answered and reached out to pick up the package.

The room was silent as Georgina slowly and carefully undid the knot in the string. Then she folded back the brown paper, which revealed another layer of brown paper tied with more string. Georgina went through the same process to find yet more brown paper and string.

'Flamin' 'ell, it's like pass the bleedin' parcel,' Ned said.

'The sick bastard likes his games,' Johnny added with disgust.

Finally, the last piece of wrapping was removed and Georgina lifted the lid. Her face drained of colour and she screamed in horror, 'No... no... no... no... no...'

Johnny jumped up to take a look and he too paled. 'Fucking hell!'

Ned looked next, and heaved. When Charlotte saw what was in the box, vomit rose and burned the back of her throat. She had to swallow it back down. 'Is – is – is that a heart?' she asked tentatively.

When Johnny nodded, despite feeling sick, Charlotte quickly sat down next to Georgina, while avoiding looking again at the greying, strange-looking lump of flesh. She rested her hand on Georgina's arm. 'I'm so sorry,' she said gently. 'Let me take this away.'

'No,' Georgina protested. 'It's David's heart and this,

with a couple of his fingers, are all I have of my husband. They're all I have of him to bury. I'm going to give him a proper burial.'

'I know you will, but until then, let's put this somewhere safe.'

Charlotte was pleased when Georgina agreed, though she wasn't looking forward to handling the package. Johnny must have sensed how uncomfortable she felt and stepped in. Without saying a word, he gently picked it up to carry it through to the kitchen.

Though deathly white, no tears fell from Georgina's eyes. Charlotte assumed that she was in shock, but her grief was sure to break. When it did, she hoped she'd be able to comfort her. Christ, it was ironic. There was Charlotte's husband coming round from his coma while Georgina's husband's heart had been cut out. Life could be a bitch sometimes.

'Read this to me,' Georgina said and handed Charlotte an envelope.

Charlotte pulled out the note. Her eyes quickly scanned the message and she baulked. She couldn't read this to Georgina, it was too awful. She took a deep breath and said, 'I don't think you should hear this.'

It was no surprise when Georgina barked, 'Read it!'

Charlotte's hands shook as she held the note. The words, clearly scrawled in capitals, were written with callous hatred.

YOUR HUSBAND CRIED AND SCREAMED LIKE A BABY WHEN I CUT INTO HIS CHEST. HE BEGGED ME TO STOP. HE PISSED HIMSELF, WHICH WAS UNPLEASANT BUT MADE WORSE WHEN HE SHIT HIS TROUSERS TOO.

THEY SAY THAT THE BEST WAY TO A MAN'S HEART IS THROUGH HIS STOMACH. I FOUND THAT IT WAS EASIER TO GO THROUGH HIS CHEST AND CRACK HIS RIBCAGE OPEN TO YANK IT OUT.

YOU'RE NEXT.

Georgina said nothing as she rose to her feet and stumbled through to the bedroom. Charlotte went to follow.

'Leave her be,' Johnny advised.

Charlotte sat back down on the sofa and asked quietly, 'What's gonna happen now?'

'I don't know, sweetheart. But one thing's for sure. Thomas Kelly has just signed his own death warrant.'

13

It had been four days since Georgina had received David's heart. In that time, she'd barely left the bedroom and Johnny was worried about her. The few times that she'd emerged from the room, Johnny had noticed that her clothes were dishevelled and her hair dirty and unkempt. She didn't speak. She hadn't uttered a single word except 'NO' when declining the offers of food.

Charlotte breezed through the door with Ned in her wake and Johnny tried to smile as he said, 'Hello, love. How's Tim?'

'So much better, thanks, Johnny. He doesn't say much but he knows that I'm there. I'm sure he squeezed my hand today.'

'That's smashing, that is. You'll have him home soon.'

'We've got a long way to go yet but he's on the mend.' Charlotte then lowered her voice. 'How's Georgina?' she asked, flicking her head towards the bedroom door.

'Gawd knows. I ain't seen her all morning. I'm really worried about her.'

'Yeah, me an' all, but I don't know what to do. I should have come back sooner but to be honest, I stayed at the hospital longer than usual because I feel so flippin' useless here.'

'I know what you mean. I don't want to intrude on her grief but she needs to eat something. I was thinking about calling Molly, get her up here. What do you reckon?'

'I considered that too but I think Georgina would do her nut. She won't want my sister around, not when Thomas Kelly is still out there and a threat to us all.'

'Oh, yeah, good point.'

The telephone trilled and Charlotte rushed to answer it before the noise disturbed Georgina. Larry was on the other end of the line.

'He's here. Thomas Kelly is back in Bristol.'

'Kelly? You're sure? Have you seen him?'

'I ain't seen him with my own eyes, but I'm sure. I've heard from a reliable source that he turned up this morning in a flash motor, showing off and bragging about bringing down London's top gangster. I need to speak to Miss Garrett.'

'That – that's a bit difficult at the moment,' Charlotte said uncomfortably. But then she was surprised when she heard Georgina's voice behind her.

'Give me the telephone.'

Charlotte handed her the receiver and listened to the one-sided conversation.

'No, Larry. Don't kill him. Leave that pleasure for me...' Georgina paused to listen and then said, 'Yes, find out his whereabouts. Keep an eye on him. I want to know his every move and who he has working for him.' There was another pause, then: 'Yes, I'll be in Bristol tomorrow. What, not Bristol, but a small town outside the dock, you say?'

When Georgina finished making the arrangements she replaced the receiver and turned around. Charlotte was pleased to see a fire in her eyes again.

'You heard that. Johnny, you're driving us to a place near Bristol.'

'All of us?' Ned asked.

'No, you're to stay here with Charlotte.'

'For fuck's sake, why have I got to babysit her? Why can't it be one of the twins?'

Georgina didn't respond to Ned's questions, she just glared angrily at him and he nodded, mumbling, 'All right, I'll do the babysitting.'

Charlotte fumed. She stomped over to Ned and spat angrily, 'You ain't *babysitting* me. You're protecting me. It's your job to make sure that no one hurts me. Have you got a problem with that?'

Ned held up his hands, and shook his head.

'Good. Now keep your ugly trap shut and let Georgina get on with what she has to do,' Charlotte snapped, proud of herself for putting Ned in his place. With David dead, Georgina needed their support, not bickering around her. And though Charlotte realised that she was being selfish, she couldn't help feeling relieved Georgina would be away for a while. She was finding the oppressive and gloomy atmosphere in the flat hard to live with. Yes, she was mercenary, but she wanted to celebrate Tim's hopeful return to good health and she couldn't do that with Georgina in mourning.

After parking his stolen vehicle directly outside the pub entrance, Thomas Kelly swaggered in, looking down his nose at the pub's customers as he sauntered towards the bar.

The landlord was quick to put a pint of ale on the counter.

'I heard that you were back, Mr Kelly. Nice car. I take it that business was good in London?'

'Can't complain, my man, can't complain.'

Thomas had a reputation in the area – one that he was proud of – but he desired more. He wanted his name to mean something in London too and even more so in Liverpool. Yet things hadn't panned out as he'd planned in London, and in order to take over the Portland Pounders, he needed control of David Maynard's businesses.

He supped his ale as Titch ambled through the door in his usual clumsy manner. It irked him. How was he supposed to build his empire with useless great lumps like Titch around him? Ralegh wasn't much better. The pair were acceptable as a bit of muscle but he didn't think that they had half a brain between them.

'Boss,' Titch greeted, his hands stuffed into his trouser pockets as he glanced around the pub.

'Do I need to ask if there were any problems?'

'No, Boss. We did exactly what you said.'

'Right. Now go and check on the girls. I bet the slags have been slacking while I've been away. Tell them I'm back. Warn them. Slap a few of them around to remind them who they work for.'

'Yes, Boss,' Titch answered with a nod of his head.

'Well, don't just stand there.'

Titch hurried out. Thomas was glad he'd had the forethought to send the man to sort out his prostitutes. Thomas felt sure that his whores working the docks would have taken the piss while he'd been away. But a swift backhander from Titch would keep them on their toes. They earned him good money so he didn't want them roughed up too much. But Titch knew how much pressure to put on the women without going over the top. After all, a tart battered black and blue would be no good for business.

'One of your girls was in here last night,' the landlord said.

'Touting, was she?'

'No, nothing like that. She was flashing her cash and saying she'd had a windfall.'

'What sort of windfall? I hope it weren't my money that she was throwing around.'

'I don't know, but she had too much to drink and said she doesn't work for you anymore. She had a few choice words to say about you too. Swearing like a navvy and dragging your name through the mud. I threw her out in the end.'

'She fucking what? What silly little slag was it?'

'That little redhead, the one with an upturned nose.'

'Clara?'

'Yes, that's her. Mouthy little thing.'

Thomas slammed his pint down on the counter and stormed out of the pub. He leapt into his car and sped towards the docks. He saw Titch en route and stopped beside him. 'Get in.'

'What's wrong, Boss?'

'Clara. That's what's fucking wrong,' Thomas seethed.

He put his foot down, impressed with the speed he could get from the car. Within minutes, he arrived at the Avonmouth docks, which sat on the Bristol channel. It was a place where Thomas had always felt comfortable, probably because his father had owned a big house on the Liverpool docks. The burly, mostly rough men who loaded and unloaded the boats, the different smells from the goods being imported, the hustle and bustle and heavy lifting machines, the grand cargo ships – all these things were familiar to Thomas.

Though he had an inherent fear of the water that had derived from an incident he'd witnessed when he had been about five years old. He remembered it clearly: the woman, only young, about his age now, floating face down, her arms gracefully swaying in the water above her head. His father had punched the woman, catching her hard under her chin, which had lifted her feet from the ground. She'd tumbled backwards and fallen off the wharf and into the flotsam of the River Mersey. The woman hadn't cried out for help. She hadn't even struggled to try and keep her head above water.

Thomas could remember peering open-mouthed over the edge and down at the drowned woman until his father had dragged him away by the scruff of his neck. 'Shouldn't we pull her out of the water, Dad?' Thomas had asked. His dad had nonchalantly replied, 'No, son, she isn't worth getting wet for. Come on, let's get home for our tea.' Thomas wondered if that early, vivid memory was the first time that he'd witnessed a murder. He couldn't be sure but he did know that he'd been wary of water since that day.

Thomas pulled up alongside two of his prostitutes. He noticed how they both almost stood to attention when they saw him.

'Where's Clara?' he asked through the car window.

'I don't know, Mr Kelly. We haven't seen her for a few days.'

'If you see her, tell her I'm looking for her.'

'Yes, sir, Mr Kelly, we will.'

He drove on, unsurprised to see that soldiers were still

heavily present on the docks and doing the work of the striking dockers. He'd been wary of the soldiers when they'd first arrived, but had soon come to realise that the young men had just the same needs as the dockers. Business hadn't declined as he'd expected. In fact, his tarts had never been busier. If he had any say in the strike, which he didn't, he'd like the dockers to stay out for as long as possible. The longer the soldiers did their jobs, the more his pockets were lined with their hard-earned pay.

He soon spotted another woman who he pimped. This one – he couldn't recall her name – was a slovenly cow and partial to the booze and drugs. When he stopped beside her and she turned to look through his window, he recoiled at the grotesque sight of scabs around her mouth. Again, he asked after Clara. But the woman claimed ignorance.

As Thomas drove away, he said to Titch, 'Get rid of that one. She's filthy.'

'I'll tell her to move on.'

'No, I said, *get rid* of her! Sling her in the drink for all I care. I don't want her filthy disease associated with my name.'

After a fruitless search of the docks, Thomas left Titch to continue to look for Clara on foot, while he drove back to the pub. Once again, the landlord was ready with a pint of ale. But the thought of Clara soured the taste. The woman needed finding, and when she was found, Thomas would cut out her dirty tongue. Clara would never again bad-mouth the name of Thomas Kelly. He'd make sure of that!

14

Clara Coxon held her hand out expectantly at Larry and fluttered her lashes that were thick with mascara.

'Bugger off, Clara. You ain't told me nothing new.'

'Oh, go on, Larry. Just see us all right for a few shillings. I've got five hungry kids at home and now I'm out of a job because of spouting my mouth to you.'

Larry sighed, rolled his eyes and pulled out the coins from his pocket. ''Ere, now bugger off until you've got something worthwhile to tell me.'

Clara shoved the money into her jacket pocket and cooed, 'Aw, thanks, Larry. You're a proper gent. I'll see you soon, darling.'

'Only if you've got info. I don't want to hear no more of your sob stories.'

Clara blew Larry a kiss and sashayed away, glancing over her shoulder to offer the man a wink before she snuck out of the boarding house. Cor, she fancied Larry something rotten but he didn't seem interested in her. Well, he was for what she could tell him about Thomas Kelly but that seemed to be as far as the man's attraction went. Not that she could blame him for turning his nose up at her. He seemed like a nice bloke, well-off too, with his shiny shoes and smart suit.

He was nothing like the beer-swigging, stinking, toothless men who she had opened her legs to for money.

Larry was different. He wasn't posh, not like the king. Yet he had style and manners, whereas she, at just twenty-three years old, already had five young kids and not two ha'pennies to rub together. Of course, her kids' fathers were nowhere to be seen. One had been in the merchant navy and probably had a girl in every port. Her middle child's dad was in gaol and would be for a long time to come. The twins' father had buggered off with a woman from Wales.

Clara scuttled along the street, her thoughts still turning. When it came to her eldest daughter, well, God only knows what happened to her father. She hoped that he was dead. She prayed that she'd never bump into him again. Not that she was even sure that he was the father – it could have been either of her attackers. The encounter, nearly ten years ago, had been terrifying. Clara was just thirteen at the time and running an errand for the man on the coffee stall at the end of the dock. While she was happily skipping along on that summer's day, without a care in the world, strong hands had suddenly grabbed her and shoved her into an alley, behind some pallets.

Before she could regain her wits, two men were on top of her. One held her down to the ground, pinning her arms, as the other had pulled down her knickers. She'd tried to fight, kicked really hard, but at less than five feet tall, she'd been no match for the brute who had climbed on top of her and raped her. Clara still cringed at the memory. The pain had been intense. She hadn't been able to scream out for help because a big hand that stunk of tobacco had covered her mouth. And then, just when she'd thought it was over, the men had swapped and she'd been raped a second time. That had been Clara's introduction to sex.

Life hadn't got any better after the rape. Clara had been too ashamed to tell anyone about it, and when her belly had started to swell with child, her father had thrown her out of the house. Her mother, a fragile woman, never dared to defy him. So, with no shelter and no money and nobody to turn to, Clara had been forced to do what she'd seen so many women do in the Bristol docks – she'd sold her body for cash.

Clara jingled the coins in her pocket that Larry had given her. There was enough to feed her kids for at least a week. They were in for a treat tonight! She'd be more careful this time. The last lot of cash that she'd earned from Larry was already gone. She cursed herself for knocking back too much beer the night before and now, not only was she suffering with a thumping headache, but somehow, drunk, she'd managed to either lose her money or some sly sod had robbed her and she hadn't noticed. Probably the latter, she assumed, knowing that the area was steeped in poverty and frequented by plenty of unsavoury characters. And to be fair, she'd pinched a fair few bob in her time from unsuspecting drunken sailors. *What goes around, comes around*, she thought bitterly.

Clara came out of the greengrocer's loaded with potatoes, cabbage and carrots. She also had a few bananas that she'd hidden under her skirt when the grocer wasn't looking. She called into the butcher's and bought half a dozen sausages. When she'd asked for an extra one for free, the butcher told her to clear off, but that was no more than she expected. Now, laden with food for a good meal tonight, Clara paused to look up the steep hill that led to home. It was quite a trek to the top and she knew that by the time she reached the top, she would have worked up a sweat and her calves would be burning. But she liked living up there, especially on a clear day when the views across the sea were spectacular. Oh, there'd been many, many times when she'd daydreamed about sailing away across the blue oceans to a better place, to a land of milk and honey.

'You're brave walking around here as bold as brass.'

Clara was snapped out of her thoughts and turned to see Rosie, an older woman, who worked the docks for Thomas Kelly. Rosie had taken on the role of *mother* to Mr Kelly's whores and had been the person who'd shown Clara the ropes. Back in those days, it was Mr Roland Harris they'd all worked for. Clara had thought him bad enough, but when Thomas Kelly had taken over, she'd soon discovered that in comparison to Kelly, Harris had been a pussycat.

'Kelly's looking for you and he's none too happy.'

'You haven't seen me, Rosie, right?'

'No, my dumpling, I haven't seen you, but keep your head down.'

'I will, thanks, Rosie.'

'If you spot a classy-looking black and cream car, hides yourself. It's him. He's sitting behind the wheel like he thinks he's royalty or something. I wouldn't mind but he probably bought that car with money earned from us lot lying on our backs.'

Rosie's country Devon drawl was more pronounced than that of the locals. It gave her a homely and warm sound that matched her plump pink cheeks and deep brown eyes. But Clara knew that behind that maternal image, Rosie could be a fierce woman who wasn't afraid to jump into any brawl outside the pubs.

As Rosie walked off, Clara lowered her head against the wind that always blew straight down the hill. Never up, always down. That had baffled her since the day she'd first moved into the house, three years ago. Nevertheless she climbed to the top, thankful that Kelly didn't know where she lived, and outside her small home, one of her twins pulled open the front door, running out to meet her.

'Mummy, Mummy,' four-year-old Humphrey squealed. Clara had named him after her favourite film star, Humphrey Bogart. In fact, all of Clara's five children had the namesakes of a star from the silver screen. Humphrey's twin brother was named Gregory. She'd called her six-year-old son Clark and her nine-year-old daughter Greta. The baby of the family, one-year-old Ginger, named after Ginger Rogers, was the only name that she regretted registering. Because of the docks and the goods brought across the ocean from exotic lands, everyone assumed that Ginger was named after the spice. Clara wished she'd opted for the name Judy instead.

'Have you all been good for Greta today?' Clara asked as she handed Humphrey the cabbage to carry.

'I have, but Clark and his friends took Ginger's pram out and rode it down the hill. Greta shouted at them to bring it back but they didn't and it got a bit broken and Clark has cut his head.'

Clara sighed. A broken pram was all she needed. It had been second-hand but as she couldn't afford to buy another one, she hoped it was still usable.

Inside the two-roomed house, Greta was standing with

her arms on her hips and her young face was creased into a frown. She looked like a miniature mummy with her brood around her. 'You've heard then?' Greta asked with attitude.

'Yes. Is Clark's head all right?'

'He's got a nasty bump and a big scratch but he's fine. But the same can't be said for the pram. It's fucked.'

Clara was used to hearing her daughter use foul language and had given up on reprimanding the girl. Greta had picked up the swear words from Ginger's dad. At first, Clara had found it amusing, but when Greta started dropping *fuck* into every sentence, it wasn't so funny.

Greta, being a headstrong and mature girl for her age, hadn't taken any notice of Clara chastising her. So she'd given up and turned a blind eye instead. 'I've brought some food, so give me a hand in the kitchen.'

Greta huffed and trudged through to the tiny kitchen that had a stove with only one gas ring that worked, a stone sink and one tall cupboard where their food was stored, though most of the time it was empty. Upstairs, the sound of Clark and Gregory fighting reached Clara's ears. It was Greta who went to the foot of the stairs and hollered, 'Keep it down up there. You'll wake Ginger.'

And right on cue, probably due to Greta shouting, Ginger began crying. Greta stamped up the bare wooden steps to fetch the baby and Clara began peeling the potatoes. She loved her children, each one of them unique, but all with strong characters. Though it was Greta who was more of a mum to them. The girl had grown up fast with the burdens of motherhood on her shoulders. Clara, instead of bathing and seeing to her children's needs, felt more like the man of the house. The one out working and bringing home the housekeeping. It wasn't an ideal situation but it seemed to work for them and they were a happy family. And that's how Clara wanted to keep it.

But at the back of her mind, the thought of Thomas Kelly niggled. Rosie had been warned that he was looking for her, which had left her with a feeling of foreboding. Something was telling her that she'd never be free of him – unless Larry delivered on his promise to take the life of the man. If he did, she'd never have to worry about Thomas Kelly again, but that felt like a far-off dream.

'Bloody hell, this ain't like any of the bridges in London that cross the Thames,' Johnny exclaimed as they passed over Brunel's Clifton Suspension Bridge. 'And we ain't gotta pay to cross the likes of Albert Bridge or Battersea Bridge. Bleedin' liberty this is, charging us to drive over this one.'

Georgina looked to her left and out of the car window. The Avon Gorge was a sight to behold, yet the stunning outlook saddened her as realised that she would never be able to share this view with David. She'd never share anything with him again. They passed over the River Avon below.

'Shit, how high up do you reckon we are?' Nobby asked.

'I don't know, mate. Two hundred, maybe three hundred feet. Whatever it is, it's a bleedin' long way down,' Johnny answered.

Georgina noticed a crack in his voice and wondered if Johnny was scared of heights. She also saw that he was gripping the steering wheel as if his life depended on it. Who'd have thought that Johnny, full of banter and happy to pull his gun and shoot any man, would be afraid of heights! If she wasn't so deeply wrapped in sorrow over David's death, she might have found the energy to tease Johnny about his fear.

They had arranged to meet Larry in a small country pub away from the bustling docks and wagging tongues. Georgina wanted the element of surprise when she'd finally get to confront Thomas Kelly. She didn't want to be seen and for word to travel to him that she was in town.

As they pulled into a country lane, she began to wonder if they were lost. She couldn't believe that a pub would be situated along this narrow, winding road, seemingly in the middle of nowhere. But as Johnny steered the car around a tight bend, she saw the picturesque public house set back from the lane. Larry was standing outside the whitewashed stone building with a thatched roof, a red-painted door and pretty window boxes blooming with geraniums. She thought he looked very out of place.

'You found it all right then,' Larry said to Johnny, shaking his hand.

'Yeah, thanks to your directions. Fucking hell, Larry, you couldn't have found a place further out in the back of beyond.'

'Quaint, ain't it?'

'It's a bit different from our normal watering hole.' Johnny chortled.

Larry led them inside and to a large, dark-stained oak table. 'What can I get you to drink, Miss Garrett?' he asked tentatively.

'Just water.'

Larry offered his condolences. 'Sorry about Mr Maynard.'

Georgina managed a small smile, but the smile didn't reach her eyes.

Larry soon returned with a tray of drinks and the group huddled around the table.

'What's the plan then? Are we gonna drive to the pub where Kelly drinks and shoot him there?'

'No, God, no!' Georgina blurted, shaking her head. 'We've got to be a lot more discreet than that! Remember, I don't know the Old Bill down here. We can't afford to make any mistakes and get nicked for this. I'm not going back to prison, especially for the likes of Thomas Kelly. And I don't want to be swinging on the end of a rope either.'

'I hadn't thought of that. It's not so straightforward, is it?'

'No, Larry, it's not. And apart from anything else, I want Kelly to suffer, just like David did. I'm not giving that man the benefit of dying quickly. So, tell me what you've found out about him.'

'I've been paying one of his tarts for information. I know where he drinks. But I don't know where he lives... yet. He's been seen driving around in that stolen motor so he shouldn't be difficult to track down. But I've been laying low, like you told me. Good job an' all. That town is quiet, really quiet, and I get the feeling that Kelly controls it.'

'I can't believe that he's stupid enough to be driving around in that car. He might as well be waving a red flag. What an idiot.'

'Clara reckons that he's a right braggart. He likes to show off and thinks he's the big man.'

'Clara is the woman you've been talking to?' Georgina asked.

'Yeah.'

'Make sure it's a one-way conversation, Larry. Find out what you can but don't tell her anything about yourself, or us. We don't know if she can be trusted. She might be playing one up against the other so keep your mouth shut.'

Larry looked down into his pint and Georgina's eyes narrowed. 'For fuck's sake, what have you said to her?'

'Nothing. I haven't mentioned you. But she was so scared about telling me anything about Kelly that I had to offer her some reassurance. I told her that I was gonna kill him.'

Georgina clenched her teeth. 'Great,' she seethed. 'I hope she hasn't gone running back to Kelly with that nice little titbit!'

'No, Miss Garrett, she wouldn't have.'

'You don't know that,' Johnny spat. 'You can't trust a woman, especially a brass.'

Georgina turned to Johnny and glared at him. 'All women?' she snapped.

'Sorry, that came out wrong. But you know what I mean. Look what happened with me and Elsie Flowers. The cow stitched me – us – right up!'

'Johnny's right, Larry. You don't know Clara so let's assume the worst. We'll have to keep her quiet.'

'What, kill her?' Larry asked incredulously.

'No, of course not!' Georgina said impatiently. 'Just hold her for a while. Keep her with us and off the streets. Once the job has been done, we'll release her.'

'But she's got five kids to look after, Miss Garrett.'

Georgina raised her eyebrows. 'You seem to know quite a bit about her personal life and since when have you ever given a shit about a working woman's kids?'

Larry leaned back in his seat and said smugly, 'I don't give a shit about her kids but *you* will.'

Georgina shrugged. 'Fair point, I suppose. Do you know where she lives?'

'Yeah. I made sure that I found out.'

'Good. Well, we ain't taking on five kids so you'll have to keep her indoors.'

'Eh?'

'You'll have to hold her in her own house... with her kids.'

'You're fucking kidding me?'

'No, Larry, do I look like I'm joking?'

'Why do I always get the crap jobs? First you had me getting dolled up like a bird and now you want me looking after some tart's sprogs!' Larry turned to look at Johnny and continued, 'See what happens when you work for a woman. You end up doing women's work.'

'Watch your mouth,' Johnny warned.

'If you ain't happy, Larry—' Georgina began.

But Larry cut in. 'It's fine, I'll do it. Of course I will. I'm just letting off some steam.'

Georgina sipped from her glass of water. She knew full well that Larry would do as she asked. He always did. *Good old Larry*, David used to say about him. Christ, she missed her husband. But there was no time to dwell on that at the moment. 'Drink up,' she said, 'we've got work to do.'

As Georgina scraped her seat back and her men downed their drinks, she had only one thought on her mind – Thomas Kelly had to die.

★

As Thomas Kelly drove up the steep hill that led to Clara's house, he was grateful for the stolen car. 'Bugger walking up this,' he said to Titch beside him. He pulled up outside the narrow terraced house and climbed out, stopping to inhale a large lungful of the fresh air and momentarily looking out at the vista. 'Nice view,' he said flippantly, before marching to Clara's front door.

Titch knocked heavily on the shabby wooden door. Thomas could hear kids crying and sounding like they were causing havoc in the house. He'd heard that Clara had a few children but he was surprised when a young girl answered the door with a baby on her hip.

'Is your mother home?' he asked, keeping his voice light.

'No. She's working.'

'Who does she work for?' Thomas asked.

'I don't know, you'll have to ask her.'

The girl's tone was defensive, spoken like a woman rather than a child. He noticed that she was craning her neck to get an eyeful of his car, which made him feel smug. 'When is she due home?'

'When she bloody feels like it. You can see I've got my hands full here so do you want me to give her a message or something? If it's about the rent or some other debt that she's in, forget it: She can't afford to pay you so don't bother wasting your time.'

Well, this little madam really is a cheeky one, thought Thomas, almost laughing at her. 'You can give her a message. Tell her that Thomas Kelly is looking for her. Did you get that? Thomas Kelly.'

'Yeah, all right, I'm not deaf or the village idiot. I heard you the first time.' With that, the girl slammed the door in his face.

Thomas exchanged a smirk with Titch. 'Can you believe her? What was she, nine or ten years old? Give it half a dozen years and she'll be working the docks for me. You watch.'

'What now?'

'Back to business. Despite what the kid said, I think Clara's in there, but I'm not in any hurry. She'll be shitting herself so let her rot in her own fear for a while.'

Thomas sauntered back to his car. As he opened the door, he glanced over at the narrow house with dirty windows. He'd left his threat hanging in the air. It was all over town that he was looking for Clara and the thought of her squirming in fear left a smile on his face. Maybe she'd come to find him and beg for forgiveness. Maybe not. But either way, Clara would be regretting slagging him off. No matter how much the woman pleaded, he wouldn't let her off the hook. He'd use her to set an example to the other tarts: Thomas Kelly was not to be crossed.

15

Johnny listened as Miss Garrett booked three rooms above the country pub. She paid the landlord for his discretion about his guests from London and also persuaded the man to sell her a pair of trousers, a shirt, braces, boots and a flat cap.

When they ambled up to their rooms, he was pleased that he didn't have to share with Nobby and Eric. The pair of them were capable of turning his stomach with the vile smell of their farts. Larry would be a much more welcome roommate.

Johnny threw his trilby hat on to a coat stand in the corner as Miss Garrett handed Larry the clothes she'd bought, saying, 'Get changed into these. You'll look less conspicuous. Johnny will drop you off. Leave your car here.'

Larry didn't look keen on wearing the second-hand outfit but at least the items were freshly laundered. When she left the room, Johnny flopped down onto one of the single beds and lay with his hands resting behind his head, grinning.

'It ain't funny, mate. First she had me dressing up like a woman and now this,' Larry complained, holding the trousers in front of him.

'Miss Garrett is right though, Larry. You don't look like a local in your suit.'

'Yeah, I get that, I suppose. But I ain't relishing the thought of keeping Clara and her kids out of the way. I hope Miss Garrett sorts Kelly out sooner rather than later.'

'She won't hang about,' he said, then added quickly, 'watch your head!'

Too late. Larry had stepped forward and into the trousers but when he stood upright again, he clonked his head on the eaves of their small room. 'Ouch, shit,' he moaned.

'That might have knocked some sense into you.'

'If I had any fucking sense, I'd get out of this game. Me shoulder's still sore from that last bullet I took.'

'Last... how many times have you been shot?'

'Seven. But I reckon me luck is gonna run out one of these days.'

'Blinkin' 'eck, Larry, seven holes in you! I'm surprised that you don't leak like a tea strainer.' Johnny laughed.

'Mr Maynard used to laugh an' all. He reckoned I've been used as target practice. I liked and respected the man and I'm sorry he copped it.'

'Yeah, me too.'

'I ain't happy about having to go to Clara's. I'd rather be there to see Kelly getting his comeuppance.'

'You've still got a part to play.'

Larry scowled, but then said, 'Right, Johnny, I'm ready. Let's go.'

Johnny dropped him on the outskirts of town and kept his eyes peeled for Kelly's car. 'Are you sure you know where you're going?' he asked.

'Yeah. I know me way around. I made a point of

familiarising meself with the area. Don't worry, it was in the middle of the night. No one saw me.'

'All right, mate. I'll see you soon. In the meantime, have fun.'

'Fun? Fat chance of that, especially in these,' Larry said, pointing at his boots. 'They're fucking uncomfortable and weigh a bleedin' tonne.'

'Stop moaning like an old woman.'

'That's all right for you to say. You ain't gotta put up with Clara and her kids.'

'It won't be for long. I've got the directions of where she lives so I'll pick you up when we're done with Kelly.'

Larry clumped off, looking miserable while Johnny headed back to the country pub. The sun was getting low in the sky. It would be dark soon. He felt weary and was looking forward to getting into the comfortable bed in his room. It had been a long day and he had a feeling that tomorrow would be even longer.

Hiding under her bed, Clara's heart had pounded at the sound of Thomas Kelly's voice. He had found out where she lived. Someone she knew had probably told him, and she hoped he hadn't given whoever it was a beating to get the information. But now that he had been at her front door, she realised that he really *did* mean business. But the man couldn't know that she'd spoken to Larry. At least she hoped he didn't!

Clara had held her breath, and had listened carefully to every word on her doorstep. She'd been relieved that Mr Kelly hadn't forced his way in. After all, in her sparsely furnished home, he'd have easily found her. She imagined him dragging her out by her hair from under her bed and then giving her a good hiding, or worse.

Greta had been her usual insolent self. Clara was horrified at the way her daughter had spoken to Mr Kelly. The girl had no idea of the man's power or of how violent he could be.

When Clara had heard the front door close, she'd finally let out her breath. And when she heard his car pull away, she had sighed with relief.

'Who was he?' Greta asked.

Clara remained under the bed for a moment to compose herself. 'My boss,' she answered. 'Actually, my old boss. I used to work for him.'

'Did you rob him?'

'No.'

'Then why is he after you?'

'I don't know, Greta. But knowing him, it won't be good news.'

She was just about to slide out from under the bed but froze when she heard Greta shout, 'Who the fuck are you?'

Clara caught her breath again, fearing that Mr Kelly had sent in one of his thugs. She was pleasantly surprised when she heard Larry answer in his distinct London accent.

'Don't be scared, love. I'm Larry, a friend of your muvver's.'

'Not another *uncle*! You'd better not get my mother in the family way.'

'Erm, nothing like that. Is your muvver here?'

At this point, Clara, lying on her back, popped her head out from under the bed. 'Hello, Larry,' she said cheerily, smiling up at him.

'What you doing down there?' Larry asked, sounding amused.

'I was playing hide-and-seek with the kids.'

'More like hide-and-seek from Mr Kelly,' Greta added.

'He's been 'ere?'

'Yes. He's just this minute left. How did you get in?' Clara asked as Larry offered his hand and helped her to her feet.

'I hopped over the back wall and your boy let me in the back door. What did Kelly say?'

Clara smoothed her dress down and patted her red hair as she answered, 'Nothing. I was under there. Greta saw him off. But he'll be back.' She looked Larry up and down, noting that he was considerably underdressed compared to his normal attire. 'Anyway, it's nice to see that you made an effort.'

Larry looked uncomfortable and cleared his throat before replying. 'This, yeah, I, erm, wanted to *blend* in.'

'Why, Larry? What's going on and why didn't you come to the front door?'

'I didn't want to be seen.'

Puzzled, Clara asked, 'What's going on?'

He looked swiftly around the room and seeing all the kids, said, 'I need to talk to you in private.'

It was Greta who spoke again. 'There's nowhere private in this house and I'm not leaving you alone so that you can be disgusting with my mum.' She placed the baby on the floorboards and then her hands on her small hips as she glared at Larry with defiance.

'Don't be cheeky, Greta,' admonished Clara. She began to usher Greta out of the door, urging, 'Go and put the kettle on, there's a good girl.'

'You're not getting rid of me that fucking easily,' Greta protested.

'Just do as you're told and stop showing me up!'

'Huh, you don't need me to show you up. You do a good enough job of that yourself.'

'You cheeky little pig. Go on, get on your way.'

Greta threw Larry a filthy look before scooping up the baby and strutting haughtily from the room. 'And you're too *old* for my mum,' she spat, before slamming the door behind her.

'She's a character,' Larry commented. 'You've got your hands full there.'

'Yes, nine years old going on twenty-nine, that one,' Clara replied, rolling her eyes. She sat on the edge of her bed and patted beside her. 'Come and sit down,' she purred.

Larry stayed standing in the middle of the room. Clara gazed up at him, longing for him to pull her into his strong arms. Even in his scruffy clothes, she still found him to be a magnificent sight.

Larry remained where he was and said, 'Listen, Clara. I'm gonna tell you as it is… You and the kids have got to stay home. You can't leave, not for nuffink. And I'm gonna stay here with you to make sure you do as you're told.'

Clara's eyes stretched wide. She rather liked the idea of Larry staying with her, but *do as you're told*. She hadn't done that since she was about fourteen years old. Granted, her disobedience had earned a few slaps, but after the way men had treated her, she had vowed not to take orders from any of them again. 'I beg your pardon?' she said, her eyes narrowed.

'There's no need to get out of yer pram, and this ain't

open for debate. You're staying indoors until you're told otherwise. All right?'

'No, Larry, it's not all right. It's not all right at all! What's this all about? And if I can't go out, how am I supposed to earn a living to feed my kids?'

'I told you. It won't be for long, and you don't have to worry about money. You'll be taken care of.'

That information softened Clara a little, yet she still wanted to know why she was being kept a virtual prisoner in her own home. 'Well, I suppose I could stay home for a while but I shall expect to be well compensated for this. But why? I don't understand.'

'You don't need to worry about it. I just want you to stay away from Thomas Kelly.'

'Huh, I knew it had something to do with him. What if he comes back looking for me?'

'I'll deal with him.'

Clara felt herself swoon as she gazed up at him. Larry was everything that she wanted in a man. Good-looking, strong and heroic. He was a good ten years older than her, maybe more, but she knew from earlier conversations with him that he didn't have a wife waiting for him in London. And now, with him staying in her home, she had time to win his affections. Though with five screaming brats around, it wasn't going to be easy. 'Where are you going to sleep? We've only got the two rooms. I sleep down here and Greta sleeps upstairs with her brothers and sisters.'

Larry looked around the small room and she saw him take in the single bed, a rickety rocking chair and a sideboard where Clara stored her clothes. There weren't many options for Larry to choose from. She smiled wryly.

'I'll, erm, I'll have to kip on the floor.'

'No, you don't want to do that. All sorts of bugs come out of the woodwork at night. You'll be better off squeezing in with me. I don't mind sharing.'

The door burst open and Greta stood there with a baby in her arms and two boys chasing each other around her. 'Are you going to feed this lot? They're driving me mad.'

'Yes, Greta, I'll be there in a minute. Larry is going to be staying with us so don't give him any cheek.'

'I fucking knew it. It's going to happen again. He's going to leave you with another baby and I'll end up having to look after it.'

'How many times have I told you to watch your language? And if you must know, it's not like that. Larry won't be here for long, but while he is, none of us can go out.'

'What? Why not?'

'You don't need to know why, you just have to do as you're told.'

'But what about school? You've already had a warning. If we don't go, you'll get in trouble, Mum.'

'We'll be in a lot more trouble if you or your brothers and sisters go out of that door.'

Greta glared at her, but was then distracted by the twins who were using her as a shield as they threw punches at one another. Clara knew her daughter would sulk at being confined, but she would do as she was told. Her daughter might swear like a navvy, but she wasn't disobedient – just argumentative.

Clara walked towards the door, calling over her shoulder to Larry, 'Make yourself at home. I'll cook us all some dinner.'

In the kitchen, she was grateful to find that Greta was already preparing the vegetables. However, it was clear from her dark expression and the way that she was banging things on the side that she was in a bad temper. Clara was in no mood to pander to her daughter and hissed, 'You'd better get over whatever it is that's bothering you, young lady! I won't have Larry made to feel uncomfortable because of your tantrums.'

'It's always the same, Mum. A man comes into the house, and then us kids get pushed aside. The man leaves and then we know what always happens next: another baby comes out of you. I'm fed up with it.'

'I've already told you, it's not like that with me and Larry. He isn't going to be here for long so you've nothing to worry about. And once Larry has gone, I'll treat you. I mean, *really* treat you.'

'Promise me, no more babies.'

'I promise. And you promise to be nice?'

Greta still looked belligerent, so Clara pulled her into her arms. She stroked the child's greasy red hair, the same colour as her own. 'You're my best girl, Greta, and I don't know what I'd do without you.'

'Huh, you'd have to find someone else to look after your kids.'

Clara smiled, relieved to see that Greta also had a slight smile on her face now. 'You know, one day, when you're all grown up, you'll be a movie star, rich and famous just like Greta Garbo.' It was a fantasy that Clara had cultivated since the first day she'd noticed that her belly was full with a child. Clara had believed that the baby growing inside her, the one who'd been so cruelly and viciously seeded, would

RAVEN

have a better life than her own. She had convinced herself that the way out of poverty and whoring was through the silver screen. And daily, since Greta was first-born, she'd reminded her daughter that she would be a beautiful movie star. It was Greta's destiny.

But Greta was right – the last thing that Clara needed was another mouth to feed. Though she told herself that Larry didn't seem the sort of man who would abandon a pregnant woman. He had honour and a sense of responsibility. Perhaps getting pregnant would be a way to keep him. A plan began to formulate in Clara's head. She'd drag the tin bath out later, clean herself up. And hopefully, Larry would wash her back. She had just a few days to tempt him into her bed and she'd make sure to get his London address before he left. If she did get pregnant, she'd write to tell that he was going to be a father. He was sure to come rushing back, and then they'd get married. There's be no more whoring for her, not when she had got herself a good man.

In London, Charlotte sat on the sofa with her feet tucked underneath her and with a book resting on her lap. She'd been trying to read the final chapter but had given up because Ned kept interrupting with his inane comments about a program on the wireless. She'd been able to block out the sounds of the BBC man's clipped voice, so the program had gone right over her head. However, Ned's voice wasn't so easy to ignore, especially when he kept pushing her for an opinion.

The doorbell rang, which startled Charlotte and seemed to make Ned jump too.

'Who the bloomin' 'eck is that?' he asked.

'I've no idea. I can't see through walls, but I'm not expecting any visitors.'

'Stay put. I'll go down and see.' Ned's gun was on the sideboard and Charlotte noticed that he picked it up as he opened the front door of the flat that led down to the back of Mary's shop.

Unable to *stay put*, Charlotte sneaked over to the door and strained her ears to listen. When she heard Molly's voice, her heart leapt with joy and she eagerly ran down the stairs to greet her older sister.

'Molly… what are you doing here?' she asked, embracing her.

'Well, when you said that Georgina had gone to Bristol, I thought I'd better come and be with you.'

'I'm so glad you're here! Come in, Ned will carry your bag.'

'I'm your protection, not a bloody porter,' Ned moaned as he took Molly's bag. 'Does Miss Garrett know you're here?'

'No, of course she doesn't. And don't you go telling tales on me, Ned.'

'My lips are sealed. She'll do her bleedin' nut if she finds out that you've come here when all this shit is going on.'

'I know. That's why you're not to tell her. But I couldn't leave Charlotte all alone.'

'She ain't alone. I'm here,' Ned said.

'But you're not her big sister.'

In the flat, Molly threw herself onto the sofa. 'I'm knackered. That was a long train journey and it was horrible when the tube went through Balham underground station.

I thought of all those poor people who drowned when that bomb landed on the High Street and burst the water main,' she said. slipping her shoes off. 'So, how's Tim?'

'He's doing really well, considering. We still don't know if he will be left with any permanent damage but he's awake and he's saying a few words, sort of. Well, he's trying. The doctor said it's a good sign. But it's going to be a long and slow road to recovery.'

'Where do you want this?' Ned asked, indicating to Molly's bag.

'Pop it in my room,' Charlotte answered.

'Any news from Georgina?' Molly whispered.

'No, nothing yet.'

'How was she before she left?'

'Not good, Molly. I've never seen her like it before. She hardly spoke or came out of the bedroom for days. I've not seen her cry either.'

'She got like that when Lash was killed. So full of hate and anger. It broke my heart to see her go through it with him. I can't believe she's having to face it all over again.'

'I know. And to be sent David's heart like that. It was a terrible way to find out that he's dead.'

Molly shuddered. 'It's awful.'

'She'll get her own back on Kelly,' Ned said as he came out of the bedroom.

Molly nodded as she replied, 'Oh, I know she will! Georgina won't rest until David's killer is dead too. But it won't take away her pain. She thinks that murdering Kelly will make her feel better. But it won't. She still needs to grieve for her husband's life but Georgina isn't very good at dealing with those sorts of emotions.'

'I don't know what to say to her,' Charlotte said wistfully. 'It's horrible. I'm scared she will bite me head off.'

'She will. But she doesn't mean to, so don't take any notice. It's just her way. She tries to hold in all her pain and she thinks that crying and sadness is a sign of weakness. But she will crack eventually. And when she does, that's when she will need you. She'll need all of us.'

'I'll be there for her, Molly.'

'I know you will, sweetie. You love her just as much as I do. Do you know, I used to be a bit jealous of your relationship?'

'Jealous? I didn't know that.'

'Yeah, well, for as far back as I can remember, Georgina has always been my best friend. When you two got close, I didn't want to be envious, but I couldn't help it.'

'There's no need to be jealous. You'll always be her best friend. I think she looks at me more like a little sister rather than a friend.'

'Ha, yes, that sounds like Georgina. She likes to protect people.'

Ned piped up, 'She does. That's why she pays me to look after you.'

'And Molly now.'

'I'm gonna need a pay rise.' Ned chortled. 'A bloody big one an' all if I'm expected to have to listen to you two prattle on.'

'Take the blinkin' wireless and go and sit in the bedroom,' Charlotte suggested curtly.

Ned rolled his eyes but remained in the armchair.

'Is there any tea in the pot? I'm gasping,' Molly said.

'Yeah, of course, sorry, I should have already offered you

one but I was so surprised to see you,' Charlotte said and went into the kitchen. As she stood and waited for the kettle to come to the boil, she wrestled with herself about whether she should tell Molly about the baby she'd lost. She decided against it. The brutality of the way she'd miscarried would always be hard to come to terms with and no amount of talking about it would ease her pain.

Soon returning to the front room with a cup of tea and three digestive biscuits, she fixed a smile on her face and asked, 'How's Mum? Is she minding the boys?'

'Yes she is and she's fine, sends her love. I thought, you know, under the circumstances, it was best to leave Edward and Stephen with Oppo and Mum.'

'And the boys – they're fine too?'

'Yes, of course,' Molly answered sharply, looking down into her cup of tea.

Charlotte got the impression that her sister was hiding something. 'You're sure?' she challenged.

'Yes. Why wouldn't they be?'

'What's wrong? I know you, Molly. I know when you're not telling me something,' Charlotte pushed.

Molly looked around the room as though avoiding looking at Charlotte, and then placed her cup of tea on the coffee table. She held her hands on her lap, wringing them, and tears pricked her eyes. 'There is something. I don't know, it's probably nothing, but...'

Charlotte waited for Molly to continue but instead of explaining the problem, her big sister sniffed and began to cry. Charlotte instinctively placed her arm over Molly's shoulder and gently asked, 'What on earth is upsetting you so much?'

'It's just me being oversensitive, I suppose. Oppo says that there's nothing to worry about but I can't help it.'

'What are you being sensitive about?'

'Edward,' Molly answered. Her shoulders heaved as she cried and through juddering breaths, she said, 'I'm worried he's going to turn out like his father.'

Even the thought of Edward turning out like his father was enough to make Charlotte gasp.

Ned interrupted, saying coldly, 'I've always said the same. Billy Wilcox's son, well, Edward might just as well be the spawn of the devil. Billy and the devil are as evil as each other. I'd be worried an' all if young Edward was my lad.'

Molly sobbed harder and Charlotte glared at Ned. 'Shut up, you stupid old man!' she seethed.

'Oi, I ain't *that* old!'

'Just clear off, Ned. You ain't helping so get out of my sight.'

Ned huffed and picked up yesterday's newspaper before sloping away to the bedroom. Charlotte pulled a handkerchief from the sleeve of her blouse and handed it to Molly. 'Take no notice of anything that Ned says.'

'But he's right, Charlotte! There's no getting away from the fact that Billy is Edward's dad. I heard something the other day that really made me think. There was a vicar on the wireless and he was saying, *"The sins of the father shall be visited upon their sons."* What does that mean, eh? Is Edward going to have to pay for all that Billy did wrong? Or is my son – my beautiful boy – is he going to inherit Billy's wickedness?'

'I ain't got a clue about that Bible stuff, Molly, but I think you're reading too much into it. Edward's a good boy and he's never even set eyes on Billy.'

Again, Molly hung her head, as if in shame. 'But he's not a good boy.'

'What makes you say that?'

'He's sly, Charlotte, really sly. He tries to hide things from me but I see them. I know what he does. And, I can't lie, it scares the life out of me.'

Charlotte shuddered as she asked, 'What things?'

'Loads of things and it unnerves me. Like, when Oppo kills us a chicken for the pot, he chops its head off. It turns my stomach. I can't watch it, but Edward finds it funny.'

'He's been brought up on a farm, Molly. Things like that won't upset him.'

'I know, but he seems to enjoy watching the chickens die. And it's not just that. There's the time he took Stephen and the dog down to the stream. I don't know what happened but Stephen came home bawling his eyes out. I rushed down there and Edward was pulling the dog out of the water. He said the dog had drowned, but – but I think he was holding it under the water and only pulled him out when he saw me coming. I can't prove it, but there was something in his eyes. Something that sent a shiver down my spine and reminded me so much of Billy.'

'Did you tell Oppo or mum about this?'

'Yes, but they both think I'm being paranoid. I'm not, Charlotte. Something *very* wrong happened that day and Stephen refuses to talk about it. In fact, he gets really upset at the mention of the stream and won't go near it anymore. To tell you the truth, I think he's scared of Edward.'

'I understand what you're saying, but Stephen is bound to be upset if he saw his dog drown.'

'That dog was a good swimmer. He was always playing in the stream. I can't see how he could have drowned unless… unless Edward held him under.'

'Are you sure, Molly? I can't believe that Edward would do such a terrible thing.'

'I don't want to believe it either, not of my own flesh and blood, but there are so many things that don't add up.'

'Like what?'

'I think Edward is hurting Stephen. It seems that every time they're alone together, Stephen comes home with an injury and he seems… I dunno… withdrawn. He's had a broken arm, several bumps to the head, a twisted knee – Gawd, the list goes on. I used to think that he was accident-prone but he only ever has these *accidents* when he's with Edward.'

'Have you asked Stephen about it?'

'Yes, of course I have. I asked him outright if Edward is hurting him.'

'And what did he say?'

'He denied it, but he looked terrified. I know fear when I see it and Stephen was scared, really scared.'

Charlotte had wanted to dismiss Molly's accusations but now she was beginning to think that maybe her sister was right to be concerned. The thought of Edward turning out even remotely similar to his father was absolutely stomach-churning and spine-tingling. Billy Wilcox had been so despicable that his own mother had shot him dead.

Molly ran a hand over her face, and choked out, 'I'm right, ain't I? There's something very wrong with Edward. He's wired up wrong, just like Billy was.'

'I don't know, Molly, but Edward's childhood is very different to how his father's was. Billy grew up with a gangster for a father and running wild on the streets of Battersea. Edward is surrounded with love so surely that will make a difference.'

'Billy was loved too, especially by his mother, but he still turned out to be a monster. Oh, Charlotte, I can't stand the thought of Edward taking after him.'

Molly began sobbing again as Charlotte's mind turned. Her sister had painted a worrying picture, but surely, if Molly's fears were founded, Oppo or their mum would have concerns too. 'Why does Mum think that you're being paranoid?' she probed.

'I dunno. Probably because Edward is the apple of her eye. She spoils him rotten and makes it quite clear that Stephen ain't her own blood and that he's adopted. As for Oppo, well, he's always so busy on the farm. He doesn't really notice stuff and thinks that I'm over-reacting. But too much has happened and... and I can't believe that I'm going to say this out loud but – I think Edward tried to kill Oppo.'

'What? No, surely not.'

'Do you remember when there was a fire in the barn and all our hay bales were destroyed?'

'Yeah, I remember – it happened last year.'

'Oppo was in the barn working on the tractor at the time and he swears blind that he left the doors open. When the fire started, it spread so fast, and when he ran to escape the flames, the doors were closed... and... and locked from the outside.'

Charlotte's eyes widened. 'From the outside?' she parroted.

'Yes, the drop bar was across the doors. Oppo said it must have dropped down on its own, but I think that's very unlikely. It's never happened before or since. Oppo was lucky to get out alive.'

'Blimey, Molly, that's really sinister!'

'It breaks my heart to think that Edward is responsible but I feel sure that it was him. Billy Wilcox killed his own father and now I'm sure that Edward is trying to do the same to Oppo. I'm scared... Really scared of my own son and I don't know what to do.'

Charlotte slumped back, horrified. 'Christ, Molly,' she muttered.

'I know. It sounds so unbelievable. But what if Edward *really* hurts Stephen? They aren't real brothers and Edward knows that I'm not Stephen's real mum. What if he—' Charlotte broke off, sobbing and unable to continue.

'Kills Stephen and Oppo,' Charlotte finished for her.

'Y – yes.'

'I would have suggested sending him to Georgina. She might be able to sort him out, but with what's happened, now ain't the time.'

'I've racked my brains and I just don't know what to do,' Molly sobbed, 'but I can't carry on living on a knife's edge. My nerves can't handle it.'

'You need to send him away. How about a boarding school?'

'What? No! Never! I can't do that.'

'Why not? It's the best place for him.'

'Those places are full of toffs. He'd be like a duck out of water.'

'Molly, it ain't safe to keep him at home. You said yourself that he isn't wired up right. What's he now, eleven?'

Molly nodded. 'But what if he hurts someone at the boarding school?'

'I doubt that. From what you've told me, Edward's anger is directed at his family. They have strict rules in those schools, discipline, and that might be just what he needs to sort him out.'

'No, Charlotte, I can't do it.'

'You must. You've got to face facts. Edward isn't safe to be around and you need to get him out of the house and off the farm before he seriously hurts one of you.'

Molly took a long time to answer, but finally, after blowing her nose, she said, 'I think you're right. I don't have a choice. Edward can't live with us anymore. As hard as it's going to be, I have to protect the rest of my family, which means Edward needs to go to boarding school.'

Charlotte heaved a sigh of relief. She'd been too young to remember much about Edward's father, Billy Wilcox. But over the years, she'd learned a lot about him from Georgina and Johnny, and from the things that Molly had told her. And from what she'd gleaned, it was sounding like Edward was walking in his father's footsteps and that history was going to repeat itself. It was clear that Molly had bred a beast with Billy and Molly had to rid her life of the child, for the sake of her own and all those around her that her sister held dear.

He needed sorting out, and now.

16

When Georgina woke up in the unfamiliar surroundings of her room, her first thought was of David. Her throat constricted as an overwhelming painful sorrow engulfed her and she fought to hold back tears. She wouldn't cry. Not yet. Not until Thomas Kelly had paid for taking her husband's life. Until then, she would hold her grief in and fill her mind with hate and anger. A light tap on the door snapped her from her thoughts. 'Yes,' she called.

'Breakfast, Miss Garrett.'

'Just leave it there, thank you,' Georgina called. She was groggy from a restless night, but got out of bed to retrieve the breakfast tray from outside the door. Though they looked perfectly cooked, the poached eggs on toast didn't appeal. Her stomach was too knotted to entertain the idea of food. But the strong aroma of coffee was welcoming and she drank a cup, feeling revived.

Once dressed, she knocked on Johnny's door. He opened it looking refreshed and ready to face the day, which was more than she could say for herself. As he stood aside she walked into his room and sat on Larry's empty bed. 'Did you sleep all right?' she asked casually, masking her sadness.

'Like a log. It's so quiet here, but the birds woke me up at the crack of a sparrow's fart.'

'Yeah, it's nice, but we ain't on holiday. I need you to keep focused.'

'Don't worry, Miss Garrett. I'm ready for anything. Have you got the plan worked out?'

'Almost. I'm not driving Kelly back to London so we need a place to take him to.'

'I saw an old barn a few miles back. It looked abandoned. I can drive there and check it out?'

'Yes, do that now. I'll come with you.'

Georgina slipped out of the back door with Johnny. The sun was shining, the sky blue with a few cotton-wool clouds, but she was too intent on her plans to appreciate the beauty of the surroundings. Her heart was heavy with David's loss, her mind fixed on revenge. Ten minutes later, Johnny turned onto a dirt track, and trundled towards a barn in the distance. Georgina thought it looked ideal: remote and isolated. No one would hear Kelly's screams.

When Johnny pulled up outside and they climbed out of the car, she noted the tall grass and weeds that had grown all around the area. It didn't appear that anyone had visited the barn in a long time. They walked to the entrance that was around the other side, away from the view of the road. Johnny yanked hard a few times on the wooden door and it eventually opened. She peered inside. The place was dusty and large cobwebs hung from the rafters. Georgina felt a shiver run up her back. She didn't like spiders. But then her eyes fell on some old farm tools that hung on hooks along the walls. She saw an array of scythes, hoes, pitchforks and chains. A smile slowly spread across her face. 'Perfect,' she said, thinking of Kelly wrapped in those rusty chains.

Back at the pub, Georgina found Nobby and Eric playing cards in their room. They seemed apologetic.

'We was bored and asked the landlord for them,' Nobby explained.

'That's fine. I'm glad you're keeping out of sight. I've got a job for you. Johnny will drop you at an old barn up the road from here. I want the place cleaned up.'

Nobby and Eric looked confused.

'Get rid of the spider's webs. There's brooms and stuff in the barn. Just make it so that nothing with more than two legs is going to creep up on me.'

'Oh, yeah, all right,' Nobby said, clearly trying to hide his amusement.

'Have it ready for lunchtime. I'll be bringing a visitor.'

'Are we going to get Kelly?' Johnny asked.

'That's why we're here.'

'Hold on, does that mean it'll be just the two of us to grab him?' Johnny asked.

'Yes, that's right,' Georgina told him.

'But what about his blokes? Wouldn't it be best for all of us to go together?'

'Aw, Johnny, are you scared? Are you losing your bottle?'

'No, Miss Garrett, nothing like that. I just thought—'

'Leave the thinking to me,' Georgina cut in. 'Right, let's get a move on. All pack your stuff and I'll meet you at the car.'

'But you've paid for three nights.'

'Like I said, Johnny, we ain't on holiday. I want Kelly to die today. Every minute that he walks and breathes feels like a knife twisting in my gut. We're getting it done with no more messing about.'

Georgina left Johnny open-mouthed as she went to her room to gather her belongings. It was unlike her to not have a clear and well-thought-out plan, though she'd given her men the impression that she knew exactly what she was doing. The trouble was, every time she tried to concentrate and work things through in her head, she kept coming back to the same place... Kill Kelly. And that's as far as her thoughts went. One way or another, with little idea of how she was going to nab him off the streets, Thomas Kelly's life would be ending today.

'Can't you shut the kids up?' Larry moaned.

Clara had failed miserably at enticing Larry to wash her back. In fact, he'd insisted on staying in the backyard while she'd bathed. She'd been equally unsuccessful at luring him into her bed last night.

She sat on her bed, leaning against the wall with her knees pulled up to her chest and watched Larry pace the floor. Back and forth he went, then over to the window, a quick glance left and right and then back to pacing. She could see that he was bored stupid, and the children's incessant yelling, fighting and crying was obviously getting on his nerves. Not that she could blame him. Her children's unruly behaviour narked her too.

'Shall I put the kettle on?' she asked.

Before Larry could answer, Greta burst into the room.

'Humphrey and Greg are ganging up on Clark,' she snapped, sounding exasperated. 'I've had a fucking stomach full of them this morning. Can't I sling them out in the backyard?'

Clara looked at Larry for an answer. 'Surely a couple of hours in the yard won't do any harm?'

He ran his hand through his hair and sucked in a long breath. 'I suppose not, but tell them they'd better keep the noise down.'

Greta smiled at Larry. It was the first time that Clara had seen her daughter show him anything but contempt, and she was pleased to see that Larry smiled back. It was a small breakthrough, which she hoped would work towards her plans of winning Larry's heart.

Greta dashed off, calling the boys' names, who responded by pounding down the stairs. There were cries of glee when she informed them that they could play in the yard but had to be quiet. Moments later, Greta came running back into the room.

'This was on the floor inside the front door,' she said, holding an envelope towards Clara.

Larry hurried forward and grabbed it from Greta's hand. 'Have you read it?' he asked.

'No,' she replied, fervently shaking her head.

'Greta isn't good with her reading and writing, but she's really clever with numbers,' Clara said. She wondered why Larry had been so quick to grab the letter. It probably wasn't important, maybe just another reminder that her rent was overdue or something similar. No one ever wrote to her unless they were demanding money. 'I think you'll find that's addressed to me,' she said, holding out her hand.

'No, it isn't. It's for me. I recognise this paper. It's the same envelopes that Miss...'

Larry had stopped mid-sentence and Clara got the impression that he wasn't supposed to talk about this *Miss* whoever she was.

'What does it say?' she asked, as Larry ripped open the envelope to read the contents.

Larry looked at Greta, who also seemed to be curious about the letter. 'Go and put the kettle on,' he told the child, getting rid of her. Once Greta had gone to the kitchen, Larry quietly closed the door behind her. 'It's just Kelly throwing his weight around. There's no need for you to worry your pretty little face about it,' he said, stuffing the letter into his trouser pocket.

Clara was about to demand to know what the letter said but hearing Larry refer to her *pretty little face* gave her other ideas instead. She jumped from the bed and held her skirt hem in each hand as she swung from side to side. With her head held at a cheeky angle, she asked sweetly, 'Do you think I'm pretty, Larry? Do you?'

He looked taken aback and seemed unsure of how to answer her. Clara slowly stepped towards him with lust in her eyes. 'You think I'm pretty,' she purred, pouting her lips. 'It sounds as though you like me, Larry, and I feel the same about you,' she cooed and placed her hands on his firm chest.

He stepped back, but she moved forward again to press against his taut body and husked, 'I could be *your* pretty girl, Larry. I'd be a good girl and do *anything* you want.'

Larry stared down at her, his eyes at last dark with passion. Clara's stomach flipped at the thought of bedding

SAM MICHAELS

him. She stood on the tips of her toes and moved her lips closer to his, ready to feel his warm tongue in her waiting mouth.

'I bloody knew it!' Greta suddenly screeched.

Larry leapt back and Clara spun around to see her daughter standing in the doorway looking furious and with Ginger in her arms.

'Get out!' Clara shouted.

'No, I won't! I'm going to stay right here.' Greta marched across the room and laid Ginger on the bed before sitting herself firmly on the edge. 'You promised me, Mum. You promised no more babies.'

Larry, his face flaming red, avoided eye contact with Clara as he walked past her and out of the room.

'Larry... wait...' Clara called after him. When he ignored her call, she turned back to Greta. 'See what you've done! That was my only chance with him and you've gone and ruined everything.'

'Good! I'm glad.'

'You stupid girl. Larry was our ticket out of here. Do you think I want us living in this dump, with me working all hours to feed you all? I want a better life and we could have that with Larry.'

'You've said that about all the men, but they never make it better. They only make it worse.'

'Larry's different,' Clara said.

'Huh, you say that about all of them too.'

'Larry *really* is. I know you've heard it all before but please, Greta, give the man a chance. With Larry, we could live in a nice big house and never have to worry about money. You and your brothers and sister wouldn't go hungry ever again. You'd have smart new clothes too and lots of toys. Wouldn't you like that?'

Greta looked at her sister lying on the bed and kicking her skinny legs out. The child looked as though she could do with a good meal. With obvious reluctance, she answered sulkily, 'I suppose.'

'Right then, go and apologise to Larry… and stop swearing!'

When her daughter left the room, Clara fussed over Ginger and less than five minutes later Greta returned with Larry in tow. He had two cups in his hands.

'He made a pot of tea, Mum,' Greta said, obviously surprised.

Clara met Larry's eyes and smiled. 'Well, I never. I don't think she's ever seen a man make himself useful in my kitchen. Most prefer to be waited on hand and foot.'

'It's only a cup of tea,' Larry replied, and then added, 'Me and Greta have had a chat. We've cleared the air.'

'Good, I'm glad to hear it.'

'I'm going to put Ginger in her cot,' Greta said. She gathered the baby from the bed and threw her mother a *knowing* look. 'Say night, night,' she said as she left the room and closed the door behind her.

'She's a good kid,' Larry commented.

'Yes, she is. To be honest, I don't know how I'd manage without her.'

'She told me that she can't read.'

'No, not very well at all. She's missed most of her schooling because I've needed her at home to care for the little ones. But it doesn't matter because she's going to be a film star, just like Greta Garbo.'

SAM MICHAELS

Larry looked thoughtful as he said, 'But she'll need to be able to read to be a film star.'

'Don't be daft, of course she won't.'

'How will she learn her lines? She'll have to be able to read the scripts.'

'My Greta will be so rich and famous that she'll have people to read the scripts for her.'

Larry scratched his head and looked as though he was about to ask her another question but Clara cut in and changed the subject. 'Enough about Greta. Come and sit beside me. I do believe that you was about to kiss me earlier.'

'Yeah, erm, about that… Sorry, it won't happen again.'

Clara jumped to her feet and ran over to him. She threw her arms around his neck. 'But I want it to happen. I want you to kiss me, Larry.'

He stepped back and held Clara's wrists, removing her arms. 'No, love, it ain't happening. I'm here to do a job and then I'll be gone.'

'I saw it, Larry. I saw it in your eyes. You want me, you know you do.'

'Stop, Clara, please, love.'

'But it's true! You want me just as much as I want you.'

'You're a smashing girl but I'm not the bloke for you.'

'Yes, yes you are, Larry.'

'No, I'm not. I'm sorry if I gave you the wrong impression.'

'You can't do this. You can't come in here and turn my life upside down and then flounce off back to London. Take me with you. I would make you happy, I swear I would.'

Larry sighed and turned away. Clara stepped towards him again and from behind, she tentatively rested her hands on his back. As she slowly moved her hands over his body, she felt the gun that he had tucked inside the back of his trousers. Ignoring it, she slowly moved her hands up his tense back and began to rub his shoulders. 'We could have a good life, you and me.'

'You've got five kids. I can't take them on an' all.'

Clara felt that she was losing the opportunity to be with him and panicking, she blurted, 'You wouldn't have to be a father to the kids. It'd be just me and you, Larry. The kids can stay here.'

'Oh yeah, and who would look after them?'

'Greta. You've seen for yourself that she's capable. She already looks after them most of the time. As long as we send her money, she'll be fine.'

Larry spun back to look at her but Clara was disappointed to see that he appeared shocked at her suggestion and said hurriedly, 'I wouldn't expect you to pay for their keep. I'd get a job in London to provide for them. They wouldn't be your responsibility.'

'Slow down, woman. Think about what you're saying. You can't leave a nine-year-old girl to bring up the rest of your children.'

'She's a better mother to those kids than I am. They'd be fine.'

'No, Clara, it wouldn't be right to lay that responsibility on a child and I can't believe you're suggesting it.'

'But I'd do anything to be with you.'

Larry turned back to the window and Clara hoped that he was mulling over her suggestion. But then she heard him mumble, 'Shit.'

She looked past him and saw Thomas Kelly's car pulling

up to the kerb. 'Oh, no! I bloody knew that he'd be back. What shall I do?'

'Stay calm. Gather the kids and go upstairs. Shut yourselves in the bedroom and don't come out until I tell you to.'

'What are you going to do?'

'Stop asking questions and get the kids out of the way.'

Clara ran to the back door and urged the boys inside 'Quick as you can,' she said and then ushered them upstairs.

In the bedroom, Greta was looking over Ginger asleep in the cot. 'What's going on?' she asked when Clara burst in with Humphry, Gregory and Clark.

'Shush. Don't say a single word. There's a bad man at the door but Larry is going to sort him out. Just keep quiet, all of you,' Clara said urgently, pulling her children into a huddle around her and then she yanked the thin blanket over them. 'You're so good,' she whispered. 'Remember, not a word.'

Humphrey and Greg, her four-year-old twins seemed to think that it was a game and were both smiling. But Clark, her six-year-old, was shaking with fear. She pulled him closer towards her and Greta sat on the other side of him stroking his small hand. Clara looked over Clark's head and locked eyes with her daughter. 'You're my wonderful, brave girl,' she whispered as she was filled with guilt. How could she have considered running off to London with Larry and leaving her beautiful children behind? It had been a moment of madness and now she was glad that Larry hadn't taken up the offer. From now on, she would always make it clear that she and the children came as a package. If a man didn't want her kids, then they couldn't have her either.

She tensed at the sound of heavy thudding on the front door. Thomas Kelly was back and with him came trouble!

Thomas was slightly taken aback when a big bloke pulled open Clara's front door. He guessed that she'd brought the man to her house to protect her, but big or not, Thomas wasn't worried. It was clear from the bloke's wide stance and threatening expression, that he had no idea who he was coming up against. Well he was about to find out and Thomas growled, 'Who the fuck are you?'

'None of your fucking business. What are you doing on my doorstep?'

The man was bold and menacing. Thomas admired that. He was just the sort of person he'd like on his payroll. 'I've no issue with you, my man. I'm here to see Clara.'

'I ain't your fucking man and anything you want to say to Clara goes through me.'

'Do you know who I am?'

'I couldn't give a fuck.'

Thomas adjusted his jacket, deliberately flashing his gun that was tucked into his waistband. He was sure the man had seen it. 'You're obviously new to the area so I'll give you a chance. But me – Thomas Kelly – I *own* this town so don't go up against me or you'll regret it. Now, I said that I want to talk to Clara, so get out of my way. I'm coming in.'

'No you're not. Piss off,' the man growled and slammed the door.

Thomas couldn't believe he'd had the audacity to shut the door in his face! The man would pay for that.

'What now, Boss?' Titch asked.

'Kick it in.'

'What, the door?'

'Yes, you fucking idiot, the door! Kick it in and then kick the life out of that brazen bastard too.'

Clara had sneaked from under the thin blanket and crept to the top of the stairs, her heart hammering as she listened to every word. She jumped when the door slammed, but then Larry appeared at the bottom of the stairs and hissed, 'Quick, get the kids and leave by the back door.'

Clara ran back into the bedroom to see four sets of terrified eyes staring at her. Greta had already picked up Ginger from the cot and was holding the sleeping baby close to her chest.

'Out, now, through the back,' Clara commanded.

Her children seemed to sense her panic and obeyed without argument. Clara followed behind them, but they were only about halfway down the stairs when it became clear that Kelly or one of his thugs was trying to kick in her door. She knew the old and worn wood wouldn't hold for long and that it would only take a few good thuds for it to splinter.

'Hurry,' Larry urged.

As Clara passed him, their eyes met. She wanted to stop and tell him how much she adored him, but there was no time for words. As she hurried through the kitchen, she grabbed a large knife from the side. It was blunt but it was better than nothing. The children ran out into the backyard and paused, their faces pale with fear. Clara yanked open the yard door and hissed, 'Run... keep running and don't look back.'

'Come with us,' Greta cried.

'I'll be right behind you,' Clara told her.

Greta turned and ran, while at the same moment, Clara heard the front door crash open. She spun around and looked through the kitchen to see one of Kelly's men pounding into Larry, both of them fists flailing, and then Larry fell to the floor. Titch, the heavier, younger man, took advantage, and with big boots, he kicked Larry's head.

'Stop! Please, stop!' Clara screamed, running into the kitchen.

The man ignored her and she looked past him to see Thomas Kelly watching the scene with a wicked leer of satisfaction on his face. He was enjoying seeing Larry being repeatedly kicked, his face now a gory mess and blood pouring from his skull.

'Please, make him stop, Mr Kelly. It's me you want!' she begged.

Larry's eyes were closed, and she wondered if he was unconscious. She hoped he was and that he wasn't feeling any more pain as the thug continued to kick him again and again.

'I don't think I want him to stop,' Kelly said. 'The man deserves a good beating.'

The thug paused, panting, with sweat running down his face, but then, as he lifted his foot again, Clara saw that Larry's eyes had opened and he was reaching for something behind his back. His gun! Yes, Larry had a gun! A fierce kick smashed into Larry's eye socket and another to the side of his head, yet somehow he'd managed to pull his gun and aimed it up at Titch.

Kelly had seen what was happening and acted quickly as he pulled out his own gun and fired. Clara heard a tremendous bang and, horrified, she felt as if time stopped still as she gazed at the hole in Larry's head. He was still now, perfectly still, while Kelly stood over him looking triumphant.

She was frozen, trembling with the blunt knife held at her side, unable to believe what had happened. Larry had a bullet in his head. He was dead. She saw Thomas Kelly coming towards her, and knew that she should run. Follow her kids. But her legs wouldn't work. All she could do was wait, shaking from head to toe, as Kelly, still holding his gun, used his other hand to pull the knife effortlessly from her grip.

'There's a good girl,' he said and slipped the knife into his pocket.

Clara couldn't stop shaking and, unable to hold herself up, she sank down onto the dirty linoleum on the kitchen floor, her hands held over her face as she sobbed.

'Who was he?' Kelly asked. 'Your new pimp?'

Clara couldn't talk. She felt as though she was drowning in her own tears. Larry was dead, and all her dreams had died with him.

'I don't suppose it really matters who he was. It's you I wanted a word with.'

Clara looked up to see him standing with his gun pointed at her head. Her bladder released and she felt a warm sensation under her legs. Vomit rose, burning her throat. She turned her head to one side and was sick on the floor.

'Look at you, a filthy whore covered in piss, snot and puke. You'd have saved yourself a lot of trouble if you'd turned up at the pub as ordered.'

Clara looked up at Kelly with no idea what he was talking about. 'What... when...' And unable to formulate her thoughts coherently, her words trailed off.

'You must have got my note?'

Clara shook her head, confused, but then she remembered an envelope and the note inside that Larry had stuffed into his pocket. He'd said it was addressed to him, and she hadn't questioned that. 'I – I didn't see the note.'

'Really, that's a shame, but never mind, I've finally caught up with you.'

'Wha – what do you want?'

Kelly signalled to Titch, who pounded across the kitchen and pulled her roughly to her feet. He then yanked both arms behind her, so forcefully that she felt they were going to pop out of her shoulder sockets. 'No... please... you're hurting me.'

As though she hadn't spoken, Kelly said, 'I've heard that you've been shouting your mouth off about me and throwing your money around. I can't have that, Clara. I can't have my tarts thinking that they can swan off with any new pimp. I won't have dirty slags like you slating my good name.'

'I don't know what you're talking about,' Clara cried, and then howled as Titch pulled tighter on her arms, causing a surge of excruciating pain.

'Let me remind you,' Kelly snarled.

To Clara's horror she saw him pull a knuckle duster from his pocket and slip it onto his hand. Fear snaked through her veins. She knew that the heavily fortified metal structure was going to cause a lot of pain and if he used it on her face, a lot of damage too. 'Please, Mr Kelly. I promise you, Larry wasn't my pimp. I work for you, only you and I can't earn you money if my face is smashed up.'

'You don't work for me now, Clara, and by the time I'm finished with you, you'll never work for anyone else.'

Clara closed her eyes in terror as she saw Kelly's fist and the metal rings of the knuckle duster coming fast towards her face. She tried to turn her head away but the first blow caught the edge of her eyebrow. Her head snapped back with the force of the blow, her brain rattled and she felt woozy, but before she could recover her wits, another punch smashed into her mouth. Intense pain was followed by the coppery taste of her own blood and she was sure that she'd swallowed a tooth or two. Her mouth fell open as blood pumped from a wide split lip, exposing raw flesh. The third punch landed on the side of her nose, and she screamed in agony as her bones crunched.

'Look at you. You're not so pretty now,' Kelly said, smiling with satisfaction.

Clara could feel the room spinning around her as she began to slip into welcome oblivion. If Kelly's thug hadn't been gripping her arms so tightly, she would have fallen unconscious onto the floor. Something cold was thrown in her face – water – bringing her back from the brink and she opened swollen eyes to see Kelly pulling her blunt kitchen knife from his pocket.

He barked an order, 'Keep her still.'

Her head still swimming, Clara was barely aware of him lifting her skirt. But she cried out in excruciating anguish as he sliced the knife in a criss-cross fashion across her stomach and inner thighs.

The pain tore through her and as she drifted into darkness, and the last thing that Clara heard was Kelly's mocking voice as he crowed, 'I've really fucked you up now. No man will ever pay you to stick his dick anywhere near that mess.'

17

Charlotte cleared away the dinner plates with a warm feeling inside. She was really enjoying having Molly to stay and wished that she saw more of her sister. Nothing more had been said about Edward, but Charlotte could tell that Molly was still wrestling with the idea of packing the boy off to boarding school.

The phone trilled and Charlotte's heart skipped a beat. Every time the bloody thing rang, it caused her anxiety. It would either be the hospital with news of Tim, or Georgina with an update from Bristol.

When Charlotte put the receiver to her ear, she was surprised to hear her mother's voice.

'Hello… Charlotte… Is that you?' Fanny shouted.

Charlotte pulled the receiver away from her ear and then spoke slowly and clearly into the mouthpiece. 'Yes, Mum, it's me. There's no need to shout. Just talk normally – I will still hear you.'

Molly came to stand beside her and Charlotte rolled her eyes with a smile.

'Is Molly there?' Fanny asked.

'Yes, she's here. We've just finished our tea. Do you want to speak to her?'

'Yes. Put her on.'

Charlotte, disappointed that her mother hadn't called to speak to her, handed the receiver to Molly. She hadn't even asked how Tim was. With a huff, she sat on the sofa and listened to the one-sided conversation. Her eyes widened. She could tell by Molly's alarmed face that their mother hadn't called with good news.

'Oh no, Mum. Is he all right?' Molly asked anxiously. 'He's had to have a plaster cast? Is he in a lot of pain...? Oh, right. Was he on his own when it happened...? No, Mum, it's not a strange question... Right, so what did Edward say about it...? What do you mean nothing? He must have said something... All right, calm down. I'll be home tomorrow... Yes, I'll get an early train. Bye, Mum,' Molly said and as she replaced the receiver, she drew in a long breath.

'What's happened?' Charlotte asked.

'It's Stephen. He's had a nasty crash on his pushbike. It seems that Edward took him up the big hill behind the farm. On the way back down, the brakes on Stephen's bike didn't work so he couldn't slow down or stop. He rode straight into a big oak tree. He's knocked out his front teeth, has a nasty lump on the front on his forehead, and a broken wrist.'

'Oh, the poor boy!'

Molly shook her head. 'I doubt this was an *accident*, Charlotte. I think Edward did it. I bet he tampered with the brakes and that's why they didn't work.'

'How can you be sure?'

'I just *know*. Like I said, something always happens to Stephen when he's with Edward. But I can't prove it. The boy is too clever, just like his father was. But he did it, I'm sure. God, Charlotte, Stephen could have been killed! To be honest, I don't like the thought of sending Edward away, but I don't think there's any other option.'

'There isn't, love,' Charlotte said gently.

'Mum won't be happy about it.'

'She hasn't been happy about anything since our Ethel was killed.'

'True. But she will fight me over this.'

'He's *your* child, Molly, not Mum's. You have to protect Stephen and Oppo, regardless of what Mum says.'

'I know, but I'm not very good at standing up for myself, especially against Mum. There's no way that she'll believe that Edward is wicked like his father. It's going to cause ructions.'

'It's better to have a fall-out with Mum than for any more *accidents* to occur.'

Ned sniffed and then cleared his throat before saying snidely, 'The boy should have been drowned at birth.'

Molly looked horrified at his words and close to tears, so Charlotte snapped, 'Shut your nasty mouth! In fact, why don't you bugger off home!'

'I'd love to do just that, but I've had orders from Miss Garrett to look after you.'

'I don't need you to look after me. I'm more than capable of taking care of myself.'

'I ain't budging.'

'In that case, flippin' button your gob.'

Molly heaved a sigh and said, 'See, I need to be more like you, Charlotte. I wish I had the guts to speak to Mum like that.'

'Bloody women,' Ned mumbled.

Charlotte chose to ignore him. She took Molly's hand in her own and said, 'I got my guts from Georgina. I've seen the way she looks after her own and won't let anyone stand in her way. You need to take a leaf out of her book. I wish I could go to the farm with you. I don't have a problem with speaking up to Mum. But I can't, not right now with Tim in the hospital.'

'I know. Don't worry. I'll do what I have to do.'

But Charlotte was worried. If Molly failed in having Edward packed off, Charlotte feared what might happen to her precious family. She'd never been close to her mother but she loved the woman. And though Stephen was the child of a dead prostitute, Charlotte was ever so fond of the boy. And Oppo, well, he was like a big brother to her. She hated the thought of any of them being hurt. But strangely, though she'd tried to love Edward, she'd always found that there was something about the boy that gave her an unsettled feeling. Nothing that she could put her finger on. Just something odd, almost creepy, about him. She felt awful admitting to herself that she wouldn't miss him one little bit once he was gone.

Clara's eyes opened and she quickly peered around her grimy kitchen. Relief washed over her when she realised that Thomas Kelly and his thug had gone. But with the relief came the unbearable pain. And then her eyes fell on Larry's lifeless body lying in a pool of blood.

She managed to heave herself onto all fours and slowly crawled across the kitchen. Every movement sent shockwaves of agony through her body. The sight of Larry's gun beside him spurred her on. She couldn't believe that Kelly had left it behind. It must have been an oversight on his part.

Kneeling next to Larry, she took a moment to study his greying face. There was nothing peaceful in his death and it showed in his broken features. He didn't deserve this. She had no idea how Kelly had come to the conclusion that Larry was her new pimp, but even if he had been, that was no excuse for murder.

Clara reached for the gun. It felt heavier in her quivering hands than she'd expected. She held it unsteadily and imagined pointing it at Kelly's head and pulling the trigger. But in reality, she wouldn't go chasing after the man to take his life. She only wanted to protect herself and her children. Her children! She had to find her children!

Clara crawled across to the sink, gasping with unbearable discomfort as she pulled herself up to her feet. After pausing for a moment, she stumbled to the back door and out into the yard. The back gate was still open, and with her jaw clenched against the agony of every movement, she staggered through it in search of her children. Thomas Kelly was a vindictive man and she was terrified that he may further punish her by hurting the children.

Halfway down the hill, two boys playing with marbles in the kerb, glanced up at Clara and then ran into their homes, screaming. She realised she must look a hideous sight, her face probably mangled beyond recognition, and her clothes covered in blood, puke and piss, but her focus was on her children. She wasn't sure for how much longer she could carry on and bear the pain. She had to locate them before she collapsed and so she staggered on.

At the bottom of the hill, Clara leaned against a wall and looked up and down the street. Everywhere was eerily quiet. No one was carrying home their shopping or chalking their doorsteps. No windows were being cleaned and no boys in short trousers were kicking a football around. Was the town always this sleepy? Or had Clara never noticed before?

She had no idea where Greta would have taken them. *If only I knew the girl better*, she thought with regret. But Clara would rectify that. Once she had her children safe in her arms, she promised herself that she would be a better mother to them. *Please, Lord. Let my children be all right. I'll be a good mum. I won't ever let them down again*, she silently prayed.

A woman pushing a pram came around the corner and gasped when she set eyes on Clara. Clara lowered her head. The woman dashed to the other side of the road. That's when Clara realised that she was swinging the gun by her side. She quickly shoved it into the back of the waistband of her skirt and pulled her blouse over it.

Her head throbbed, but worse was the agonising, fiery pain from her inner thighs. Every step she took caused the open wounds to rub together and she could feel blood trickling down her legs. Her face and lips pulsated with pain too. But Clara couldn't rest until she found her children. Then what? How could they go home? Larry was sprawled dead across her passageway. And why hadn't the police turned up? Someone must have heard the gunshot. The noise had been deafening and had reverberated around her small house. She knew that Kelly had a lot of power in the town but was shocked to think that he could get away with daylight murder. Well, once she'd found her kids, she wouldn't be going to the police in case they were Kelly's puppets.

Foggy and dazed, barely able to put one foot in front of the other, Clara staggered on until she found herself close to a pub that Kelly frequented. With her head swimming, she wasn't even sure of how she'd got there. She could remember struggling down the hill. The lady with the pram. But then blank. She stopped for a moment and tried to focus, but agony racked her body. She wondered if Kelly was in the pub and her hand moved to feel the cold metal of the gun she had tucked into her waistband. She could walk into the pub, catch Kelly unawares, and shoot the bastard down. Yet even as this thought crossed her mind, Clara knew she wouldn't be able to do it. She wasn't a cold-blooded killer like him, but if he hurt her children it would be a different story – then she wouldn't think twice about gunning him down. Her children. Yes, her children. She had to find them, so Clara pushed herself on. All she wanted was to find them safe and unhurt.

18

Georgina's heart was as cold as stone. She'd managed to bury her sorrow and now had only one thing on her mind – Thomas Kelly. She knew they were heading into danger, and her thoughts turned to Alfie and Selina. If anything happened to her, she knew that they'd be fine and happy with their grandparents, while loved and watched over by the whole gypsy community. Georgina forced her thoughts back to the present and as Johnny drove, she surveyed every street they passed through. Larry had said that Kelly used a local pub and they were on their way there, hoping to find the man.

Georgina had only seen one copper so far. A bobby on his bicycle. The man looked close to retirement age, and she wondered if Kelly had him on his payroll. She knew the game and was clued up about how these things worked. Years of running her own business and then helping David with his had taught her every trick in the book. And one of the things that she'd been quick to learn was the importance of keeping the Old Bill close and on side. A backhander went a long way to persuade a low-paid copper to turn a blind eye. Kelly would know that too.

Johnny's astonished voice snapped her from her thoughts. 'What the bleedin' hell has happened to her?' he said.

Georgina followed Johnny's gaze and saw a young woman staggering unsteadily along, her face battered and bleeding, her clothes drenched in blood. 'Stop the car!' she demanded.

Johnny hit the brakes and the car screeched to a halt. He wound down his window and called to the woman. 'Are you all right, sweetheart?'

'Of course she fucking ain't!' Georgina snapped, tense and wound-up like a coiled spring. She jumped out from the car and ran across to the woman, finding her close to collapse. 'It's all right, love, you're all right,' Georgina soothed as she placed her arm over the pitiful sight. 'My name's Georgina. Come and sit in my car, eh? We'll take you to a hospital.'

The woman lifted her head and Georgina had to hold back a gasp when she saw the full extent of her horrific injuries.

'No, my kids... got to find my kids,' the woman mumbled.

'All right, but come and sit down before you fall down,' Georgina urged, gently guiding the woman to the car.

With each, obviously agonising step, the woman repeatedly muttered, 'My kids.'

'Don't worry, we'll help you to find them,' Georgina assured her. She managed to ease the woman onto the back seat and slid in beside her.

Johnny turned around, his eyes full of sympathy as he asked, 'What happened to you, sweetheart?'

The woman looked confused and said again, 'My kids... where are they?'

'Were they with you when you were attacked?' Georgina gently asked.

'No... they ran off. I have to find them.'

'What's your name?'

'My kids...'

'We'll find them. What's your name, darling?'

'Clara... where are my kids?'

Georgina shot a look at Johnny and her pulse quickened. 'Do you know a man called Larry?' she asked.

Clara's puffy and swollen eyes widened with fear, and she tried to get out of the car. Georgina put a staying hand on her arm and said gently, 'It's all right. We're not going to hurt you. We're Larry's friends. We just need to know where he is.'

After a painfully long pause, Clara sobbed, 'He's at home.'

Georgina took in the state of Clara and asked, 'Is Larry all right?'

The woman shook her head, and then with a groan, she passed out.

Johnny rummaged in his jacket pocket and pulled out a piece of paper that Larry had given him. He studied the crudely drawn map of directions to Clara's house. 'I know where she lives.'

'Quick as you can, Johnny,' Georgina instructed firmly.

Johnny turned the car around and put his foot down hard on the accelerator. After two wrong turns, they found themselves on a steep hill lined with small, terraced houses on one side and uneven, green fields on the other. The car revved in groaning strains as they climbed the hill to Clara's house.

Clara came round and Georgina asked, 'Who did this to you?' But she was met with Clara's continuing cry for her children before she drifted into unconsciousness again.

As they got closer to the top of the hill, Georgina's heart raced faster and faster. She felt sure that something terrible must have happened to Larry. There was no way he would have left Clara alone to wander the streets in this state.

Again, Clara came round, and seeing where they were she cried, 'No, no, not going in there.'

Georgina's jaws tightened. Something terrible must have happened in the dilapidated, narrow house.

'Look, the door's been kicked in,' Johnny said before he climbed out of the car.

'You stay here,' Georgina told Clara and then followed him. She glanced down the hill, but there wasn't anyone to be seen, the place disturbingly quiet.

Johnny walked into the house, and then his voice rang out, 'Fucking hell!'

Georgina ran inside to see him bending over Larry's body. He looked up at her and said flatly, 'He's dead. He's been beaten and shot.'

'It had to be Kelly.'

'Fucking bastard! Larry knew, you know. He knew his luck was running out and that the next bullet he took would kill him.'

Georgina was sickened by Larry's death, but knowing that they had to act quickly, said, 'We need to move him.'

'Where to?'

'We need to get him back to London. We can't leave any trace of us being here. When we kill Kelly, I don't want any clues leading back to us.'

Johnny looked mortified. 'But – but – we can't drive all the way back to London with a dead body in the car!'

'Why not? You've done it before, Johnny. Remember Augustus Rice, the bloke who's house you robbed the paintings from that Lord Hamilton had put us on to? You drove his corpse back to my house.'

'Yeah, I know, but that was different. Larry is me mate!'

'I realise that, Johnny, but we've got to cover our tracks. There's no way I'm going back to prison or hanging for killing Thomas Kelly.'

'Yeah, I see what you mean. But couldn't we bury him somewhere here?'

'It's too risky. We don't know the area and what if he's found? There'd be a manhunt – one that would lead to us. It's best that Larry comes home and then the cleaners can take care of him. In the meantime, let him rest in peace here for a while. Close the door and we'll come back for him once we've dealt with Kelly.'

'What about Clara? What are we gonna do with her?'

'Let's see if I can get her to talk to me.'

Back in the car, Georgina was pleased to see that Clara was awake, though the woman looked terrified. Georgina offered a gentle smile. 'We will look after Larry. You don't have to worry about him. And we will find your children. Did Thomas Kelly do this?'

Clara nodded.

'Do you know why?'

'He – he thought that Larry was stealing his girls from the docks. He thought that Larry was my pimp.'

'Did Kelly mention me?'

Clara shook her head. She then buried her face in her

hands, her voice muffled as once again she cried that she had to find her children.

'Yes, love, I know. Have you got any idea where they might be?'

'No.'

'Listen to me. You're not well. You've been seriously injured and you need to see a doctor. Let me take you to the hospital and I promise you, I will find your children.'

'No, I have to see them with my own eyes. I'm so worried that Mr Kelly will hurt them.'

'He won't. I'll find them before he does. And I'm not being funny, but you look a right mess. You'd likely frighten the life out of your kids. You don't want them seeing you like that. Get cleaned up first, eh?'

Clara thought for a moment and then replied, 'You're right, they shouldn't see me like this. But how do I know that you'll really look for them?'

Georgina opened her handbag and pulled out six five-pound notes which she pushed into Clara's hand. 'Take this. And when I bring your children to the hospital, I'll give you ten times that amount of money. You helped Larry, which helped me. I'm a woman of my word. You can trust me to help you now.'

'Thank you.'

Clara winced in pain with every word that she spoke. Blood seeped from her wounds and her exposed flesh looked raw. Georgina knew that the woman required urgent medical attention – attention that was now offered free with the new National Health Service. 'Take us to the nearest hospital, Johnny,' she instructed.

'I dunno where it is.'

'I do,' Clara murmured.

On the way to the hospital, Georgina could see that Clara was trying to stay awake and was peering through the window in search of her children. Georgina managed to get a description of them, but Clara now seemed to be worsening and drifting in and out of consciousness again. Georgina looked through the windows too, saddened to see that like the London streets, there were scars from German air raids. Damaged buildings and ruins were a familiar sight but they always reminded Georgina of the many lives lost. They drove past a large church where only the bell tower remained standing, the rest of the building just rubble.

She recalled an article that she'd read about Bristol being heavily bombed and how the government had set up decoy sites in an attempt to lure the Luftwaffe away from the city and its docks. But just like London and the Thames, the River Avon had been a guide to the German bombers, its water twinkling in the moonlight and leading them directly to their targets. The damage had been heavy and was evident to see even in this small town just outside of Bristol.

'Clara, we're here,' she said, wondering if the woman could hear her.

Her eyes fluttered open. 'You will keep your promise?'

'Yes. I'll bring your children here. Now, go in and tell them that you was attacked by one of your customers. Don't mention Larry or me or Johnny. Is that clear?'

'Yes.'

'Can you walk in there?'

'I think so.'

Johnny rushed around to the door and helped Clara from the car. As she staggered towards the hospital, Georgina was amazed that the woman could walk. She dreaded to think what wounds had been inflicted to her under her skirt. But from the blood that was left behind on the back seat of the car, she could tell that the injury was serious.

Johnny got back into the car, slamming the door closed as he said, 'Kelly did a right job on her, the sick bastard!'

'I think it's only the need to find her children that has kept her alive. I know that feeling.'

'Are we really gonna look for them now?'

'Yes, Johnny, of course we are! Let's go. The sooner we find them, the sooner I can get back to destroying Thomas Kelly.'

As they drove through the small town, it was Johnny who spied Clara's five children wandering up a side street. He saw an older girl carrying a baby in her arms with three younger lads dragging their feet behind her.

'There they are,' he announced, pleased with himself as he turned into the street.

As Johnny pulled up behind them, Miss Garrett got out of the car first and approached the kids.

'Am I glad to find you,' she said, smiling widely.

The oldest girl, Clara had said her name was Greta, eyed them suspiciously.

'I'm Georgina and this is Johnny. Your mum sent me to find you.'

'Piss off. You don't know my mum!'

'Yes, we do, darling. Your mum had had a bit of an accident but she's all right. I'll take you to the hospital to see her.'

'Did a man hurt her?'

'I think so but now your mum is desperate to see you, so come on, get into my car and I'll take you to her.'

'We're not going anywhere with you. If you come near me, I'll scream and I can scream really loud.'

Johnny leaned forward and grinned at the girl. 'Yeah, I bet you can. Larry told me that you're a right little madam. You're Greta, ain't you?'

Greta didn't answer and swiftly handed the baby to the biggest of the lads. She then turned back to glare at Johnny, hands on her hips. 'I'm warning you. You're picking on the wrong kid.'

'No one is picking on you, sweetheart. We just want to take you to the hospital to see your mum.'

'How do I know you aren't the man who was kicking down our door?'

'I promise I wasn't. You don't have to be scared of us,' he cajoled as he put his hands in his pocket to pull out some coins. 'Here, take this and you can by some sweets, or some flowers to take to your mum.'

Greta looked down at the two boys, one who was holding her skirt and the other the baby. She took Ginger from his arms and then yelled, 'RUN!' She turned and legged it up the narrow, cobbled street, calling over her shoulder, 'You dirty old git.'

'Nice one, Johnny,' Georgina said with a roll of her eyes. 'Kids are always warned about taking sweets from strangers. Don't just stand there. Go and catch them!'

Johnny had no idea how he was supposed to round up five small children, though found that his large steps soon caught up with their little legs. 'Hold on, Greta. I'm not gonna hurt you.'

She ignored him and kept running. The two smaller boys were struggling to keep up with her, and he was able to grab the pair of them, holding them both by the backs of their jumpers. They wriggled and squirmed and kicked at his shins.

'Are you gonna run off and leave your brothers?' Johnny called.

Greta looked over her shoulder and when she saw the twins struggling to get away from him, she skidded to a halt. 'Let them go or I'll scream.'

'I ain't messing about no more. Get in the car, the lot of you. You're going to see your mother. Any more lip from you and I'll give these two a right good hiding.'

Greta's eyes widened and then narrowed. 'You said that you wouldn't hurt us.'

'I won't so long as you do as you're told. Stop mucking me about and get in the car.'

Greta scowled, but at last stamped to the car, giving Johnny a dirty look as she passed him. 'If you hurt my brothers, you'll be sorry,' she warned.

'Blimey, you're a stroppy little cow,' he said, and could see now why Larry hadn't looked forward to spending time at Clara's house.

'Come on then,' Greta snapped before climbing into the back seat. 'You're supposed to be taking me to see my mum.'

Johnny had to smile. Greta might be stroppy, but he couldn't help finding her amusing.

'Well done,' Georgina mouthed as Johnny bundled the two boys into the back seat.

'There's blood on this seat,' Greta cried out.

'No, love, it's just some blackcurrant juice I spilled this morning,' Georgina told her.

Greta didn't look convinced and in a small voice asked, 'Is my mummy going to be all right?'

'I won't lie to you,' Johnny said. 'Her face is a bit of a mess, but the doctors will sort her out.'

'Is Larry there with her?'

Johnny looked at Miss Garrett, unsure of how to answer the girl. Thankfully, she replied for him. 'No, Larry isn't with your mum. He's had to go back to London to work.'

Johnny knew that after seeing their mum they couldn't go back home, not until Larry's body had been removed. He glanced across at Miss Garrett to see that she was rubbing her finger, a sure sign that she was worried or deep in thought. When she spoke, he knew that she'd been thinking along the same lines.

'Greta, have you got a daddy, or grandparents you can stay with until your mummy gets better?'

'No, there's just us.'

'I see, well, we can't leave you at home on your own.'

'Why not? Mum does. She leaves me to look after the others while she's at work.'

'Right, well, we'll have to see about that,' Georgina said as they drew up outside the hospital. 'We're here now. Go in through those doors and tell them who you are, and who you've come to see. If they won't let you see your mum, tell them that they've got to let her know that you're all there and safe. Can you do that?'

'Of course I can. I'm not stupid.'

'I'm sure you're not,' Georgina said, 'but if they won't let you see your mum, I want you to go to the waiting room. Wait for me there and I'll be back as soon as I can to take you home.'

Johnny watched the children troop into the hospital and then turned to Georgina. 'What the fuck are we gonna do with them?'

'Well, if they haven't got anywhere else to go, we'll have to do what I said and take them home. It means we'll have to move Larry.'

'Now?'

'Yes, I'm sorry, Johnny. I don't like the idea of dragging his body around with us but we don't have any choice.'

Johnny shrugged. He could see that it was their only option but the thought of his mate's corpse sitting in the back seat left him feeling sick to his stomach. 'How are we gonna pick the kids up if we've got Larry's body in the car?'

Georgina sighed heavily. 'You won't like it, but we'll have to get rid of everything in the boot and put him in there.'

'No way, that ain't very dignified!'

'I realise that but we can't drive around with him on display. What if we get stopped by the Old Bill? *Oh, yeah, him in the back, Officer, he's feeling a bit under the weather and is dead to the world.*'

'That ain't funny, Miss Garrett.'

'I know. But you see what I mean?'

'Yeah, I suppose,' Johnny agreed, though shoving Larry in the boot of the car felt like a betrayal to his mate. Larry had been a good bloke and deserved better.

The car engine went into high revs again as it climbed up the steep hill to Clara's house and they parked outside. When they walked into the house, Johnny nearly fell backwards in disbelief. 'Where the fuck has he gone?'

Georgina pushed past him and stared open-mouthed

at the smears of blood on the floorboards but no sign of Larry's body. 'Are you sure he was dead?' she asked.

'Yeah, absolutely fucking sure!'

'It looks like someone had made a crude attempt of clearing up. It must have been Kelly or one of his men.'

Johnny ran a hand through his hair. 'Shit! What now, Miss Garrett?'

'I don't know, Johnny. There's not much we can do. Christ, I hope it was Kelly and not the police.'

'Nah, if it was the Old Bill, they'd be swarming all over the place now.'

'Yes, of course, you're right. It must have been Kelly. I don't know what he intends to do with Larry's body, but I doubt he's got a clean-up crew. As I've said before, we don't want any trace of us left behind. If Kelly just dumps the body and it's found, the police are bound to investigate.'

Johnny went through to the kitchen to look for something to use to clean up the blood. His mind turned with thoughts of Larry's disappearing body. He was certain that Larry had been dead but now he began to doubt himself. But if Larry was alive, where was he? And if he weren't, why would Kelly have returned to the house to collect a corpse? As Johnny wiped the floor with a few old rags and a bucket of water, he tried to push all thoughts of Larry from his mind. Trying to fit the pieces together and work out what was going on was giving him a headache. He'd leave the thinking to Miss Garrett. After all, she was much better at it.

19

Charlotte had said goodbye to Molly but she couldn't shake the worry that gnawed in the pit of her stomach. Molly hadn't said much but she was worried too. It was etched all over her face. But at least her big sister was going to sort out the problem and send Edward away from the family home. Gawd, Charlotte didn't envy Molly. What an awful thing for a parent to have to do. And no doubt, their mother, Fanny, would likely kick up a right stink!

Ned fetched in a cup of tea and put it on the coffee table in front of her. She didn't bother to acknowledge him. She was still angry about the things he'd said in front of Molly; that Edward was the spawn of the devil and should have been drowned at birth. After the things Molly had told her about Edward, Ned was probably right, but he shouldn't have voiced his opinions in Molly's hearing.

'Do you really think that evil is passed on through families?' she asked. She'd thought out loud and wasn't bothered or interested in Ned's opinion.

'Yeah, I do. You've only got to look at Billy's father. Norman Wilcox was a ruthless bastard. You never knew him, but he had an evil streak. He used to have a belt with a sharpened buckle and had many an eye out with it. Miss

Garrett's dad, Jack, he bore the brunt of it once. Jack had a bloody big scar from one end of his face to the other. It was before your time but you'd often see blokes in Battersea walking around with nasty scars on their faces and you knew that Norman Wilcox had done it. He ruined women's faces an' all. He didn't care.'

'He sounds like a nasty piece of work.'

'Billy took after him, though he turned out to be ten times worse.'

'Blimey,' Charlotte remarked. 'It's funny, I always thought that Norman was a bit of a gent. I remember his wife, Jane. She was nice.'

'Nah, Norman weren't no gent. He'd happily kill anyone to get what he wanted. Most people did what they could to stay out of his way but Lord help you if you had something that Norman was after. He was a right bastard. I never liked him.'

'What a family, Ned! What Billy got up to was horrendous. He murdered his father, and then Billy was shot dead by his own mother. Cor, you couldn't make it up!'

'I know you ain't happy with what I said about Edward, but he's already turning dangerous, just like his father.'

Charlotte shuddered at the thought. 'I hope Molly doesn't hang around and gets Edward sent away as soon as possible.'

'It'll keep them safe for a while, but don't forget there's school holidays.'

'Yes, I hadn't thought of that. Maybe I should tell Molly not to let him come home. It would be safer to keep him in the school.'

'Safe my arse. When he leaves school, what then? He'll

probably be full of resentment at being sent away. Mark my words, there'll be a blood bath at that farm one day.'

'Please, don't say that, Ned,' Charlotte said, and shook her head as horrifying images flashed through her mind. She could picture Edward, grown up, strong and angry. He was searching the farm for Molly to pay her back for sending him away. 'He'll slaughter them all,' she whispered as her blood turned icy cold in her veins.

'That lad needs putting in the ground like his father and his grandfather. I never thought that I'd advocate killing a kid but Edward ain't normal. He's pure evil, just like his dad.'

'No, Ned, killing a child would make us the evil ones.'

'Fine, you make your bed, you lay in it. But don't say I didn't warn you.'

Charlotte reached for her cup and sipped on the now almost cold tea as her thoughts turned. Once Edward was out of the way, her sister and family would be safe. But if Ned was right and sending him away would fill Edward with resentment, she feared for their future.

Georgina and Johnny dropped Clara's children back at their home. It broke Georgina's heart to see the little ones with their solemn, mucky faces and their shoulders heavy with the burden of worry about their mother's injuries. It made her think of her own children. She'd tried so hard to keep thoughts of Alfie and Selina out of head but now her arms ached to hold them.

Georgina took Greta to one side, and while they had a chat, she told Johnny to keep an eye on the other kids. She was impressed with Greta's intelligence, and though she was an endearing, cheeky little madam, she felt sure that the girl would follow her instructions. She then gave Greta some money to feed them all, and turning to look at the rest of the children, she thought that they could all do with a good meal.

'When's our mum coming home?' one of the boys asked Greta.

'I don't know,' she told them, 'but we'll be all right until she does.'

They looked a little reassured, but Georgina hated leaving them.

'Are you all right?' Johnny asked as they climbed back into the car.

'Yes. I'm sure that Greta believes that she can look after the other children, but it doesn't seem right. As soon as we're back in London, I'll arrange for someone to come to stay with them until their mother comes out of hospital.'

Johnny smiled. 'I sort of guessed you'd do something like that.'

'Yes, well, I wouldn't leave my kids to fend for themselves.'

'I bet your two are 'aving the time of their lives with Lash's family.'

A small smile spread on Georgina's lips. Yes, her children would be having a wonderful time and wouldn't be missing her half as much as she missed them. If anything, Alfie and Selina felt more at home with their gypsy grandparents, especially Selina. Georgina's heart felt heavy. All she'd ever wanted for her children was to offer them a happy home and a secure future, one where they'd never know poverty and what it felt like to be hungry. She'd worked hard and risked her life in order to achieve a better life for her kids, a life out of the slums, and a good education. She thought she'd achieved that too, with their lovely country home in Kent. But then Thomas Kelly had come along and turned everything upside down. He'd kidnapped and killed the man she loved. Her smile turned into a grim line and her heart hardened. 'Let's get him. No more fucking about. I want Kelly.'

Johnny turned the car and drove back down the hill towards the pub where they hoped to find the man.

'How are we going to get him?' Johnny asked.

'You'll see,' Georgina answered as she went over her plan in her head. It wasn't one that she'd thought through and it had only began to formulate an hour ago. But she wanted Kelly at the end of her gun. The plan was simple, nothing complicated. Straightforward, no mess, no mucking about and best of all, no drawing attention to themselves.

Johnny trundled through the quiet streets with his heart pumping. His blood rushed through his veins, his jaw clenched and his hands gripped the steering wheel. This was it. They were finally going to do what they'd come here for. But he wished he knew what his boss had in mind. Miss Garrett had kept her ideas to herself, which had infuriated Johnny. He wanted to know the risks. Maybe they were high and that's why she hadn't divulged anything to him. But Johnny still felt perturbed. She must know that he would do anything for her, no matter what the cost to his health. He'd proved it often enough. So why wouldn't she tell him now?

Unable to keep quiet, he asked again, 'How are we going to do this, Miss Garrett? I need to know the details.'

'Let's see if his car is outside the pub.'

'Then what?'

'Then we are going to leave our car around the corner and break into his.'

'What for?'

'To hide in the back seats, and when he gets back in his car, we'll be waiting for him.'

Johnny punched the air in front of him, hissing, 'Yes,' but then said, 'Hold on, what if he ain't alone?'

'It's a chance we've got to take, but we can take two on if we have to.'

'Yeah, no problem.'

'Once we've got control, we'll force him to drive to the barn. That'll be when the fun *really* starts.'

'What if he sees us in the back of the car?'

'He won't. The back windows are blacked out, and I've arranged a little surprise for him. He'll be so keen to jump behind the wheel, he won't see us waiting for him.'

'What surprise?'

'You'll see.'

'No, Miss Garrett. Don't do this to me again. I bloody hate surprises. Just tell me.'

'I've had a word with Greta and I've paid her to distract Kelly.'

'How?'

'She's going to settle down the kids and then get her best friend to sit with them so that she can run down to the pub with her brother's catapult. Once I give her the thumbs up, she'll wait down the road for Kelly to come out of the pub. When he does, she'll lob a stone at him and shout something rude, which, let's face it, will come naturally to her. Kelly will jump in his car to chase after her but we'll be waiting for him.'

Johnny ran through the scenario in his head and then asked, 'But what if he chases her on foot?'

'He won't. Think about it. She's like a little whippet. She'll already have a head start on him. If a kid in the street catapulted a stone at you, would you run after the kid or jump in your car?'

'I'd jump in me car.'

'There you are. Kelly will too. And he'll be so bloody eager to catch Greta, he won't notice us. Not until he feels the metal of the barrel of my gun on the back of his head.'

'Are you sure you can trust her?'

'Yes. I know I can. She reminds me a lot of me at that age.'

'What, you was a gobby little brat?'

'No, Johnny, far from it. But I was brave and determined, just like her. And I would have done anything to protect my family. Greta knows that's exactly what she'll be doing now; protecting her family.'

'Blimey, Miss Garrett. It sounds straightforward enough but I'm still worried that he'll spot us in the back of the car. Why don't we just gun him down as soon as he comes out of the pub?'

'I know that would be the easier option, and if he spots us, that's what we'll have to do. It's not what I want though. I don't just want the man dead. I want to see him suffer first, just as I'm sure he made David suffer.'

'Yeah, well, I can understand that.'

'I hope we can get him to the barn, but at the end of the day, my objective is to finish Kelly. One way or another the man is going to die today.'

Johnny slowly nodded. He pictured them hunkered down in the back of Kelly's car, ready to capture the man. It could work, he could see that, and if it did, it would be easy and seamless. Though it had been many years since Johnny had broken into a car without causing any obvious damage. They couldn't smash a window or crowbar open a door. He wondered if he'd unearthed a flaw in Georgina's plan. 'How are we gonna break into his car without him noticing?'

'It won't be locked. Kelly stole the car in the first place. He won't have the keys for it.'

'Oh yeah, course. It'll be a piece of piss.'

'Yep. And look, there it is.'

Johnny saw the flash motor parked outside the pub and once again, his heart began to hammer. He turned off the road and went to pull over.

'No, not here. Around the next corner.'

Johnny followed her instructions and as he turned into a narrow lane, he saw that there were only a few cottages scattered along one side and a large building at the end. Johnny drove towards it and realised that it was some sort of dairy.

'Park here. It's less conspicuous.'

Before they got out of the car, they both checked their guns.

'Right. Let's get this done,' Georgina said.

Together, they walked briskly and didn't see anyone until a chap rode past them on a bicycle. He didn't take any notice of them and, thankfully, when they neared Kelly's car, there was nobody else about. Miss Garrett looked swiftly around, and then opening the back door, she climbed in, urging him to do the same.

'Get down, Johnny. He could come out at any moment.'

He hunkered down, hoping that this audacious plan was going to work. He just wanted this over with now and to go back to Battersea. He was even looking forward to finding Kathy in his bed, assuming the tart hadn't cleaned him out and run off with everything he owned. He wouldn't put it past her. She was good between the sheets but with the scruples of an alley cat.

'We're in the clear – nobody saw us,' Georgina whispered.

Johnny's mind snapped back to the present and the job in hand. He knew there were risks, which meant that he had to be on the ball. Thomas Kelly had already brought down the most powerful man that Johnny had ever known. David Maynard's heart had been sent to Miss Garrett and most of his men had been gunned down. Larry was dead, Victor too, so Johnny was under no illusions. He was well aware that Kelly was a nasty piece of work, and realised that once again, he was going to find himself in danger.

It wasn't new to him; he'd been in dangerous situations with Miss Garrett before. So far, they'd survived, but death had been close a few times. He'd been shot by Temi Zammit and almost killed. That Russian bloke, Olag, had been a close call too. Lord Hamilton had copped it that time. Christ, the list went on. There was Wayne Warner and his gang, the Portland Pounders, Mickey the Matchstick and even a woman had had a pop at him. Johnny unconsciously rubbed his neck where Nancy Austin had ordered a noose to be put around it. He'd never forget clawing at the rope, kicking his legs, feeling his windpipe being crushed. The experience of nearly being hanged had been a lot more chilling than being shot. Yet he'd never once considered the idea of not standing beside Miss Garrett. He'd always said he'd put his life in the line for her, and nothing had changed – he still would.

'I hope he comes out soon,' Georgina said quietly. 'I want this over with.'

'Me too,' he murmured. Of all the times he'd stood by her, this was the first time that Johnny had a niggling bad feeling. He tried to push it aside and told himself that he was being daft. Maybe he felt uneasy after seeing that Larry's luck had run out. Or maybe it was because they were in an unfamiliar area. Perhaps he was just getting older and wiser. Whatever was unnerving him, he knew that he didn't want to die in this sleepy town. But something was telling him that tragedy was close by.

20

Georgina had been pleased to see Greta ready and waiting up the road with her catapult poised ready to fire at Thomas Kelly. She'd known that the girl wouldn't have let her down. She knew it wasn't the best of plans, in fact a bit daft really, but it was all she could come up with in a short time. She made a mental note to remind herself to arrange a regular payment to Clara and the kids. No children deserved to grow up in the conditions that Greta and her brothers and sister were living in. Their home, their sunken eyes and skinny, undernourished little bodies had put her in mind of Molly and her sisters when they'd been kids. Molly's family had lived in two rooms, just like Clara and her children. Molly had been deprived of a good meal for most of her childhood and had dressed in little more than rags.

Georgina had never told Molly, but her best friend was part of the reason that she fought so hard to make a better life for Alfie and Selina. She couldn't abide the thought of them being dragged up in the way Molly had been. And it upset her to see Greta and the younger ones having to live in that way now. But not for much longer. Georgina would see to it that their lives were improved a little.

'Its bleedin' uncomfortable crouched down like this. It must be closing time so I hope Kelly makes an appearance soon.'

'Shush, Johnny. No talking. Don't say a word. And don't look up.'

Georgina's back ached and her left foot tingled with pins and needles. She gritted her teeth and hoped her foot didn't go completely numb.

'How much longer?' Johnny whispered.

'As long as it takes. Just shut it!'

Georgina's ears pricked. She was sure that she heard Greta's voice. She fought the urge to lift her head and held her breath instead.

'You cheeky little shit!' Kelly shouted.

This was it. Greta had fulfilled her part in Kelly's downfall and now Georgina prayed that he'd jump into the car. Just as she'd hoped, she heard the door open. Seconds later, as Kelly plonked himself down in the driver's seat, the passenger door also opened. Georgina waited until she heard both doors bang shut and then Kelly started the engine.

'That was Clara's girl. She needs a fucking good hiding, just like her mother. Wait 'til I get my hands on her,' Kelly growled.

Georgina nodded to Johnny and in unison they both sat up, Georgina shoving her gun against the back of Kelly's head, and Johnny doing the same to his passenger. 'Don't move or I'll blow your fucking brains out,' she ordered, her calm tone shrouding her internal panic.

'What the fuck…?' the fat passenger spat.

'Shut it,' Johnny barked and Georgina noticed that he drove the barrel of his gun harder against the man's head.

SAM MICHAELS

'Put your hands where we can see them,' she commanded. 'Both of you.'

The men slowly raised their arms. And then Kelly spoke. 'I knew it. I fucking knew that you was in town. Nice to finally meet you, Georgina.'

'It's Miss Garrett to the likes of you,' Johnny snarled.

She ignored Kelly and reached forward to frisk him and remove his gun. She felt safer with the man's weapon in her hands, yet still held her own gun at his head.

Johnny did the same to the passenger, but when he didn't find a gun, he demanded, 'Where is it?'

'I don't have one.'

'Knife?'

'In my sock.'

'Give it to me... slowly.'

The man did as he was told, then Kelly spoke again, and though being held at gunpoint, he showed no fear. 'Have you enjoyed your trip from London?' he asked.

'Drive,' Georgina snapped.

'Where to?'

'Just fucking drive or I'll shoot you right here.'

'Can I put my hands back on the steering wheel?'

'DRIVE!' she yelled. His sarcasm grated on her to the point of almost making her teeth ache.

The car lurched forward, but then the engine stalled. Kelly started it again and he licked his dry lips. Georgina smirked. It was a clear sign that he was more nervous than he was letting on.

Johnny gave the directions to the barn, which Kelly carefully followed without saying a word. The fat bloke was sweating. Though Georgina hardly took her eyes off

236

Kelly, she could see perspiration beads on the fat bloke's balding head. To be fair, it was hot in the car and she was sweating too. Her hand felt clammy and her pulse raced. She wouldn't relax until she had Kelly secured.

When they arrived at the turning for the barn, Johnny told Kelly to follow the uneven road. The car bumped and jolted over the uneven ground, rattling Georgina's bones. But she still held her gun firmly at Kelly's head. Outside the barn. Georgina ordered Kelly to stop the car, and once he did, she snapped, 'Right, put your hands up again.' As he did as he was told, she told Johnny to get out first while she kept her gun aimed at both Kelly and his passenger. She hoped he wouldn't try to escape because then she'd have to kill him quickly. She didn't want that. Kelly needed to die slowly and in agony, just as David had.

Georgina and Johnny pushed the men towards the barn. Johnny heaved the doors open yet when Georgina walked in with her gun in the nape of Kelly's neck, she couldn't see any sign of Nobby and Eric. But then the twins emerged from behind an old cart, both of them also pointing their weapons at Kelly.

'You got him,' Nobby said, smiling broadly.

'Yep. Strip them, sit them and tie them,' Georgina answered.

'Shall we gag 'em an' all?'

'No. I want to hear them bawling and begging for their lives.'

Nobby and Eric moved towards the fat man first. 'You heard the lady,' Nobby said. 'Strip.'

The fat man didn't protest and began to quickly remove his clothes. He stood in just his grubby underwear and socks, looking terrified.

'Take everything off,' Georgina ordered. She looked at the man with revulsion and wondered if he'd been one of the blokes who had punched Charlotte in the stomach, causing her to miscarry.

The man stepped out of his underwear and stumbled sideways as he pulled off his socks. Georgina avoided looking at his revolting body and told Nobby, 'Tie him to the wheel of the cart.'

Once he was secured, she turned her attention back to Kelly. 'Now you,' she demanded.

Kelly held out his hands in an open gesture and asked disbelievingly, 'You can't be serious?'

'Oh, believe me. I'm dead fucking serious. Take off your clothes or Nobby will cut them off and I can't guarantee he won't slice your flesh while he's doing it.'

Kelly grinned, showing no sign of fear. 'All right. If that's what you want. I never had you down for a dirty cow, Georgina. But if you want to see what a *real* man looks like, then I'm happy to oblige.'

Georgina didn't respond. She wouldn't sink to Kelly's level and play his games. Instead, she nodded at Nobby who stormed across from the cart and punched Kelly on the side of the head. Kelly's trilby hat fell off as he staggered sideways, took several stumbling steps but remained on his feet.

Johnny moved forward and poked his finger in the man's face. 'I told you. It's *Miss Garrett*. And don't fucking speak to her unless you're asked to,' he snarled.

Kelly, looking a bit dazed, turned his head and glared at Georgina with contempt.

'Now strip,' Nobby spat.

He removed his jacket and folded it before placing it on the dirt floor beside him. Then his tie, braces and shirt followed and he folded those too. Kelly next took off his shoes and socks, along with his watch, which he put inside one of his shoes. With a sardonic smile, he then fixed his eyes on Georgina as his trousers fell around his ankles.

Her only reaction was too look at him disdainfully.

He shrugged, then folding the trousers neatly, he placed them on the pile of clothes. Fixing his eyes on Georgina again, he began to pull down his pants.

She decided to bait him and said, as she wiggled her little finger at him, 'I bet you've got the tiniest dick.'

'I don't think so,' Kelly drawled. Stark naked he stood with his chest puffed out and his hands on his hips. He was trying to be blasé but Georgina knew that he must be feeling humiliated.

Nobby went behind Kelly and grabbed his arms, pulling them tight behind his back and asked, 'Where do you want him?'

Georgina knew exactly where she wanted him. She'd already done a quick recce of the barn and was fully aware of what tools and utensils were at her disposal. 'Bang four pegs into the ground. Here will be perfect,' she answered, pointing to a spot that was about six feet in front of the fat bloke. 'Then spread-eagle him.'

Nobby and Eric wasted no time in hammering the wooden stakes into the ground. After tying rope around Kelly's wrists and ankles and securing him to the stakes, they stood back and smiled admiringly at their work.

Ever so slowly, Georgina menacingly walked around the man, and then she leaned over his stretched-out body and spat in his face. Kelly tried to avoid her spittle by turning his head to the side but her phlegm dripped into his ear.

'Oh, very ladylike,' he said, with a scowl of disgust.

'I don't pretend to be a lady. Make no mistake, Kelly, you *will* die, but in agony. I'm going to hurt you badly, and your death will be a slow and unbearable one.'

'Is that right?' he asked, showing no fear.

It angered her and she shouted, 'By the time I'm finished with you, you'll be crying and screaming, begging for me to kill you.'

'You'd best get on with it then.'

Nobby, his voice thick with hatred, growled down at Kelly. 'You was told not to speak to Miss Garrett unless you're told to,' and with that he kicked Kelly's head in the same spot as he'd previously punched him.

'Not too hard,' Georgina warned. 'I want him conscious.'

Kelly's head had sagged to one side so he was looking towards the barn door. 'Turn his head so that he's looking at the ugly bastard tied to the cart,' Georgina told Nobby.

The man nodded and forced Kelly's face towards the fat bloke. Kelly didn't protest.

Georgina addressed the fat bloke, asking, 'What's your name?'

'Titch,' he quickly replied.

'Well, Titch, you are surplus to my requirements.'

'Eh?'

Georgina rolled her eyes. He didn't look the brightest of tools in the box and probably didn't understand words of more than two syllables, so she explained, 'I mean, I don't need you, but tell me, Titch, did you beat up my friend Charlotte and her husband?'

'What? Who?'

'Tell me the truth and I'll ensure your death is an easy one. Lie to me and you'll suffer.'

Titch swallowed hard as his panicked eyes flitted from Georgina and then to Johnny, Nobby and Eric. 'Yeah – yeah, I did but it was on *his* orders,' he answered and nodded his head towards Kelly.

Kelly closed his eyes and shook his head as he moaned, 'You fucking turncoat.'

'Sorry, Boss, but if I'm going to die, I want it to be quick.'

'Shut up, you pathetic lump,' Kelly seethed. 'You should have taken it like a man and kept your trap shut.'

Georgina stepped between Kelly's spread legs, pulled her foot back and kicked him hard in the balls with as much force as she could muster. Kelly screamed, a long, high-pitched wail that sounded like an injured animal.

'I've been looking forward to doing that,' she said, brushing her hands together. 'Nothing is going to give me more joy than hearing you crying out in sheer bloody agony.'

Kelly was still groaning, his face crumpled in pain.

'Right. Let's deal with him first,' Georgina said and pointed at Titch. 'Nobby, get the scythe and cut open his stomach.'

'Can I do it?' Johnny asked.

Georgina looked at her right-hand man. They'd both seen Charlotte being stoic as she'd lost her unborn baby. And Georgina knew that it had upset Johnny. He was ever so fond of the girl and wanted revenge on the man who'd hurt her. 'Yes, Johnny. This one is yours,' she answered.

As Kelly lay grumbling on the ground, Johnny went to the barn wall and took down the old, rusty scythe. He marched determinedly towards Titch and then lifted the scythe over his head. With both hands on the handle, he brought it down across the man's large stomach.

Titch screamed, a low and reverberating rumble, unlike Kelly's squeal. But the skin stretched across his belly hardly broke. Deep red and purple bruises began to manifest instantly but there was no blood.

'You said you'd make it quick,' Titch moaned at Georgina.

'I lied.'

Titch dropped his head to his chin and his shoulders began to jerk as he cried like a baby. For a fleeting second, and only a fleeting second, Georgina felt sorry for him. But then she quickly reminded herself of Charlotte's heartbreak.

Johnny lifted the scythe over his head again, but Nobby stepped forward and stayed his hands. 'Step aside, pretty boy. It's gonna need a bit of muscle to get through that blubber. You're better with a gun.'

With a nod, Johnny handed over the scythe, but Nobby threw it to one side and then surveyed the other tools on the wall. He walked up and down, looking at each one in turn.

'Please, don't do this,' Titch cried. 'Please, I don't want to die… Please, I'm begging you.'

As Titch begged, Kelly's whimpering had quietened down but Georgina could see the man was still in discomfort. She didn't care. She wanted his suffering to last much longer. He was going to regret cutting out David's heart and sending it to her in a box.

Nobby took a three-pronged pitchfork with thick tines off the wall and asked, 'How about this?'

'Hmm, to be honest,' Georgina said, 'I'd prefer that his stomach is sliced open rather than jabbed.'

'Use this,' Johnny offered and pulled a knife from his pocket that he'd taken from Titch earlier. He tested the blade. 'It's nice and sharp.'

'Good thinking, Johnny,' Georgina praised.

Nobby took the knife and leaned over Titch. 'How do you feel about your own knife being used to slice you open?'

'No, please, no, no, no, no, no. Please don't so this,' Titch implored.

Nobby, unaffected by Titch's pleas, stabbed the knife into the side of his belly. Titch screamed in horror and pain, and continued screaming and crying as Nobby pulled the knife across his stomach in a sawing motion. Titch's body jerked and shook uncontrollably but Nobby dragged the sharp blade from one side of his stomach to the other.

Georgina wasn't squeamish but she couldn't bring herself to look at the wound. She heard Johnny say, 'Blimey, that took a long time to start bleeding.'

Titch's screams had died down to sobbing. In between his sobs, he voice weak, he pleaded again. 'I'm dying... Fuck... I'm sorry... Please, help me...'

'Shut up,' Nobby growled.

'I can't stand it. Just finish me off,' he begged.

'What do you think, Miss Garrett, shall I finish him off?'

Georgina gritted her teeth. She'd made a promise to Charlotte and she intended to keep it. 'Pull his guts out,' she ordered.

'What? You're telling me to pull out his intestines?'

'You heard me.'

'Come off it, Miss Garrett. I ain't sticking me hand in there!'

'I'll do it,' Johnny said, 'after seeing the state that Charlotte was in, it'll give me great pleasure.'

Georgina nodded and Johnny removed his coat and then turned up his shirt sleeves. He rolled his shoulders, sucked in three rapid breaths and then shoved his hand into the man's gaping wound.

Titch cried out and thrust his head from side to side. 'No... No... No...' he screamed. 'Kill me...' Titch begged as tears streamed down his face. 'Just kill me.'

Johnny retched as a slimy lump of pink and bloodied mess flopped from Titch's stomach and onto his lap, spilling over to the dirty ground. Even Nobby had to avert his eyes at the revolting sight of the man's insides.

Georgina stood over Kelly again, and when a scream of agony filled the barn, she said, 'You're going to suffer a lot more than that.'

Johnny, looking satisfied, picked up some old rags to wipe the blood from his hands.

'Shut him up. He's giving me a bloody headache,' Georgina ordered.

Johnny didn't hesitate. He grabbed his gun and pulled the trigger, putting a bullet in Titch's head. The barn instantly fell silent and after taking a deep breath, she told the twins, 'Sort him out. Cover him.'

The twins threw an old tarpaulin over Titch's body.

'What's this? Are you too squeamish to look at your men's handiwork,' Thomas Kelly asked, somehow managing another of his supercilious smiles.

Johnny walked over to stand beside her and pulled a lighter from his pocket. He flicked it alight and held the flame to Kelly's cheek. 'I'd take great pleasure in setting your face on fire and then shoving it in Titch's stomach to fill the hole where his guts are missing.'

Kelly's cheek began to burn and turn crimson from the heat. The smell of singed hair reached Georgina's nose. 'No, Johnny, I want him to suffer more than that.'

With obvious reluctance, Johnny killed the flame. 'Yeah, all right, but if the bastard doesn't show you a bit of respect, I'll light him up like a torch.'

She nodded. Thanks to Johnny, she had had fulfilled her promise to Charlotte and now, at last, she could turn her attention fully to Kelly.

Johnny walked away from Miss Garrett's side. Blood and guts had never bothered him but he'd challenge the strongest of men not to feel sick at the sight of a man's guts hanging out. He'd been glad that Nobby had chucked a tarpaulin over Titch, and now wondered what Miss Garrett hand in mind for Thomas Kelly. She'd never really been one for torture. She'd always been quite straightforward with her killings, but since being sent Mr Maynard's heart, something in her persona had changed. Granted, anyone who knew her would guess that she'd be hell-bent on revenge but this was different. He couldn't put his finger on it, but even the look in her eyes had changed. The sparkle had gone to be replaced with dullness, as if a part of her had died with the man she loved. She'd ordered Titch's agonising death without a qualm, so he knew that Thomas Kelly was going to suffer... and badly.

The daylight that streamed through the two broken windows in the barn was beginning to fade. Eric had found a couple of gas lights, which he'd managed to get working, but for how long was anyone's guess. He wished they had his car with them, instead of Thomas Kelly's flash stolen one. He had a torch in his glove box, but maybe Kelly had one too.

He told Miss Garrett what he was going to do and then stepped outside of the barn. The setting sun hit his eyes and a soft breeze brushed his cheeks. Johnny sucked in the clean air, grateful to be outside the barn for a few minutes and away from the stench of death and fear. Maybe Larry had been right about getting too old for this game. Maybe it was time for him to get out of it before he had his life snuffed out like Larry. Yet, as he rummaged through Kelly's car, he knew that he could never leave Miss Garrett. What would be the point? If he did, he'd end up spending the rest of his days worried sick about her.

He couldn't find a torch in the car so he walked to the back and opened the boot. When Johnny saw the sickening sight of Larry's body, he recoiled in shock. He closed the boot and ran back into the barn. Taking hold of Miss Garrett's arm, he pulled her to one side and hissed, 'You ain't gonna believe this.'

'What?' she asked, searching his face.

'It's Larry. He's in the boot of Kelly's motor.'

Her face darkened with fury. 'Well, at least we know what happened to the disappearing body. But I don't get it. Why would he go back for Larry?'

'I dunno. Let's ask him.'

They marched over to Kelly and, glaring down at the man, Georgina asked, 'Would you care to explain why one of my men is in the boot of your car?'

'No, not really.'

Johnny placed his shoe on Kelly's neck and pushed down hard. The man gurgled and squirmed, his face contorted. 'Miss Garrett asked you a question. Answer her.'

'Can't… Br… Breathe.'

Johnny released the pressure on Kelly's neck and Miss Garett repeated the question, only for Kelly to say, 'Work it out for yourself.'

Johnny glowered and said to Miss Garrett, 'He's a bit too fucking brazen, but he'll break. They all do.'

'Yeah, well let's start breaking him now. Nobby, get that pitchfork.'

The man fetched her the old farm tool and without any hesitation, Georgina slammed it down into Kelly's leg.

As Kelly screeched, Johnny examined the injury. One of the prongs had missed Kelly's leg but the other two had gone right through his thigh, probably to the ground. 'Nice work, Miss Garrett,' he said, impressed with her strength.

It didn't take long for Kelly to quieten down so Georgina gave the fork a little wiggle. Once again, Kelly yelled out in pain.

'Anything you'd like to say now?' she asked.

'BITCH!'

Without saying a word, Georgina leaned heavily on the fork handle and ground it down. Now Johnny was sure that it had gone clean through Kelly's thigh.

'I don't know about you, Johnny, but I'm a bit peckish and could do with a drink. Let's leave him here to have a think about what he wants to tell me. The twins can watch over him. We'll go and get a good night's kip and then come back in the morning.'

Johnny was about to agree but his voice was drowned out by the sound of Kelly's cries as Georgina rocked the fork back and forth. She told the twins, 'Nobby, Eric, take it in turns to get your heads down. Me and Johnny will be back first thing. While we're gone, take one of his fingers every hour. He should still have a couple left by the time we get back.'

Johnny tried not to smile at how flippant she sounded. He knew she was good at putting on a front and, though brutal, only those who really deserved it suffered at her hands. He tried to imagine what must be going through Kelly's mind. He hoped the man was shitting himself. He knew that he would be if he were in Kelly's position.

Outside, Johnny was once again grateful for the fresh air but then he looked at Kelly's car and baulked at the thought of Larry in the boot. His disgust must have been written all over his face.

'I ain't being funny, Johnny, but we were going to put Larry in the boot of our car and drive him back to London.'

His guvnor knew his so well. She could read him like a book. 'Yeah. I don't know why I'm letting it bother me. I mean, Larry's dead. He ain't gonna give a flying fuck about being shoved in the boot, is he?'

'No, he isn't, so try not to dwell on it.'

Johnny got into Kelly's car and used the hot wires that were still in place to start the engine. Once Miss Garrett was sitting beside him, he headed back to the country pub that they'd checked out of earlier and asked, 'Do you think it's a bit risky staying around here for another night?'

'Nobody saw us taking Kelly and Titch. The barn is

isolated, and with any luck, nobody will notice that they're missing until tomorrow.'

'Yeah, all right,' Johnny said, but then another thought crossed his mind. It was all very well planning to take Larry home with them but what did Miss Garrett plan to do with Kelly and Titch's bodies?

21

The following morning, Charlotte awoke with Tim on her mind. He'd survived the attack, but it was becoming apparent that he would be left with permanent damage. The doctors couldn't say to what extent, yet it was clear that his speech had been adversely affected. He'd spoken a full sentence yesterday but his words had been slurred and a few of them jumbled. It made no difference to Charlotte. She'd love her husband no matter what. Her wedding vows were sacred to her. *In sickness and in health. Anyway,* she thought, *them doctors don't know everything,* and she was determined that she'd nurse Tim back to full health.

As she trudged to the kitchen to put the kettle on the stove, she yawned and stretched her arms over her head. Ned was fast asleep on the sofa, snoring loudly. *Some bloomin' protection he is,* she thought.

The telephone trilled, and suddenly Ned shot up, a confused look on his face. 'Wh... what?

'I'll get it,' Charlotte said and looked at the clock. It was half past seven. Georgina had never been a late sleeper. But she was surprised to hear Molly's voice on the other end of the line.

'Charlotte... it's me, thank Gawd you're up.'

'Molly, what's the matter?'

'It's Edward. He's gone.'

'Gone where? Do you mean you've already got him into a boarding school?'

'No, not yet. Edward has run away. He could be anywhere. Oh, Molly, I'm worried sick about him. Edward ain't street smart like we was. He's a country boy. He's clever but he won't have a clue how to look after himself.'

'Hang on, Molly, slow down. Why has Edward run away?'

'It was horrible. I can't believe he did it. But I caught him red-handed trying to make Stephen take a load of pills.'

'What sort of pills?'

'Sleeping pills that Mum has. I walked into the bedroom and found him in the middle of getting Stephen to swallow them. Luckily, Stephen had only taken a couple but Edward had another dozen on the side. He was trying to kill Stephen; I know he was!'

Charlotte felt the hairs on the back of her neck stand on end. It felt dreadful to accept the fact that her eleven-year-old nephew could be so calculated.

'He tried denying it. He said that Stephen had a headache and he thought the pills were aspirins. He said he was giving Stephen the pills to make him feel better.'

'Maybe he's telling the truth.'

'No, no way. You should have seen the look on his face, Charlotte. Honestly, it was just like staring into the eyes of Billy Wilcox.'

'Bloody hell! That must have been awful for you.'

'It was. I confronted him. I asked him if he was trying to hurt Stephen. He got upset at first and cried. But when I told him that I *know* the truth, he got angry and it turned into a right old shouting match. Mum came into the room so I told her what I'd found him doing to Stephen.'

'I suppose she jumped to Edward's defence.'

'No, to my surprise, instead of sticking up for Edward she went bloody mad! She said her sleeping pills are kept in her bedside drawer and that Edward had no right going through her things. For the past few weeks, she's been sure that her pills have been going missing, but it never occurred to her that Edward was nicking them. She couldn't believe it.'

'So her blue-eyed boy had blotted his copybook. Yet how did Edward even know about giving someone an overdose?' Charlotte asked.

'I dunno. Maybe he heard something about it in school.'

'I suppose that's possible.'

'It was horrible. Mum was shouting at Edward, I was shouting at Mum, telling her to calm down, Oppo was shouting at me, trying to find out what was going on. And then Edward blurted out how he knew everything about his father!'

'Billy? How?'

'I wrote it all down. Years ago. It was silly of me really but I was struggling with me feelings so I thought it would be a good idea to spill it all out on paper. I put it away after and forgot about it, but Edward must have found it. He will have read everything that Billy Wilcox did to me, and others. I didn't hold back; it was all there in black and white; the way Billy had blackmailed me into sleeping with him. The fire that killed Hilda. The beatings that Georgina took. The prostitutes forced to work for him. Even about him murdering Norman, his own father.'

'Bloody hell!'

'I feel awful, Charlotte. It's all my fault! I think Edward is trying to be like his dad. He's copying Billy.'

'No, Molly, it's not your fault. A *normal* kid wouldn't try and kill his younger brother. He ain't trying to *copy* Billy. He *is* Billy. Edward is the double of his father. Don't blame yourself.'

'Maybe you're right. My head is all over the place and I just don't know anymore. Anyway, once Edward saw how upset and furious Mum was, he ran off. I thought that once he'd calmed down, he'd come back, but he hasn't. He's been gone all night now and I don't know what to do.'

'Let him go,' Charlotte said bluntly. 'You're best rid of him.'

'He's my son!'

Charlotte could hear the pain in her sister's voice and felt guilty for saying something so callous. 'I'm sorry, that just came out without me thinking. What does Mum say?'

'Oppo called the police and Mum agreed it was the right thing to do. But if they find him, they're gonna bring him back here. I can't tell the police that I don't want my child home because he tried to kill Stephen. But I'm scared and I can't think straight.'

'Where do you think Edward has gone?'

'I don't know. I've been all through this with the police. I gave them a list of his friends from school and any places where I thought he might be hiding. But to tell you the truth, I really I ain't got a clue. I don't know my son. I don't understand how his mind works or what he might be thinking.'

'The police will find him, Molly, I'm sure. When they do, you must get him sent to a boarding school, and as soon as possible.'

'Yes, yes... I will,' Molly choked out. 'But he'd have to come home for the holidays.'

'One thing at a time. Get a place sorted for him somewhere. Anywhere that's not under your roof. We'll worry about the holidays later. He can always come and stay with me.' The moment the words had passed Charlotte's lips, she regretted her offer. She had Tim to think about.

'It's so hard, Charlotte. I love Edward, but at the same time I'm frightened of him.'

Charlotte listened, heartbroken to hear Molly sobbing and said, 'I wish I could be there with you.'

'I'm trying to hold it together but I can't stop crying and I... I'm so tired.'

'It's all right, sis. You're allowed to be upset. Listen to me, put the telephone down now and get straight on to finding a boarding school.'

'All right, I'll do that now. After what he tried to do this time, I really haven't got any choice.'

'It's for the best, love,' Charlotte said softly.

'I know. Bye, Charlotte.'

'Bye, love, and keep me updated.'

'I will.'

Charlotte put the phone down and turned to see Ned holding a cup of tea towards her.

'I only heard one side of that conversation, but enough to know that Billy's spawn is causing trouble again.'

Charlotte nodded and told him what was going on, ending with: 'The sooner they find Edward, the better.'

'If he's found out about his father, he could turn up in Battersea,' Ned suggested.

'I doubt it.'

'Yeah, well, I hope you're right. We're well rid of the Wilcoxes. I don't like the idea of another one on the streets, kid or not. There's a screw loose that runs through that family and it seems to get worse from father to son.'

'Yeah, I know what you mean. What was Billy like as a kid, can you remember?'

'Not really. I worked for Norman but I didn't take much notice of his kids. I thought Billy was a bit of a scamp but looking back, I'm pretty sure that the rest of the kids in the area were scared of him.'

Charlotte welcomed the cup of tea and soon drank it. Her head was spinning with thoughts of Edward, Billy and Molly. A knot of fear felt lodged in her stomach. She was no stranger to death. She'd been close to Georgina so had been around guns and killings. She'd been through the war too, seen the devastation of the Blitz and had witnessed the gruesome sights of mutilated bodies caught up in bomb blasts. But this was different. She now had what sounded like a cold, calculated, potential killer in her family. Worse, Edward was only a child. She shivered. One day he would become a man, and Charlotte knew that he was going to turn out even more dangerous than Billy Wilcox.

Georgina had hardly slept. The need for revenge consumed her. She had nearly returned to the barn several times throughout the night but, using all her willpower, had manage to stay away to let Kelly suffer as his fingers were removed. Lying in the darkness, she'd wanted to think of David, but every thought was interrupted by images of the man who had murdered him. She hated being unable to remember her husband without Kelly marring her memories. She didn't want her feelings for David to be so intertwined with Kelly, but they were. And they would continue to be until she'd eliminated the man. Only then would she be able to remember her husband with love, warmth, and sadness, instead of the burning anger that devoured her every waking moment.

She couldn't face breakfast and tapped on Johnny's bedroom door. He opened it within seconds, fully dressed and wearing his hat. It seemed that he was keen to get back to the barn too.

'Ready?'

'You bet,' he answered.

In Kelly's car, Georgina was surprised that Johnny wasn't quizzing her. She'd expected him to be bombarding her with questions about what they were going to do with the man today. Instead he was in a quiet, serious mood, and drove in silence.

'All good?' she asked.

'Yep. Fine.'

'You're sure?'

'Yeah. Good as gold.'

'You're very quiet.'

'Just preparing myself.'

'For what?'

'For whatever you're gonna do to that bastard today.'

'Is this too much for you, Johnny?'

'No, of course not. Kelly deserves everything that's coming to him. It's just a bit, you know… well, it put me off me sausage, egg and bacon.'

Georgina found herself chuckling. Then the chuckle turned into a belly laugh that brought tears to her eyes. She couldn't stop, and doubled over with mirth. It was the first time that she'd properly laughed since David's death.

'What's so bloody funny,' Johnny asked, bemused.

'I don't know,' she said, still laughing.

'You're bleedin' nuts, you are.'

'Probably. But you… you had your hands in a man's stomach and pulled out his intestines.'

'That wasn't funny.'

'I know.' She sniffed, trying to contain herself. 'Oh, I needed that,' she added, realising that she didn't feel quite so tense. She knew what had just happened. All her pent-up grief and anger had just leaked out a little in the form of hysterics. But regardless, it still felt good.

'We're here now,' Johnny said as they pulled up outside the barn.

Georgina was ready. She planned on releasing a lot more of her emotions, but this time in the form of anger and hatred towards Kelly.

Nobby and Eric greeted her with dark circles ringing their eyes. They didn't look like they'd had much rest either. She realised that she hadn't been fair in asking them to chop off one of Kelly's fingers every hour. Even if one of them had tried to sleep, the man's screams would have woken them. Georgina would make it up to them, but for now she asked, 'How's he been?'

SAM MICHAELS

'He's still got three fingers left. 'Ere, this'll make you laugh. He was crying when I sawed his thumb off so I stuck it in his mouth and made him suck it like a baby.'

Georgina didn't laugh, but she did smile. 'You two can take a break. Take the car and drive to the pub to get some breakfast.'

'Nah, we're all right, Miss Garrett. We'll stay and see the job through. You are gonna kill him today, ain't ya?'

'Yes, Nobby. He dies this morning. But slowly.'

She walked over to Kelly and stood in between his legs, keeping her eyes away from the bloodied stumps on his hands. She was pleased to see that he looked exhausted and pale, with one leg grotesquely swollen around the pitchfork prongs. 'Good morning. Did you have a good night?' she asked, her voice light.

Kelly didn't even appear to have the energy to glare at her.

'You'll be happy to know that I've got some *smashing* surprises lined up for you today. Let's start with the good old-fashioned breaking of a few bones. Nobby will do the honours.'

Kelly closed his eyes and screwed his face up as he turned his head to one side.

'Any bones, Miss Garrett?'

'Smash his kneecap and then one arm,' she answered.

When Nobby brought the sledgehammer down on Kelly's knee, the sound of the bone crunching was drowned out by the man's screams. Nobby then quickly lifted the hammer again and slammed in into Kelly's arm.

Georgina felt no compassion for Kelly's pain. He had tortured David, probably beaten him, cut of his fingers off and ripped out his heart. What Kelly was suffering so far, was nothing in comparison. He had worse to come, but for now she left him to whimper.

She turned to the twins and Johnny to ask, 'Well then, what do you think we should do to him next?'

'I reckon we should poke his eyes out,' Nobby suggested.

'Or skin him alive,' Eric snarled. 'Our muvver always used to threaten us with that, didn't she, Nob?'

'Yeah, she did. I'd happily skin the bastard. Or we could do what the Red Indians did and scalp him.'

'We ain't playing cowboys and Indians,' Johnny pointed out. 'But we could put a few bullets in him, his feet and what 'ave ya, hurt him but keep him alive.'

They looked at Georgina for her input, but she just shrugged her shoulders nonchalantly. She didn't care what happened to Kelly, just so long as he suffered. 'They all sound like suitable punishments to me. As far as I'm concerned, you can do whatever you feel is fitting for what he did to David, Victor, Larry, Tim and Charlotte. Just so long as it fucking hurts him and doesn't kill him yet.'

'Let me at him,' Nobby said wickedly with enthusiasm.

'Not his eyes,' Georgina added thoughtfully. 'I want to see his pain when he takes his last breaths. And I want him to see us messing him up.'

'Shall I slice him up a bit then? Skin him?' Eric asked.

'Yes, if you can stomach it. Remember, not too deep.'

Johnny lit a cigar and for once, Georgina welcomed the aroma. She normally didn't like the smell of his Cubans around her but this time she appreciated it as it masked the stink from the faeces that Kelly was lying in.

Eric began to meticulously slice skin off Kelly's chest.

'No… no…' Kelly shrieked. 'Wh… what are you doing?'

'Skinning you alive,' Eric answered as he removed a thin sliver of flesh.

'No more… please, I can't take any more.'

'What was that? Did you have something that you wanted to say to Miss Garrett?'

Kelly nodded weakly, crying, so Eric called, 'He wants a word.'

Georgina walked slowly to the man, and looked dispassionately at his mangled body. 'So, you're ready to answer my question now?'

'Yes. You win,' he said. 'I've had enough.'

'Why did you return to take Larry's body?'

'I thought he was a pimp and stealing my tarts,' Kelly said feebly. 'It wasn't until after Titch killed him that it struck me he could've been working for you.'

'So you took Larry's body because you suspected he worked for me. Is that right?'

'Yes.'

'No, that doesn't add up. Eric, get on with skinning him.'

'Make him stop,' Kelly screamed as another slice of skin was removed. 'I'll talk. I'll tell you everything.'

Georgina gave Eric a nod. He stopped slicing and stepped back, leaving large patches of raw flesh exposed on Kelly's chest. 'You'd better tell the truth this time,' Georgina warned.

'I will, but in return, I want your word that you'll put a bullet through my heart.'

Georgina smiled with satisfaction as she bent down and hissed in Kelly's face, 'I told you that you'd be begging to die quickly, but I didn't expect you to break so quickly. We've hardly got started on you yet.'

'Give me your word... a bullet through my heart.'

'You don't deserve my mercy. You didn't show my husband any.'

'He's not dead... David Maynard is alive...'

Georgina felt her stomach lurch. She stood, rod straight and glared down at Kelly. David was alive? No, she didn't believe him.

Kelly was crying and laughing weakly at the same time, his breaths rapid. 'You... you should see your face.'

'You bastard. You're lying!'

'I... I'm not. He's not fucking dead... your husband is alive.'

'The heart?'

'I sent you the heart of a pig,' he said, chortling, despite being in pain.

'I don't believe you.'

'It's true. It's why I took Larry's body.'

Georgina stared blankly, her mind racing as fast as her heartbeat.

'I was taking Larry to David Maynard. I wanted him to confirm that he was one of your men.'

'What difference would it have made?'

'I'd have known you were here, in this area, and looking for me.'

'No, it still doesn't make any sense. You're trying to fuck with my head, but it ain't working!'

Kelly's unnatural laughter turned to desperate sobs. 'I didn't kill your husband. I thought I could learn more from him alive than dead. But look where that's got me.'

'You're a fucking liar!' Johnny spat.

'I'll prove it. I'll tell you where he is, but only if you promise to kill me now, and quickly.'

Georgina, still unsure of whether or not to believe Kelly, shouted through gritted teeth, 'Don't take me for a fool. Tell me where my husband is!'

'Only if you promise to put a bullet through my heart.'

'I don't think you're in any position to bargain with me, but yes, I promise.'

'How do I know I can believe you?'

'I've just given you my word, so just fucking tell me!'

Kelly nodded, and his voice sounding weaker with the effort of talking, said, 'Just outside the town, the road to the docks. On the right, small lane, three burned-out cottages. The last one isn't badly damaged. He's in there.'

'How many of your men are with him?'

'Just one.'

'You'd better be telling me the truth.'

'I am,' Kelly croaked. 'Now, stick to your word and shoot me.'

'When I see for myself that my husband is alive, then I'll kill you.'

'You promised.'

Georgina dropped to her knees and leaned down to whisper sinisterly in Kelly's ear, 'I'll fulfil my promise. But only once I've seen David. If you're lying to me, I'll make you suffer like nothing you could ever imagine.'

She still didn't believe Kelly and thought that he was playing with her mind. It was just his way of trying to manipulate and control the situation. But just in case there was even the smallest of hopes of finding David alive, she had to check. 'With me,' she told Johnny and Nobby. 'Stay with him, Eric.'

Georgina shook her head, still doubtful as she raced to the car. 'Do you believe him, Johnny?'

'I don't know, but what would be the point of lying? He must know that would only cause him more pain.'

Georgina nodded, beginning to feel a spark of hope as they climbed into the car and drove off at full speed. She rubbed her finger where her mother's wedding ring had once been, repeating in her head, *Please be alive. Please be true. Please be alive.*

22

David's eyes flickered open. As his vision adjusted to the light, a ceiling came into focus, one that he didn't recognise. It was much lower than the broken roof of the warehouse where Thomas Kelly had kept him captive. This ceiling had dark oak beams spanning across it and a light fitting hanging down with a faded floral lampshade. Confused, he realised that he was lying on a sofa. He slowly turned his sore head to the side and saw Ralegh sitting on a tatty armchair. The man was reading a comic and chuckling to himself. 'Where am I?' David asked. He found it was difficult to speak, his voice was little more than a croak. His throat was dry and his beaten, mutilated body ached. But the raging fever had cleared and despite the pain he was in, he felt ravenously hungry.

Ralegh threw his comic onto the flagstone floor and pushed his large frame out of the chair. He poured a cup of water from a flask and approached David. 'You're awake,' he said, stating the obvious as he put the cup to David's cracked and sore lips.

David drank greedily from the cup. The cool liquid soothed his throat and quenched his thirst. He looked over the edge of the cup at Ralegh and was relieved to see kindness instead of hatred in the man's eyes. He remembered that he'd formed an alliance with Ralegh and persuaded him to turn on Kelly. Ralegh had agreed to help him escape in exchange for protection and a well-paid job in David's firm. Yet before they could make any plans, he had a vague memory of being moved. After that it was just a blank. What had happened? Had Ralegh helped him to escape and they were hiding out?

David's questions were soon answered and his heart sank when Ralegh explained, 'We're just outside Bristol in a small town that Kelly runs.'

He had no recollection of the journey and asked, 'Where's Kelly?'

'I don't know. He's not been back here since yesterday morning.'

David eased himself up. Every sinew in his body hurt and his hands throbbed. 'Help me to get on my feet. We need to get out of here.'

'There's no point in trying to escape now. There'd be nowhere to hide. Kelly knows everyone here and you're in no fit state to get very far.'

'We just need to get to a telephone box. I'll call my wife. She'll send people to pick us up.'

'No, it's too risky. Kelly could come back at any moment, and if he finds that we're not here, he'll have us chased down.'

David barely had the energy to argue with Ralegh but he refused to allow this opportunity of freedom to pass him by. 'Listen to me. One phone call, then we keep low for a few hours until we're picked up. We'll be home and dry then. If you want to break away from Kelly, this is your only chance.'

Ralegh paced the small room, clenching and unclenching his fits as he walked back and forth. 'I'm not sure about this. If Kelly finds us, he'll kill us. It's too risky.'

David barely had the energy to argue with Ralegh but he refused to allow this opportunity of freedom to pass him by. 'If you don't get away from Kelly, you'll end up dead like your brother. Kelly will use you like cannon fodder. He doesn't give a fuck about you or anyone else. But I'll look after you, Ralegh. You'll be all right with me.'

Ralegh finally stopped pacing and marched to the window. He pulled back the ragged curtain and looked outside. 'You're right. Kelly wants to take on the Portland Pounders and he'll send us in all guns blazing. It won't work; he's going get us all killed.'

'I wouldn't risk my men like that. They've been with me for years. I take care of them, pay them well, and you'll be better off joining me. Come on, Ralegh. We're wasting time. We could have been out of here by now.'

After a little more thought, Ralegh finally said, 'Yeah, all right. Let's get out of here.'

David grunted in pain as the man gently pulled him to his feet. His legs felt weak and the room spun. If Ralegh hadn't been supporting him, David would have fallen back onto the sofa.

'Are you sure that you're ready for this?' Ralegh asked, his brow creased in what appeared to be genuine concern.

'Yes. Let's go.'

Ralegh picked up his pistol off the arm of the armchair and stuck it in his trouser waistband.

'Is that fully loaded?'

'No, Kelly's short on ammo. He only gave me one bullet

and that was supposed to be used on you if you tried to escape.'

'I hope you're prepared to shoot Kelly if you have to. I can't do it,' David said, holding up his maimed hands.

'Yeah, I will, or he'll kill us both.'

'If you've only got one bullet, you'd better be a good shot.'

'A good shot or fucking lucky.'

David regained his strength as adrenaline pumped through his body. But at the street door, fear coursed through his veins. This was it. He was about to step outside and into freedom.

Ralegh pulled the door open and looked up and down a country lane. 'Let's go,' he whispered urgently.

Despite his renewed feeling of strength, David found he needed support. Ralegh placed a shoulder under his arm and almost dragged him along a small garden path. The rising sun was low on the horizon as he realised that he had no idea what time it was or what day. It didn't matter. He just wanted to get home to Georgina and now, seeing her beautiful face was closer to becoming a reality. A low wooden gate hung off of one hinge and David pushed it to one side. 'It's all right, Ralegh. I think I can walk now. Which way?' he asked.

'There's no telephone boxes around here. The closest one is by the railway station, but if you're seen in that state by a copper, he's bound to ask questions. I think we'll have to stay off the roads and cut through the woods, but it'll take us a good hour to get there.'

David nodded in agreement but then Ralegh stopped and stared ahead, wide-eyed and his jaw hanging low. David followed his eyeline and saw a cream and black car coming towards them.

'Fuck, that's Kelly!' Ralegh said as he fumbled in his belt for his gun.

David could see that Ralegh was shaking. 'It's all right, don't panic. You know what you've got to do.'

Ralegh held the gun in front of him but his hand was moving about all over the place.

'Take a few deep breaths and calm down,' David urged. He was worried that Ralegh would miss his target. After all, the man only had one bullet. And if he missed, that would be it for David. He wouldn't be able to outrun Kelly. As it was, he could only just about walk. His heart thudded loud and fast as the car hurtled towards them.

'I can't fucking see. The sun, it's in my eyes,' Ralegh shrieked.

'Just do it. Fire the gun.'

'I can't see.'

'Shoot the fucking bastard!'

'What if I miss him?'

'Just fucking shoot!'

BANG.

Ralegh had discharged the bullet, the noise reverberating and for a moment they stood, motionless. Relief flooded over David when he saw the car veer towards a bank on the other side of the road, but instead of slowing down, the car accelerated. The sound of crunching metal echoed as it drove at speed through a fence and came to an abrupt halt against a mound.

'Run...' Ralegh shrieked. 'We have to get out of here. He might still be alive.'

'I doubt it.' David smiled. But he wanted to know for sure. He needed to know if Kelly was dead. But Ralegh was right, they had to get away.

'Come on, we need to go,' Ralegh coaxed.

David walked as fast as he could, but saw that they were going in the opposite direction to the telephone box. 'Hold on, we're going the wrong way.'

'We can't risk walking past the car. The more distance we put between us, the better.'

David nodded, and then looked over his shoulder to see if Kelly or any of his men were pursuing them. 'Shit, someone's getting out of the back seat,' he told Ralegh.

Ralegh stopped and turned to look. 'Who the fuck is that?'

David strained to see through his swollen eyes, one lid almost closed, but then as he recognised who it was, his brain wouldn't comprehend what he was seeing. 'It can't be… It's Nobby.'

He staggered towards the car wreckage, leaving Ralegh to run off.

He saw Nobby stumble to the front passenger door and frantically yank it hard several times, but the door wouldn't open. A horrifying thought raced through David's mind. As he drew closer, he could see Johnny Dymond in the driving seat. He was leaning over the passenger, blocking David's view. But David knew it was Georgina. It had to be.

'Mr Maynard… we was coming to get you…' Nobby explained shakily. 'I can't get the door open…'

David's stomach lurched. *No, no, no*, his mind screamed. 'Georgina,' he yelled. And then he shouted at Nobby, 'Move. Go and get help.' David pulled on the door but he had little strength and dashed around to the other side.

Johnny opened the door, his face as white as lint. 'She's been shot,' he cried.

David could see Georgina slumped forward. 'Get out,' he ordered Johnny.

Johnny, clearly shaken and injured himself, fell out of the car and onto all fours. 'She's alive, Mr Maynard. She's alive.'

David crawled onto the driver's seat. He gently eased his wife back and lifted her head. He saw a large gash on her forehead and her nose was broken and bleeding. And then he noticed the gunshot wound, almost right in the middle of her chest. Her blood-soaked blouse clung to her body.

'Georgina… It's me, David. Can you hear me?'

Her chest was barely moving, but she was breathing – just.

'Georgina… wake up, darling. Please, my love, open your eyes.'

There was no response and he frantically looked for something to stem the bleeding. When he saw nothing he ripped off his shirt and held it against the hole in her chest. Georgina groaned and he felt a surge of hope. Surely that was a good sign.

'Darling, it's me, David. Can you hear me?'

'David,' she whimpered.

'Yes, darling. I'm here. You're going to be all right. Nobby has gone to fetch help. Just hold on. Stay with me.'

Her stunning violet eyes slowly opened, her voice reedy. 'Have I been shot?'

'Yes, but we'll get you out of here.'

His shirt that he'd held against her wound had quickly become sodden with her blood.

She looked into his eyes and smiled softly, her voice barely a whisper as she said, 'You're alive. I found you.'

'Yes, you did. You found me.' He gently stroked her soft cheek as his eyes filled with tears.

'I think I'm dying, David,' she gasped.

'No. No, you're not dying, Georgina. You're going to be fine.'

'I... I can't see you,' she said.

Her voice was weak; he could hardly hear her and he saw that each breath she took was slow and shallow. 'Hold on, darling. Please, hold on. Don't leave me.'

'I... I love you,' she managed to whisper. A tear slipped from her eye and rolled down her pale cheek. 'Tell my children that I love them.'

'No, Georgina. Don't you dare die!' he yelled.

Her eyes suddenly looked up, away from him, and he saw a look of awe and wonder on her face, 'Gran... Dad...' she breathed.

'Don't give in. Fight, Georgina, fight!'

'I can't... I'm sorry...'

'NO! Georgina... Georgina... NO!'

'It's all right, David. My gran is here... she looks so... so lovely... and me dad... me dad is here too.'

David looked towards the roof of the car. 'Don't take her,' he screamed angrily, though what or who he was shouting at, he wasn't sure. 'Don't you dare take my beautiful wife! She's mine! You're not having her!'

He looked back at Georgina but her eyes had closed. 'I won't let you leave me, Georgina... I need you... your children need you... please, stay with us... please... don't go, my lovely… don't die,' he begged as tears streamed down his face.

He heard Georgina's rattling breath and then her head lulled sideways onto her shoulder. He looked behind to see that Johnny was sitting on the grass, his head bowed and crying openly. 'Do something, Johnny. Get some help,' he begged desperately. She was the love of his life, the almighty Georgina Garrett; he couldn't let her die. He closed his eyes at his next agonising thought: this was his fault. He had told Ralegh to shoot. She had to live or he would never, ever forgive himself.

23

Charlotte had just put the telephone down to Molly who had called to say that the police had brought Edward home. But it wasn't all bad news because Molly had followed through with Charlotte's advice and had found a good boarding school to send him to. The only problem was that Edward couldn't start the school until after the weekend. So Molly was hoping that she could keep him away from Stephen and out of trouble until then.

Cor, Eddie Wilcox, thought Charlotte. That was going to be a name in the future that was going to instil the fear of God into people, just as Norman Wilcox and Billy Wilcox had. Only Eddie Wilcox would no doubt be ten times more wicked.

'Edward's home then?' Ned asked.

'Yes, but not for long. Molly's sending him to a boarding school.'

'Good for her. I bet the little shit won't like that!'

'No, he won't. But from what Molly said, he seemed to be taking the news in his stride.'

'What do you mean?'

'Well, Molly sat him down with me mum and explained about the school and that it was for his own good to keep him out of a home for boys who'd done bad things. And she said that he just shrugged his shoulders and went off to his bedroom.'

'Bugger that! Sounds right creepy, if you ask me. I'd be less concerned if he kicked up a stink. But quiet like that, it ain't normal. Gawd knows what he's planning in his sly head.'

'Yeah, I suppose you're right; it ain't normal, but there ain't nothing normal about that child.'

'I hope you told your sister to keep her wits about her until the boy is gone.'

'She is. Stephen is sleeping in with them and Oppo has put locks on theirs and Mum's bedroom doors.'

'I'd tie him up and put him in the barn if it was up to me.'

'Then it's a bloody good job that it ain't up to you! Edward is still a child, not a wild animal.'

'Take it from me, gal. I worked for Norman and then Billy. I know how their brains worked. And if Edward takes after them, then Molly and the rest of the family are in danger.'

'It's only for a few nights, Ned, and then Edward will be in the school.'

'I'm warning you. That boy will burn the house down with them inside. Get back on the telephone and tell your sister to lock him in his room or you'll all be sorry.'

Charlotte shuddered at the thought. But she couldn't believe that Edward would hurt his own mother.

'I can see you don't believe me but don't forget that Billy killed his father and had him buried in the cellar at Queenstown Road. And I heard that his mother shot Billy dead because she thought that he was going to murder his sisters. This ain't a fucking fairy tale, Charlotte. This is real life and these things happened, so don't ever doubt what Edward is capable of.'

Charlotte rested her head back on the sofa and closed her eyes. Ned could be right and she'd be a fool if she ignored his warning. If anything happened to her family, she'd never forgive herself. She heaved a sigh, wishing that life wasn't so complicated. So much had happened in such a short time. First the miscarriage, and though she hid her feelings, she was still grieving over the death of her unborn child. Then Tim in hospital, but at least he was no longer at death's door and was making a slow, steady progress towards recovery. There was David Maynard's death too, and Georgina's hunt for his killer.

She stood up and wandered over to the window, but barely looked at anything going on outside as her thoughts turned to Edward being a serious threat to her family. She just wanted it all to stop, to have an uncomplicated life, one that was plain and boring. Oh, how she would embrace the boredom and would never complain about it again. She pictured the scene: quiet nights with Tim, him reading the paper or listening to the wireless while she cleaned up after dinner and then did some crocheting. The picture she conjured up in her head looked like pure bliss. Instead, Charlotte was surrounded by the normal mayhem that went hand in hand with being Georgina's friend. Though she had to acknowledge that Edward's evil behaviour wasn't Georgina's fault.

Charlotte reluctantly called Molly back and told her about Ned's warning. And to Charlotte's surprise, Molly agreed with Ned and said that she'd been having similar thoughts. So that was that. Charlotte could rest easy tonight, safe in the knowledge that Edward was going to be locked in his bedroom.

'I've got to go, Molly, there's someone at the door,' Charlotte said as Ned went down the stairs to answer it.

When she replaced the receiver, she heard heavy footsteps coming up the stairs and smiled broadly when Johnny walked in behind Ned. Immediately, pleased to see him, her spirits lifted and she couldn't wait to see Georgina too.

She looked past Johnny and asked, 'Where's Georgina?'

Johnny avoided her eyes and sat down heavily on the sofa before saying sombrely, 'Well, we did it. We killed Thomas Kelly and the bloke who hurt you, but you ain't gonna believe this... David Maynard is alive.'

'What?'

'Yeah, Kelly didn't kill him. He sent a pig's heart, not Mr Maynard's.'

'You're right, I can't believe it!' Charlotte said as she sat beside Johnny. She hadn't been expecting that, but it was the best news. And now she knew where Georgina was – with her husband. 'That's brilliant, Johnny, bloody brilliant! Georgina must be over the moon. Tell me everything. How did you find Kelly? What did you do to the bloke who beat up me and Tim?'

When Johnny didn't answer her, she looked at his face and could see that something was wrong. He was normally so upbeat and she wondered why he wasn't doing somersaults about David being alive. She asked worriedly, 'Did everything go smoothly? Was anybody hurt?'

Johnny shook his head. 'I'm afraid so, sweetheart. Larry was killed.'

'Oh, shit. I'm sorry. I know you were mates.'

'Yeah, we were. Larry was a good bloke.'

'Do you want a cuppa?' Charlotte offered, the cure-all, as her mother used to call it.

'No, sweetheart, I don't want anything,' Johnny answered.

And then, to Charlotte's surprise, he made a noise that sounded like a sob.

She turned to see that his eyes were full of tears. Grabbing his hand, she said soothingly, 'It must have been awful to lose your friend.'

'Yeah, yeah it was,' he croaked, 'but that ain't all.'

He reached out and pulled her into him, crying hard on her shoulder as he tightly wrapped his arms around her. Charlotte didn't know how to respond. She hugged him back but was worried about what had upset Johnny so much. She'd never seen him like this before.

'What's wrong?' she gently asked and pulled away from him.

Johnny took a handkerchief from his trouser pocket and blew into it and wiped his watery eyes. 'There was accident, Charlotte. A bad one. We'd killed the bloke who hurt you and just like you asked, we made sure his guts were spilled. And then we were putting Kelly through the mill. He cracked and told us that Mr Maynard was alive. So me, Nobby and Georgina jumped into Kelly's car and went to get him. But Kelly's bloke, the one who was supposed to be guarding David, he helped David escape and when Kelly's bloke saw the car coming towards them, he didn't know that I was driving it and he shot at me.'

Johnny paused so Charlotte asked, 'Bloody hell. Are you all right?'

'Yeah, yeah, I'm fine, sweetheart, just a few cuts and bruises.'

'Thank the Lord the bullet missed you!'

Johnny's eyes filled with tears again. 'Yeah, he missed me... but he got Miss Garrett.'

Ned sat down now, wide-eyed and shocked. 'Fuck. Was she hurt badly?'

Johnny glanced at Ned and then back to Charlotte. He slowly shook his head, and his shoulders heaving, he cried, 'She's dead... Miss Garrett is dead.'

Charlotte felt as though a huge pallet of bricks and been dropped on her from a great height. 'No, Johnny, no. Please tell me it ain't true. If this is some sort of sick joke, it ain't funny!'

Johnny didn't answer but blew his nose again.

'I don't believe you. She ain't dead. That's ridiculous. She *can't* be dead.'

When Johnny said nothing but shook his head, Charlotte jumped to her feet. She clenched her fist and pounded him, again and again. 'You're a liar, Johnny Dymond. You're a fucking liar!'

Johnny covered his head with his arms and hunched lower on the sofa. Charlotte continued to pummel him as she yelled, 'I fucking *hate* you! Why, Johnny? Why would you make up shit like this?'

She felt arms around her as Ned pulled her away from Johnny.

'Shush, now, gal. I know you're hurting but don't take it out on Johnny.'

'He's a fucking liar! Georgina ain't dead... she ain't.'

Johnny stood up, his face a mask of sadness. He opened

his arms to Charlotte. 'I'm sorry, sweetheart. If I could have taken that bullet, I would have. I'd have lain down my life for Miss Garrett.'

Charlotte could see the truth in Johnny's heartbroken eyes. 'She's really dead?' she sobbed.

'Yes, love. There was nothing we could do to save her. She died in David's arms.'

Charlotte's legs buckled beneath her and she dropped to the floor. This wasn't supposed to happen. All Georgina ever wanted was a better life, for herself and her children. She'd fought her whole life for those she loved. Just when she had everything she wanted – a husband, her children living with her in a lovely house in the country – Thomas Kelly had ripped it all away. 'And that bastard Kelly is definitely dead?'

'He will be. We left him in a bad way. He's tied down in an old barn and badly hurt. He won't be going nowhere. We left him to starve to death. Let the fucking rats have his body,' Johnny said bitterly.

'Where is David Maynard?' Ned asked.

'He's back at his house, but he's in a right old state.'

'Well he would be,' Ned said. 'He's just lost his wife.'

'And he blames himself for her death. He told the man who helped him to escape, to shoot at the car.'

'Yeah, but you said that he thought it was Kelly in the car, not Miss Garrett.'

'That's right, Ned, and we told him that. The trouble is, he wouldn't listen.'

Charlotte heard Johnny's words but her own tears were flowing now and she could hardly breathe. 'Why? Why did she have to die? It ain't fair, Johnny.'

'I know. Life's a bastard. I had a bad feeling that something was gonna happen. But not this. I never expected this.'

A heavy knot of agonising grief lodged in Charlotte's chest. 'I loved her... I loved her like she was my own sister.'

'Yeah, me an' all. The woman was a fucking legend.'

Charlotte nodded in agreement. Georgina Garrett had lived by the sword and died by it too but there was no doubt about it, the woman was, indeed, a fucking legend.

24

Four Years Later

July 1953.

Charlotte handed Johnny a cup of tea and sat in the armchair opposite him. Johnny removed his hat and placed it beside him on the sofa.

'How are you, sweetheart?'

'Oh, you know, same as usual.'

'And Tim?'

'He's having a lie-down. He does a lot of that.'

'No change then?'

'Not really. He can look after himself well enough, but he'll never speak properly again. He still has little fits too and I know it's getting him down. To tell you the truth, we hardly communicate these days.'

'Poor bloke. It must be hard for him.'

'Yeah, it is. He managed to get up to the chippy the other week but a bunch of lads started taking the piss out of him. They were calling him awful names and spitting at him. You know how he drags his leg behind him – well, they tripped him up. Luckily, a couple of fellas from the power station came along and helped him back on his feet. They brought him home an' all, bless 'em. But he ain't left the house since.'

'Bleedin' 'ell, Charlotte, that's 'orrible.'

'I know. I said I'd get him a wheelchair but he won't hear of it. So now he spends most of his time in bed. But I can't lie, Johnny, that suits me. When he's up, he's so angry. I try to be patient but it's not always easy.'

'You're doing a great job with him, love. Are you getting on all right for money?'

'Yeah, we're fine. The rents from Miss Gray and Mr Finnegan upstairs are enough to live on. I still can't believe that Georgina left me this house. I assumed that everything would have gone to Alfie and Selina.'

'They did all right. They've got the house in Kent and the one in London, amongst other things. Miss Garrett thought the world of you and it was right and proper of her to leave you this place. It was your home, after all.'

'Yeah, I suppose. What about you? How are you getting on?'

'You know me. I do a bit of this and a bit of that,' Johnny answered and tapped the side of his nose. 'But I did pop down to Bristol way last week.'

'What on earth for?' she exclaimed but then the penny dropped. 'Oh my God, Johnny, are you mad? You've seen the papers. They've found the grizzly remains of two people in an old barn, and you know who they were, don't you?'

'Yeah, of course I bloody know. And that's why I went to see Clara. I wanted to find out what the Old Bill knew and if we're connected to it in any way.'

'And? What did you find out?'

'Not a lot really. The police ain't got a clue who the bodies are. Course, everyone else knows it's Kelly and Titch. Rumours are flying round the docks and the town but no fingers are being pointed in our direction.'

'That's good,' Charlotte said, relieved.

'That Clara,' Johnny mused. 'She's a card. She's put it about that she heard the bodies were German spies who got tortured and killed by British secret agents. It's going round like wildfire. You've gotta laugh. Anyway, most people are still talking about John Christie being hanged in Pentonville Prison and the eight bodies that they found at his house in Rillington Place.'

Charlotte smiled. She hadn't seen her friend for a few weeks and was grateful for his company. She knew that he'd been bunging Clara a few quid when he could but couldn't believe that he'd been bold enough to travel to the Bristol area in the wake of the discovery of Thomas Kelly's remains. Charlotte hated that name. The man had ruined her life. Changing the subject, she asked, 'Have you heard anything more about David?'

'Nothing new. I don't think any of us will ever see or hear from him again. Nobby reckons that he's living abroad now. Ned heard the same.'

'He was never the same after Georgina died. It broke him.'

'Yeah, it did. Shame. It weren't his fault but he never forgave himself. You don't seem yourself either, sweetheart. Is it all this business with Tim getting you down?'

'No. It's Edward, Molly's boy. He leaves school today.'

'And you're worried?'

'I am. I've been dreading this day.'

'Makes me blood run cold just thinking about a Wilcox back on the streets. You don't think he'll come to Battersea, do you?'

'I hope not. I'm more worried about him turning up at Molly's.'

'Maybe he's changed. Them things that he did, he was just a kid back then. He might have grown up into a nice young man.'

'We are talking about the son of Billy Wilcox here,' Charlotte reminded him.

'Point taken. Well, if you or Molly get any trouble from Edward, you know where I am.'

'Yeah, I know, thanks, Johnny.'

'Anyway, I popped round to remind you about Benjamin's birthday bash on Saturday night. You are coming, ain't ya?'

Charlotte wasn't particularly in the mood for celebrating but she knew that Benjamin would be disappointed if she didn't show her face at the Penthouse Club. 'Yes, I'll be there.'

'Good. The blokes are looking forward to seeing you. Nobby wants you to meet his wife and Eric is bringing his new baby girl.'

'What about you, Johnny? Who will you be bringing?' Charlotte probed, smiling as she asked. Johnny liked to give the impression that he was still a ladies' man but he'd settled down with the long-suffering Kathy for years now.

'I'll suppose I'll have to bring *her indoors*. She'll get the right bleedin' 'ump if I don't.'

'Why don't you make an honest woman of Kathy and marry her? The poor woman deserves a lot more than a gold band for putting up with you for all of this time.'

'Marry her, are you kidding me?' Johnny said, laughing.

'What's so funny?'

'Kathy ain't the sort of woman that you marry.'

'She's stuck by you through thick and thin.'

'Yeah, she's a good 'un, I suppose. But hell will freeze over before I put a ring on her finger.'

Charlotte rolled her eyes. She didn't know why Johnny was so against marrying Kathy. The woman lived in Johnny's flat, did his washing and cooked his meals. They were already living like husband and wife. A ring and a marriage certificate wouldn't make that much difference but it's what Kathy wanted. She'd said as much to Charlotte a few months ago when Charlotte had popped into the café on Lavender Hill. Kathy ran the place now with a percentage of the profits being banked for Georgina's children. It was the same with the Penthouse Club. Benjamin oversaw the general management and money was put away in trust for Alfie and Selina. Charlotte had been happy to hear about the arrangement. It's what Georgina would have wanted. She had worked to leave a legacy for her children and Charlotte took comfort in knowing that Georgina's life hadn't been in vain.

'I'd better get off. I'm meeting a fella up the Northcote Road who wants to flog me a load of fur coats. Kathy's after one. Do you want one an' all? A treat, on me.'

'Oh, no thanks, but it's nice of you to offer.'

'Go on, have one. You'll look a million dollars.'

Charlotte couldn't imagine herself dolled up or looking glamorous. She couldn't remember the last time that she'd put on a bit of lippy or mascara. Her hair needed a good trim and her wardrobe could do with updating, especially since clothes rationing had ended four years earlier. Glancing down at her flat, clunky shoes, old-fashioned flared skirt and washed-out blouse with a tatty cardigan that had lost its shape, Charlotte decided that she looked frumpy. 'Do you know what, Johnny? It's about time I did myself up a bit. Yes, please, I'd love a fur coat, thank you.'

'That's my girl, good on ya. I shall expect to see you looking your best on Saturday night.'

After seeing Johnny out, Charlotte tiptoed into the bedroom. Tim had the curtains drawn and appeared to be sleeping. She quietly opened the wardrobe and thumbed through her dresses. None of them were suitable to wear to a party. She heard Tim moving in the bed and looked over her shoulder to see that his eyes were open. 'It's Benjamin's birthday party on Saturday. Are you coming? It'll do you good to get out.'

Tim shook his head and closed his eyes, pulling the blankets up to his chin.

Charlotte sighed. She couldn't force her husband to go to the party. Just as she couldn't force him to get out of bed. But determined that she'd have a good time regardless, she sifted through her clothes again. At the back of the wardrobe she found one of Georgina's dresses. It had been a long time since Charlotte had looked at it. She pulled the dress out and held it in front of her. The bias-cut, red material, had flattered Georgina's figure. Charlotte closed her eyes and pictured her in the dress. She remembered how Georgina had teamed the dress with a wide-brimmed black hat, gloves, bag and shoes. She had looked knockout in it and had turned heads. Charlotte held the dress against herself. It was far too long and she doubted that with her wider hips, it would fit, yet recalling Georgina's glamorous yet understated style had triggered some ideas in Charlotte's mind. She was fed up and bored. It was time to brighten up her drab life and change her dowdy image.

The telephone ringing in the hallway startled Charlotte. She dashed out to answer it with a sinking feeling. As expected, her sister was on the other end of the line.

'Hello, Charlotte. You know what day it is today, don't you?'

'Hello, Molly. Yeah. I've been trying not to think about it.'

'Me too. Mum's the same and I can see her nerves are jangled.'

'Have you spoken to Stephen about it?'

'No. I know I should but I don't want to drag up any bad memories for him.'

'Try not to worry, sis. Edward will most likely get straight on the train to Brighton. He's got no reason to turn up at the farm.'

'I hope so. I've told him to write to me as soon as he arrives in Brighton. I won't rest easy until I get that letter from him and can see the postmark for meself.'

They spoke a little longer, Charlotte trying to alleviate Molly's fears. When they said their goodbyes and she replaced the receiver, it was with a long drawn-out breath. She missed Georgina and knew she always would. The world often felt like a lonely and scary place without her. Georgina would know what to do with Edward. She wouldn't have feared the boy and Molly would probably feel a lot safer if Georgina were still in their lives. Yet the fact was, Georgina was dead and it was now her job to look after her big sister. Charlotte's lips tightened. Though she would never admit it to Molly, she didn't ever want to come face to face with Edward and hoped that she never would.

'Good luck, Eddie, keep in touch!'

The school term had ended and for Edward Wilcox, at fifteen years old, it meant he never had to return to the stuffy boarding school again. There'd be no more sleeping in dormitories, strictly regulated mealtimes, monthly nurse visits or canings. Edward had hated being called to the headmaster's office for ten lashes of the whip across his backside. It had only happened the once, and after the humiliating experience, he'd been more careful. He made sure that when he broke the school rules, he wasn't caught. And breaking the school rules was something that Edward did regularly. Almost daily, in fact.

Cars filled the car park to the left of the main building and lined the long, gravel drive in front. This was a regular sight at the end of each term when parents came to collect their children to take them home for the summer or Christmas breaks. A line of boys had formed near the two minibuses that were emblazoned with the school name. These buses would take the boys to the local train station in Worthing, West Sussex. From there, a teacher would accompany the boys on the journey to London where parents would meet their children at Victoria station. The *Trainers*, they were called with affection by the staff.

Edward watched as boys ran into the waiting arms of their mothers or stiffly shook hands with their pompous fathers. The sight sickened him. With his small suitcase in hand, he crunched along the long drive and out of the school gates for the final time.

As he made his way to the train station, he pulled a piece of paper from his coat pocket. The written instructions from his mother gave the address of a room in Brighton where Edward was expected to turn up. His mother had paid six months' rent in advance and had lined up an apprenticeship for him as an electrician. Edward screwed the paper into a ball and discarded it. He had no desire to be an electrician or to live in Brighton. But he knew why his mother had arranged the accommodation and the job. It wasn't done because she loved and cared for him. It was designed to keep him away from the farm in Kent. His home. The only one he'd ever known apart from the boarding school. It had been four years since Edward had seen his home or slept in his own bed. He hadn't seen his so-called *brother*, Stephen, in that time, or his gran or stepfather. In fact, he'd only seen his mother on half a dozen occasions when she'd visited him at the school. Resentment snaked bitterly through his veins.

'Hey, Eddie, do you want a lift?'

Edward stopped and peered into the expensive car that had pulled up alongside him. His friend, Simon, was in the back seat behind his haughty-looking mother and stern-faced father.

'Sure, thanks.' Edward slid in beside Simon and offered his friend a smile.

'Eddie and I were in the same classes and dorm.' Simon volunteered the information to his parents who didn't respond. 'Are you off to Brighton now?'

'No. I've decided to go home.'

'To Kent? To the farm?'

'Yes.'

'What about the apprenticeship?'

'I don't want it.'

'What are you going to do instead?'

'I'm sure there will be plenty to do on the farm,' Edward said and then turned his head to look out of the window as they sped past cattle and horses in the fields. He'd lied to Simon. He knew exactly what he was going to do and it didn't include working as an apprentice for anyone else or on the farm.

Edward could see his future panning out in front of him. He knew where he was going and what he was going to do, the inspiration coming from his father. He'd memorised his mother's notes about Billy Wilcox. He could recall it all, almost word for word. As he'd read about his father, Edward had felt a connection that he'd never experienced before. The words had jumped from the pages and in many ways, he had felt that he was reading about himself. He realised that people, even his own mother, found him strange. They didn't understand him. He knew he was different but after discovering his mother's notes, it had all made sense and fallen into place. Edward wished his father were still alive. He felt that they would have been close. His father had built a small empire and had many men working for him. Edward wanted the same. He wanted to know everything there was to know about Billy Wilcox.

But first, he had *family* to visit.

25

Edward stood under a large old oak tree, concealed by the trunk, and gazed towards the farmhouse as memories flooded his mind. They'd told him that he had to go to boarding school for his own good. If he didn't, he'd end up in trouble with the police and sent to live in a home for bad boys. Huh, he couldn't believe that a home for bad boys could be any worse than boarding school. The memory of the Latin master flashed through his mind. He'd been kept back by the master on a detention and had been forced to write one hundred lines on the chalkboard, in Latin, *ego nuper enim genus non erit* – I will not be late for class.

As he'd scribbled away, the master had stood close behind. Too close. He'd been disgusted when the man had rubbed his back before sliding a hand down into Edward's trousers. He hadn't understood what was happening at first. But when the teacher undid Edward's trousers and then his own, he'd been confronted by the man's engorged penis and it had quickly become clear what it was that the master wanted. Edward had heard stories about how the Latin teacher had his favourite *bum boys*. He had no intention of becoming one of them. When the master had taken Edward's hand and had encouraged him to *touch* him, Edward had been disgusted and had instantly raged as a red mist had descended over his eyes. He'd grabbed the man's fountain pen from the desk and stabbed it into his belly. The teacher hadn't screamed but had stood in shock, staring open-mouthed at the dark green enamelled pen protruding from his stomach.

Edward had then fled from the classroom and as he'd run off, he'd shouted *non turpis lucre bastardis* – you filthy bastard. The irony of cussing the master in Latin had left a smile on his face for days. It was common knowledge that it wasn't only the Latin master who had his *favourites*. So had the music teacher, the religious education teacher and the physical education teacher. But none of them, nor the Latin master, ever touched Edward again.

From behind the tree, Edward's eyes narrowed when he saw Oppo limping out of the barn, laughing as he walked alongside Stephen. His *brother* was now eleven years old, the same age that he'd been when abandoned at boarding school. He remembered the long journey to the school in Oppo's truck and how the boys at the school, and some of the teachers, had looked down their noses when they'd seen him climb out of the scruffy vehicle. *Snobs*, thought Edward, the lot of them. But when Oppo and his mother had driven off, Edward could still recall the feeling of rejection as he'd watched the truck trundle away.

Stephen's blond hair glistened in the sunlight as Oppo ruffled the top of the boy's head. As they walked towards the house, the door opened and Edward saw his mother. She looked beautiful with her arms folded across her chest and a warm smile on her face. Edward's eyes narrowed as he saw his mother put her arm around Stephen and usher him indoors. She loved the boy unconditionally yet he wasn't from her womb. But Edward was. She'd grown him for nine months inside her. He had more right to his mother's love than Stephen did. Stephen, the blue-eyed boy of a prostitute, was living the life that should have been his. He could feel the outer corner of his right eyebrow twitching. It always did when he thought about Stephen.

Edward lowered himself to the ground. He sat under the shade of the canopy and opened his small suitcase. Reaching inside, he pulled out a cheese sandwich that he'd pilfered from the school canteen. His hands then felt down the inside of the case, smiling when his fingers touched the cold metal key that he'd tucked away. It was the key to the front door of the farmhouse. He'd kept it safely hidden for four years. And tonight, once the house was in darkness, he intended to let himself in and make himself at home.

Charlotte lay on the bed beside Tim and held him tightly until he came out of his fit. When she'd first witnessed his body experiencing uncontrollable spasms and his eyes rolling back in his head, she'd been terrified and had found it traumatising. Now though, his short fits had become part of her daily life. She knew that Tim would be confused when he first came round. She'd forced a spoon into his mouth to stop him from swallowing his tongue, and as his rigid body began to relax, she removed it. Then, after reaching for a damp flannel on the bedside table, she gently dabbed his brow.

'It's all right, Tim,' she soothed. 'It was just another fit.'

Tim turned his head away from her. She knew he felt ashamed.

'I do love you, you know. I realise that you find that difficult to believe, but I truly do.'

Tim shook his head.

She placed her hand over his heart. 'That in there. It hasn't changed. You're still the same man I married. The funny, caring, honest Tim is in there somewhere. I know he is. This frustrated and angry man who has replaced my husband needs to bugger off and let my Tim come back.'

'You... can't luff meee,' Tim slurred.

'I can and I do. But I'm getting a bit fed up with you feeling sorry for yourself and wallowing in self-pity. A bad thing happened to us and you've been left damaged, but you've got to learn to live with the way your body is now.'

'Naaaah... naaahthing works,' he managed to say, pointing towards his groin.

'Oh, Tim, I'm not worried about *that*. To be honest, I've never really enjoyed it. It's kind of a relief to know that I won't have to perform my wifely duties any longer.'

Tim looked at her with hurt in his eyes.

'It's not you. I just don't like, you know, sex. I never have. But I love you. Come back to me, darling.'

For the first time in a long while, Tim opened his arms to her and she was happy to melt into them. She laid her head on his chest and savoured the moment of feeling her husband's arms embracing her. She felt safe there, cosy and loved. And it really didn't bother her that Tim was unable to make love to her. After all, sex was a duty, not a pleasure. And after losing her longed-for baby, she'd vowed *never* to have a child. It was her penance for not being able to protect the one she'd carried in her womb for just a short time.

'Llll… Luff youuu,' Tim said and pulled her closer into him.

At last, she had remnants of him back. She hoped that this would be the start of his dark mood lifting and that life would become more harmonious.

'Youuu… hahahahaaaapy?'

'Yes, Tim, very happy. Though I'd be a lot bloody happier if I knew for sure that Edward had gone to Brighton. I'm worried sick that he's going to turn up at the farm.'

'G… G… Gooooo. Go toooo to farm.'

'No. I'm not leaving you.'

'Go.'

'No, Tim. I can't leave you.'

'Go.'

Charlotte pulled away from him and sat up to look at his face. She'd become accomplished at gauging his moods from his expressions and there were many times that she could understand what he wanted to say by studying his eyes. When she looked at his face, Tim was smiling and his eyes shone with affection. 'I should go, shouldn't I?'

Tim nodded.

'Thank you. You're right. I needed to hear that. I'll get the train down first thing tomorrow.' Charlotte settled back down into Tim's arms and closed her eyes. She tried to dismiss her worries about Molly and felt slightly more relaxed in the knowledge that she was going to see her sister tomorrow.

★

The waning moon was almost full and shedding a clear, bright light on the farmhouse. Edward emerged from behind the oak tree and edged closer to his home. He'd drowned the family dog nearly five years ago and was doubly pleased that the mutt was no longer around, or replaced. Had the dog still been alive, he would have been yapping now, alerting Oppo that someone or something was outside. Edward was glad that the dog was dead. Stephen had loved that dog. And the dog had loved Stephen.

The geese in the nearby pen sounded unsettled, but it didn't worry him. He remembered that the geese made a racket at anything that spooked them. A prowling cat, a fox close by, even a hooting owl had once set them off. Oppo never took any notice of the geese.

He pushed his key into the lock and slowly turned it. To his delight the door opened and he stepped inside. The last time he'd been in his home, the king had sat on the throne of England but time had passed and now Britain had a new queen. The country had changed but glancing around indoors, everything remained as it had once been. Coats hung on hooks on the wall. Muddy boots were lined up underneath on the stone floor. The only difference was that his coat and boots were missing.

He quietly walked through to the lounge and found the same sofas, chairs and rugs in place. But something was different on the mantel over the hearth. Edward stepped closer to the large wooden beam. He leaned forward and squinted his eyes in the dim light to look at the framed photographs on display. He saw two of Stephen, one of his mother with Oppo and another of a family group. A heart-warming scene that didn't include him. But there had once been a picture of him on the mantel and one on the sideboard too. He checked. The photos were no longer there. Fury rose from the pit of Edward's stomach. He felt that he'd been eliminated from the family memories. No trace of him could be seen in the family room. He wanted to smash every photo of Stephen to smithereens, but the noise would awaken them. Instead he turned every photo of Stephen face down.

He sneaked through to the kitchen and saw childlike paintings stuck on the wall alongside colourful, very old pictures of Stephen's handprints. There was nothing of him. It was as though he had never lived in the farmhouse, never existed. Edward carefully peeled one of the paintings down. He held it in front of him, studying the small figure with yellow hair holding hands with the stick lady, also with yellow hair, and the man, Oppo. Their gran could be seen waving from her bedroom window upstairs. Edward tore it in half and then shoved the painting into the rubbish bin. He picked up an apple from the fruit bowl and lifted out a seat at the large kitchen table. After three bites of the apple, he left it on the table.

Edward was keen to see his bedroom. He hoped to find it would be exactly as he'd left it, though he doubted that it would be. He crept carefully through the house and up the stairs. His bedroom was the first door on the landing. It was closed. He held the knob and cautiously turned it. What if someone else was sleeping in his room? He hadn't considered that until now. Edward pushed open the door and stared in dismay at the mop of blond hair on the pillow. Stephen had taken everything, even his bedroom!

He inched towards the bed and stood looking over his

sleeping *brother*. Right now, it would be so simple and effortless to snub out Stephen's life. Hatred for the boy filled his heart. Stephen stirred in his sleep and rolled from his side and onto his back. Edward gazed at the boy's neck and imagined his hands gripped tightly around it, strangling the breath out of him.

Before the feeling overwhelmed him, he moved away from the bed and mooched around the room. His eyes were drawn to a wooden train casually tossed on top of a pile of other toys in a box in the corner. The box had belonged to Edward. Oppo had used bright blue paint to write Edward's name on the front. He crouched down and ran his fingers over the red paint that covered his name. The wooden train had also been Edward's. He'd never enjoyed playing with the toy but now he noticed it had a wheel missing. Stephen obviously didn't take care of Edward's belongings.

Edward's eyebrow twitched incessantly. His lips snarled in disgust. His bedroom was no longer his bedroom, and seething, he walked to the window that overlooked the backyard. The curtains had been left open, probably because Stephen was too frightened to have them closed. Edward smirked. He remembered how he used to tell Stephen nightmarish stories about the monster who lived behind the curtains. The boy was easily scared.

Outside the second door on the landing, Edward paused. His gran's room. She'd be oblivious to the world, in a sleeping-pill-induced deep slumber. Until the night that he'd tried to feed Stephen her sleeping pills, he'd always believed that he'd been her favourite. But since that night, she'd never spoken to him again and hadn't sent birthday or Christmas gifts. His aunt Charlotte had remembered his birthday every year and had even sent him money in a card each Christmas. But year after year, as the celebrations had passed, he'd been left disappointed when he'd received nothing from his gran.

The third door along had been Stephen's bedroom. Edward passed that one and stood outside his mother's room. He wanted to go in and look at her peacefully sleeping face, but Oppo was a light sleeper. He pictured the scenario of standing over his mother's bed and Oppo opening his eyes to discover the outcast son had returned. A wry smile spread across his face. What was the worst that could happen? Oppo would probably want to throw him out, even wallop him, but he knew his mother would never allow that.

Edward turned the handle and crept inside. The heavy bedroom curtains were drawn, leaving the room almost in pitch-darkness. He could remember the layout and reached out in the dark. His hand touched the corner of the dressing table, and his fingers tentatively felt around until he found her perfume bottle. His mother never wore cosmetics but she always dabbed a drop of lavender water behind her ears. Edward removed the glass lid and put the bottle to his nose. He breathed in the heavenly scent. It smelt of his mother. After replacing the lid, he sneaked the bottle into his trouser pocket.

Creeping over to the bed, he strained his eyes to see his mum. Her long, brown hair draped over her cheek. Edward was tempted to sweep it back. He moved his hand towards her but snapped it back when Oppo grunted.

Edward had seen everything that he'd wanted to see tonight. He bent down and, ever so quietly, whispered in her ear, 'I'll see you tomorrow, Mum.'

★

Charlotte had taken a taxi-cab from the station and had tipped the driver. As she climbed out of the vehicle, Molly ran from the house to greet her, but Charlotte could tell from her sister's anxious face that everything wasn't well.

'What are you doing here?' Molly asked as she threw her arms around Charlotte.

'I thought I'd come for a surprise visit.'

'I'm so glad you're here.'

'What's wrong?'

'Edward's been in the house, I'm sure of it.'

Charlotte's stomach knotted. She'd had a feeling that he would show his face and she'd been right! 'Did you see him?'

'No, none of us did. Come inside, I'll tell you all about it.'

Charlotte followed her sister into the house but as she crossed the threshold, she had an overwhelming sensation that someone was watching her. She paused for a moment and turned around, running her eyes along the drive and over the grassed areas that flanked it. *He's out there*, she thought. She could sense him. Edward was close by and had his eyes on her.

'I thought I heard your voice,' her mother said as she came out of the front room. 'When are you leaving?'

'Mum! Charlotte's only just arrived. She'll leave when she's good and ready.'

'Well, I hope you ain't thinking about staying for too long. I'm sure your husband will be pleased to have you back home.'

Charlotte felt Molly's hand in hers. 'Come through to the kitchen. The kettle is on the Aga.'

'What's her bloody problem?' Charlotte spat.

'You know what she's like. Just ignore her.'

'I don't think she's ever forgiven me for being a tearaway kid.'

'Mum can hold a grudge, that's for sure.'

'Forget Mum. Tell me what makes you say that Edward has been in the house?'

Molly went to the kitchen door and quietly pushed it closed. 'I don't want Stephen hearing,' she explained.

'Is he all right?'

'Yes, he doesn't know anything so be careful what you say around him.'

Charlotte pulled out a seat at the table and Molly joined her. She leaned towards Charlotte and, her voice hushed, said, 'He was here. I woke up this morning and had a strange feeling. When I came downstairs, I found a half-eaten apple on the table.'

'Are you sure it wasn't Stephen?'

'Positive. Stephen doesn't like apples and Edward would know that. He left it there for me to find. And then I noticed that one of Stephen's paintings was missing. I found it just a few minutes ago in the dustbin. The thought of Edward sneaking around the house in the dark is just creepy.'

'Blimey, it really is!'

'That's not all. In the front room, every photograph of Stephen had been laid face down. I think that Edward still has a grudge against Stephen and I'm frightened he'll try to harm him again.'

'No wonder you're upset.'

'I haven't told Oppo this, but Edward was in our bedroom too.'

'How do you know? Did you wake up?'

'No, but my bottle of lavender water has gone. Oppo knows that Edward was down here but he doesn't know he was in our bedroom.'

'Do you think that he'll come back?'

'Yeah, I do. I don't know if I'll ever be able to sleep again. Look… look at my hands,' Molly said and held out her trembling hands for Charlotte to see. 'I'm a nervous wreck. Oppo is going to change the locks. We couldn't find any sign of a break-in so we think he must have a key. And I've told Mum that I don't care how hot it is, she's not to leave any windows open.'

'You can rest easy,' Charlotte said firmly. 'I'll stay up all night. Edward won't get past me.'

'Oppo said the same but he needs to sleep or he'll be too knackered to run the farm. Thanks for the offer, but I doubt that I could sleep, even if I wanted to.'

Charlotte placed her hand over her sister's, trying to reassure her as she said, 'Don't worry. We'll get this sorted. Edward won't be coming back into your home. I'll make sure of that.'

'How? How can you stop him?' Molly asked, fighting to hold back tears.

Charlotte wasn't sure what to say. She couldn't tell her sister that she had a gun in her handbag. Despite all that Edward had done in the past, Molly wouldn't want to see him hurt. If he attempted to break in again, she supposed she could try reasoning with him. If she could discover what it was that Edward wanted, perhaps it could be provided and he'd leave them alone. Maybe he didn't want to harm Stephen. If he'd wanted to do that, he had the opportunity last night. Perhaps his intentions weren't sinister and he just wanted to return to the farm permanently, or could it be money he was after?

But unfortunately, Charlotte suspected that Edward's reasons for being in his old home were purely evil. And no matter what precautions they took to keep him out, she felt sure that Edward would be back. 'Edward doesn't frighten me,' she said. 'If he's still around and shows his face, I'll sort him out.'

26

Edward felt quite relaxed as he sat under the oak tree. He leaned back and threaded one daisy stem through another, just like his mother had showed him when he'd been a nipper. His mother loved daisy chains. And he'd loved making them for her. He used to grin with pride when he'd see her wearing one around her neck that he had made for her.

He placed the daisy chain beside him and looked around the trunk towards the house. So his aunt Charlotte had arrived. Edward wasn't concerned about her presence in the house. Nor was he worried when he saw Oppo change the lock on the front door. Edward chuckled to himself. They were such fools! As if a new lock would be enough to keep him out. They'd probably keep all the doors and windows closed too, but Edward knew something that they didn't. The lock on his bedroom window was broken and had been for years. When he'd been in the house last night, he'd checked it and had been pleased to find it hadn't been repaired. He could shimmy up the drainpipe, easily lift the window and then he'd be in. Edward had done it many times before. He'd often sneaked out of his bedroom after being sent there for misbehaving. And no one had ever noticed that he'd gone.

Edward heard a chugging noise and saw Oppo leaving the barn on his tractor. He knew the man would be in the fields until early evening. He closed his eyes and pictured the inside of the house. His mother would be sitting in the kitchen with Charlotte, probably talking about him. His gran would be in the front room with her knitting on her lap. But Stephen, what would he be doing? Would he be in the bedroom? Or perhaps sitting next to his gran. Edward had no doubt that his brother had also stolen his gran's affections, along with everything else that had once belonged to him.

He jumped to his feet and looked down at the daisy chain on the grass. Edward was about to stamp on the thing and grind the sole of his shoe into destroying it. But he didn't. Instead, he carefully picked it up and using the cover of the trees, he snuck around the side of the house.

He surprised himself at his audacity. Edward was standing in the backyard, albeit close to the wall of the house so that he wouldn't be seen through the windows. He edged along towards the kitchen window and ducked underneath. Stealthily raising his hand, he dropped the daisy chain on top of the flowers in his mother's window box. Smiling, Edward sat there for a while. The kitchen sink was positioned in front of the window and he knew that his mother liked to look at her flowers when she did the washing up. She would see the daisy chain there and know that it was a gift from him. He was letting her know that he was still around. She couldn't get rid of him as easily as she had when he'd been a child of eleven years old.

★

'I'll make us another cuppa,' Charlotte offered.

'No, you stay there, I'll do it. You use too much sugar and it's still rationed,' Molly said, as she picked up the cups and saucers to carry them over to the sink.

Charlotte wasn't watching Molly, she was busy looking at Stephen's paintings on the kitchen wall, but suddenly she heard the sound of crashing china. Her eyes went to her sister to see that Molly was standing amidst broken cups and saucers with her hands over her mouth, peering out of the window.

Charlotte leapt to her feet and hurried across the room. 'What's wrong?' she asked, and looked through the window too, half expecting to see Edward staring back at her.

'The daisy chain,' Molly cried.

Charlotte had no idea what her sister was talking about. 'What?'

'Look… there,' Molly said, pointing to the flower box on the window ledge. 'Edward put that there. He's terrorising me!'

Charlotte didn't doubt her sister. She dashed to the back door, unlocked it and ran outside. She couldn't see any sign of Edward but the hairs on the back of her neck stood on end again. He was there, somewhere, watching her. She could feel him, just as she had when she'd arrived. 'I know you can hear me, Edward Wilcox,' she shouted. 'I know you're close by. I didn't expect you to be a coward, but that's what you are. A damn coward! Show your face. Go on, I dare you!'

Charlotte looked left and right and stretched her eyes to focus as far as they would see. Despite what she'd shouted, she didn't expect Edward to appear. In truth, she didn't think he was a coward, but he was sly and toying with them. It worried her how far he would take his *games* and she wanted to draw him out. 'Hide away, Edward. Hide away like the silly, naughty child that you are. You're not scaring your mother and you're not scaring me. Do you hear me? Come and face me like a man or bugger off!'

Charlotte almost jumped out of her skin when she felt a hand on her shoulder. She spun around to see her mother with a scowl on her face.

'Leave it. Come inside,' Fanny urged. 'You'll only antagonise him.'

With a last look around, Charlotte followed her mother back into the kitchen and locked the door. When she turned, she saw Molly sat at the table in floods of tears. She rushed over to comfort her heartbroken sister. 'I can't stand seeing what he's doing to you.'

'I'm all right,' Molly said through juddering breaths.

'You're not though. Look at you. You're shaking like a leaf.' Charlotte wrapped her arms around her sister, furious with Edward for putting her family through this. 'Wait 'til I get my hands on that boy,' she seethed.

Her mother's scathing voice asked, 'Why, what are you going to do? Take a leaf out of Georgina Garrett's book and kill him?'

Charlotte was taken aback but before she could say anything, her mother continued.

'That was Georgina's answer to everything, wasn't it? Don't like 'em, so get rid of 'em. Well, you listen to me, my girl... that ain't right. It ain't how normal folk carry on. It only leads to heartache and pain and I should know. Look what happened to my Ethel. My precious girl died a horrific death because of Georgina. I wish we'd never got involved in the madness of her guns and violent, chaotic world. And you, young lady, you need to change the way you think. You need to see that you can't carry on in the same way. I hope for your sake that it ain't crossed your mind to do Edward any harm. Whatever that boy has done, he's still my grandson, your nephew, and don't you forget it.'

Molly had stopped crying and was listening to them. Charlotte placed a reassuring hand on her sister's shoulder. There was already enough of a tense atmosphere in the house and she didn't want to make things worse. 'Mum, I'd never hurt Edward,' she said, feigning hurt in her voice.

'Is that right? So why have you got a flippin' gun in your handbag?'

Molly gasped.

'You've been through *my things*?' Charlotte asked.

'Yeah, I have. And good job I did.'

'You've no right to snoop through my stuff!'

'I've every bloody right! You've brought a gun into our home, Charlotte. It ain't normal! I'll keep saying it until I'm blue in the face... It ain't blinkin' normal. That Georgina had too much of an influence on you. You should have followed in your sister's footsteps and got out of London years ago and away from that woman.'

'*That woman* was more like family to me than you ever was! You've never had any time for me.'

'That's because you've always been trouble, Charlotte Mipple.'

'I'm not a Mipple. I'm a married woman.'

'Is that right? So how come you've left your sick husband to come down here with a bleedin' gun in your handbag?

Eh? You should be at home taking care of him. Not here, acting like some sort of gangster. Like I said, Georgina had too much influence on you. And think on, girl. Where did it get her, eh? Dead! That's where. Pushing up daisies. Ain't you learned nuffink?

'Shut up, Mum,' Charlotte snapped.

'Don't you tell me to shut up, you cheeky mare. I ain't finished. Let me tell you, what goes around, comes around. And you're heading down the same path as Georgina. You ain't a gangster, Charlotte. You don't come from that world. You're just a silly little girl who finks she's something that she ain't! It's time you grew up and started acting like a properly married woman.'

Charlotte couldn't contain her anger and shouted back at her mother, 'Leave Tim out of this. You don't know anything about our lives!'

'I know that's he's been left with brain damage because of you.'

'Because of me?'

'Yes, because of you! You and that Georgina Garrett. The pair of you living in that murky world of criminals. What happened to Tim was atrocious but can't you see that things like that don't happen in *normal* life? You dragged him into your world and now look at the poor bloke. Like I said, Charlotte, you've always been trouble. You was trouble as a kid and you've only got worse.'

'Don't talk to me about being a kid,' Charlotte snapped bitterly. 'I can't remember much about my childhood but I know I was hungry all the time. And cold. You had to sit and beg on the streets to put a measly bit of food in our stomachs. Georgina dragged us out of poverty, and it's thanks to her that you've now got this big house. The woman had the balls to stand up and do something about our pitiful lives. I dread to think what would have become of us if she hadn't, 'cos I know you wouldn't have bothered to do anything to drag us out of the mire. You would have let life beat up all of us, just like you used to let Dad beat you up. So don't lecture me, *Mother*. You're pathetic.'

Molly pushed her seat back with enough force that it fell backwards. 'That's enough,' she cried. 'Stop it, the pair of you!'

'But she—'

'I said, enough!' Molly snapped. 'I don't need this right now.'

Charlotte felt awful when Molly began sobbing again, yet she couldn't bring herself to apologise to her mum. She'd meant every word she'd said. Not that her derogatory remarks appeared to upset her mother. Molly was right, though. This wasn't the time to be fighting amongst themselves. Molly was clearly afraid of Edward, and if he really was dangerous, despite what her mother said, she might well need her gun to protect her family.

Edward slinked away from behind the shed and made his way back to the oak tree. A *coward*. His aunt had called him a coward but she had no idea of how wrong she was. In school, he'd proven that he was no coward. It had been his second week there when the older boys in his dormitory, the ones who were supposed to look after the younger ones, had ambushed him in the middle of the night. He'd woken to find a pillowcase shoved over his head and what felt like many hands holding him down. He'd been warned not to scream or cry for help or they'd force cleaning fluid down his throat. Several punches to the ribs had supported their threat.

Then they'd dragged him from his bed and into the toilets where he was subject to the customary practice of having his head forced down the loo. But they hadn't stopped there. He'd been stripped naked, tied to the pipes under the sinks and then the bullies had urinated over him. They left then, leaving him on the cold tiles, wet and battered for the rest of the night. For the next few days, he'd kept his head down and ignored their taunting laughter, along with their jibes of calling him a 'weirdo' or a 'freak.'

However, once Edward regained his strength, he'd shown them that he wasn't a boy to be messed with. After setting alight their *smoking shed*, he'd stood outside smirking as they'd screamed for help. A teacher had heard their cries and unlocked the door to let them out. The boys had been blamed for starting the fire, but how the door had been locked remained a mystery. He'd made sure that the boys suspected him, and he was never again bullied. He'd shown that he was no coward and would retaliate if anyone tried to cross him. Even if that meant playing dirty.

He glanced over to the barn that he'd also once set alight. He'd got the idea from his mother's notes about his father, Billy Wilcox. She'd written in great detail about Billy razing the Maids of Battersea gymnasium to the ground with Georgina, and a prostitute called Hilda, inside. Georgina had escaped, just as Oppo had from the barn, but Hilda had burned to death. Edward tried to imagine what that would have looked like. Her skin, blistering and melting. He wondered if her flesh would have fallen off her bones, just like the cooked meat off a roasted leg of lamb. He thought about what she would have smelled like as she'd burned, pork, maybe?

His mother hadn't said whether Billy had stayed to watch the fire, but Edward assumed that he had. Just as he'd watched the flames roaring out of barn roof. He'd also watched the smoke billowing from under the door of the boys' smoking shed. There was a fascination about fire that drew Edward in.

He took his eyes from the barn and gazed at the house, picturing it on fire. The intense heat cracking the windows. The orange glow of the beast would consume everything in its path. The curtains, the rugs, the sofas, Stephen, all burning. Edward blinked hard and rid his head of the images. His mother might burn and he didn't want that. He couldn't abide the thought of her in physical pain. But her mind, well, that was different. The woman had rejected him and chosen to lavish her affections on a boy who wasn't her own by blood. That abandonment had cut deep and had been painful for Edward to accept. He doubted that she'd ever understand how she'd made him feel when he'd been sent away to the school. But maybe if his mother lost something that she loved, perhaps then she'd know how much her act had hurt him. If everyone who she cared for was taken away from her, only then would she understand his pain.

27

Oppo came home early and was fuming when he walked in to find Molly so upset. 'That's it. I've had enough of this. I'm not having him terrorising you. I'm going to report him to the police,' he ranted.

'No, Oppo, please, you can't. Edward is my son.'

'I don't care. Son or not, he broke in and sneaked around like a bloody thief.'

'The police won't do anything. This is Edward's home too and he didn't break in. He had a key.'

Charlotte snuck out of the kitchen and left them to argue it out between themselves. She thought Molly was probably right in what she'd said – the police wouldn't be interested as Edward hadn't broken any laws.

The telephone rang, startling Charlotte. She realised just how much she was living on her nerves. When she picked up the receiver, she was pleasantly surprised to hear Johnny's voice on the other end of the line.

'Tim told me where you are. You should have said – I would have gone with you.'

'It's all right, thanks, Johnny. We're managing. How's Tim?'

'He's fine. Missing you but fine. Has Edward showed up there?'

'Yes. We ain't seen him but he's been in the house.'

'Right, that's it. I'm coming down.'

'No, Johnny, there's no need.'

'There's every bloody need! I'll be there in a few hours.'

Before Charlotte could protest, the line went dead.

'Who was that?' Molly asked, standing in the kitchen doorway.

'Johnny Dymond. He's on his way.'

'Great. Mum's gonna be thrilled to have him here, another person in the house with a gun,' Molly said sarcastically.

'Would you rather we just left you to it deal with Edward yourself?'

'No. I'm sorry. And I'm grateful, I am. But I'm worried that Edward is gonna get seriously hurt.'

'I'm more worried that one of you is going to get hurt. Or worse. Do you realise how serious this situation is?'

'Yes, of course I do. I know that Edward ain't right in the head. That's why I sent him away in the first place. But if he wanted to hurt one of us, he had the perfect opportunity when he was in here last night. But he didn't, did he?'

'Wake up, Molly! You don't *really* believe that he's just hiding somewhere so that he can go for a walk through the house every night, do you?'

Molly hung her head. 'I suppose not. But I want to believe that he wouldn't do us any harm.'

'I know you do, but you've got to face up to the reality. He turned down every photograph of Stephen and ripped his painting from the wall. I reckon that there's a lot worse to come.'

'You're right, I know you are. And I'm so scared. But I don't want my son gunned down like his father was.'

'Let's hope it don't come to that. I promise you, Molly, neither me nor Johnny will fire a bullet at Edward unless there is absolutely no other choice.'

'Please don't even talk about it, Charlotte. I can't stand to hear the words *bullet* and *Edward* in the same sentence.'

Oppo stomped past.

'Where are you going?' Molly asked, her voice desperate.

'Back to work. There's no point me hanging around here. You've got your sister with you.'

'Please, Oppo, stay at home. What if something happens to you in the fields?'

Oppo, almost out of the front door, turned around and replied angrily, 'I refuse to be intimidated by a child.'

'But Billy was only a few years older than what Edward is now when he killed his father!'

Oppo slammed the door closed behind him.

'You can't blame him, Molly.'

'I'm going for a lie-down. Me head is thumping and I'm so tired. Give me a shout when Johnny arrives.'

Charlotte idled away a few hours in the kitchen while she waited for Johnny. She hoped that Molly was getting some rest but doubted that she would be. She thought her sister was probably tossing and turning, worrying herself silly.

When Johnny's car pulled up at front of the house, Charlotte was pleased to see him swagger towards her.

'Thanks for coming,' she said.

'Sounds to me like Edward is a loose cannon. I couldn't leave you alone to face a mini Billy Wilcox.'

'Thanks, but we've got to do everything we can to sort him out without hurting him. I don't want my sister left heartbroken.'

'So how do you want to deal with him?'

'I don't know, Johnny. I wish there was an easy answer but there isn't one.'

Charlotte made Johnny a cup of tea and cut him a slice of meat pie before going up to wake Molly. As she'd expected, her sister hadn't slept and Charlotte saw that her pillow was wet with tears. Gently she said, 'Johnny's downstairs.'

The late afternoon passed into night. Everyone was fraught but Charlotte persuaded them all to go to bed, suggesting that Stephen should go in with Molly and Oppo.

Johnny sat on the stairs with Charlotte.

'Do you want to get your head down for a few hours and then we can swap?' he whispered.

'You can if you want to but there's no point in me even trying to get any kip.'

'Nah, I'll sit with you.'

'There's no need. You might as well get into Stephen's bed and get some rest. I'll give you a shout if I hear anything.'

'Are you sure?' Johnny asked.

Charlotte nodded. She'd rather have Johnny rested and raring to go rather than him being knackered and sluggish.

At least an hour passed. Charlotte pricked her ears, listening for every sound, but so far only the geese had made a bit of a racket. From her position on the stairs she could hear that Johnny was snoring softly and she found the rhythmic noise relaxing. Her eyelids began to feel heavy, so fighting against sleep, she tiptoed to the kitchen for a glass of water. After filling the glass and drinking half the contents, she pulled open a cupboard and grabbed the biscuit tin, hoping that eating something would keep her alert. Three biscuits later and with the glass of water finished; Charlotte needed to use the toilet. Not wanting to disturb anyone, especially as their sleep was bound to be light and restless, she was careful not to pull the chain.

She resumed her position on the stairs, about halfway up, alert again now. The geese had settled down. Everything was quiet. Too quiet. In fact, Charlotte realised that she could no longer hear Johnny snoring. She pulled her pistol from her pocket and ran up to the bedroom. The door was ajar. When she slung it open, her heart leapt into her mouth. In the soft moonlight that shone into the room, she saw that Edward was standing over Johnny with a knife to his throat.

'You don't want to do that, Edward,' Charlotte said, trying to keep her voice steady. Her gun was aimed directly at his head and he was only a few feet away from her. She could easily shoot him down before he had a chance to slit Johnny's throat.

'He's in *my* bed,' Edward snarled, undeterred as he looked down the barrel of her pistol.

'Yes, he is. But you know Johnny. Johnny Dymond.'

Edward knew exactly who Johnny was. He'd met him several times when he'd been a kid. And he'd read in his mother's diary that Johnny had worked for his father as part of the Wilcox gang. Yet before Edward had time to consider his next move, he felt a tight grip around his wrist.

Johnny had grabbed him and pulled a large handgun from under the bed covers, which he pushed against the underside of Edward's chin.

'What you playing at, kid? Drop the fucking knife.'

Edward heard the gun cock and knew he didn't stand a chance. He opened his hand and the knife fell to the floor.

'Smart move,' Johnny growled.

A cool breeze from the open bedroom window wafted the curtain and the fresh air swept across Edward's face. 'I wasn't going to cut his throat,' he told Charlotte. The words weren't said in defence. They were simply a fact.

'If you'd found Stephen in this bed, would you have cut his?'

'Probably.'

The door opened wider and Edward smiled when he saw his beautiful mother stood there.

'Take. Your. Guns. Off. My. Child,' she slowly demanded in a quiet, low voice.

'That's not a good idea,' Charlotte argued.

'I said, take your guns off him!'

It pleased Edward to hear his mother shouting in his defence.

Charlotte lowered her gun but Edward could still feel the metal of Johnny's gun pushed against his skin.

'He would have killed Stephen,' Johnny explained.

'But he didn't. So take your gun off my son.'

Johnny slowly pulled his gun away and tutted. 'Any man who holds a knife to my throat would normally have his brains blown out by now. You're a lucky boy, Edward Wilcox, but don't push your luck with me.'

Edward didn't acknowledge Johnny and went to step

towards his mother with outstretched arms. But Charlotte lifted her gun back towards him.

'No you don't. You stay exactly where you are,' she warned.

Edward stopped and waited for his mother to reprimand Charlotte, but she said nothing. She cast her eyes down to the floor. But then she lifted her face and looked at him with disgust, in the same way as she had when she'd caught him feeding Stephen the sleeping pills.

'That knife… is it yours?' she asked.

Before Edward could answer, Charlotte said, 'Yes. He was holding it at Johnny's throat but it was meant for Stephen.'

'So it's true. You were going to murder your brother?'

'He's not my brother.'

'Are you *that* jealous of Stephen that you'd kill him?'

'Jealous,' Edward said incredulously. 'I'm not *jealous* of *him*.'

'So why do you want to kill him?'

Edward shrugged. His mother wouldn't understand. None of them would. Even Edward hadn't understood himself for a long time. It was only when he'd been in school and he'd learned about Darwin's theory of *natural selection* and Herbert Spencer's *survival of the fittest*. It was then that everything had fallen into place for Edward. His world had suddenly made sense. All his instincts and the violent urges he'd had, it was because of biology. He had inherited his father's blood and Stephen had to die as he was the weak one. Edward, on the other hand, was the fittest and had his father's strengths.

Yet he knew his mother, Charlotte and Johnny would never grasp the idea and would think that he was mad.

'What do you want us to do with him?' Johnny asked.

Edward gazed at his mother with pleading eyes, hoping that this time, she would choose him over Stephen and not send him away again. But when she looked again at the knife on the floor, he already knew what she would say.

'Get him out of here.'

His mother's words felt like a stab in his heart. Once again, he'd been rejected. But he loved his mother and fought to find an excuse for her behaviour. He knew that she had hated Billy Wilcox, so maybe, as Billy's offspring, she couldn't bring herself to love him. Edward understood and forgave her. 'Mum,' he whispered, but she turned and walked away.

Charlotte and Johnny marched Edward down the stairs and out into the cool night air.

'What the fuck are we gonna do with him now?' Johnny asked.

'Take him to the barn.'

'And then what?'

'You'll see.'

'Christ, you sound like Miss Garrett.'

Charlotte smiled. She liked that. She'd been trying to think like Georgina too and had come to realise that she was going about things in the wrong way where Edward was concerned. But hopefully, all of that was soon going to change.

In the barn, Johnny asked, 'What do you want me to do with him? Tie him up?'

'No. Let's sit down and have a chat.'

'*Have a chat*? Are you having a laugh?'

'No, Johnny, I'm serious. Us three are going to have a long talk.'

Johnny huffed and mumbled, 'If you ask me, he needs fucking burying.'

Charlotte had originally thought the same but when she'd seen Edward standing over Johnny with a knife to his throat, she'd been jolted into a realisation. Edward was still a child and she couldn't have shot him. She remembered when she hadn't been much been older than him and she too had done some terrible things. She'd even once tried to poison Georgina!

Oppo had a small table and chairs in the barn, which they all sat around. Charlotte was pleasantly surprised that young Edward was compliant and didn't try to run off. Yet the atmosphere felt volatile, especially as Johnny was sitting there with a face like a smacked arse.

'What's this all about, Edward?' Charlotte asked.

The boy stared blankly at her. His veiled eyes unnerved her. They look so hard and cold. 'Fine. You don't have to explain anything to me. Now I'm going to tell you a few home truths and it's up to you whether you take them on board, or not.'

Again, she was met with a long, cold stare.

'You're wasting your time here, Edward. They will *never* allow you to live under the same roof as them, and let's face it, it's for good reason. I know you have your issues with Stephen not being your blood brother and Oppo not being your *real* father, but you can't just kill them. That's not how things work. You'd end up being hanged for murder, just like that Derek Bentley. He was hanged in Wandsworth Prison. You don't want to end up like that, do you?'

'Don't speak to me like I'm a child.'

'Then stop acting like one! Look, I was your age once and full of rage, just like you.'

'You're *nothing* like me.'

'Oh, Edward, you'd be surprised. There's a lot about me that you don't know. I bet you think that you take after your father, don't you?'

'Yes.'

'I don't think you do.'

Johnny interjected, 'He bloody well looks like him.'

Charlotte threw Johnny a steely look and then turned back to Edward. 'You take after me, not Billy Wilcox. You're my blood, my nephew, and just like you, I used to hate everyone. I hated my mother, my sisters, school, the farm, everything. I used to live here too, when you was just a baby. In fact, I even hated you. I ran away from here and went back to Battersea. And then I hated the woman who tried to make me come back here. I even tried to poison her. But that woman, Georgina Garrett, she took me under her wing and she showed me a different way of thinking. She gave me a new life and I want to do the same for you, if you'll let me?'

'Why?'

'Yeah, why?' Johnny parroted.

'Because you're a clever young man, Edward, and you're my nephew. You have so much potential and I'd like to see you achieve something. With me and Johnny by your side, you could become very powerful.'

'What the fuck are you going on about?' Johnny asked as he lit his cigar.

'I've got a plan, Johnny.'

'Oh, shit. Now you *really* sound like Miss Garrett,' he chortled.

'Edward has a cruel streak – that's not in question. But I think that we can harness that and channel it in the right direction. I'd guide him, every step of the way.'

Johnny and Edward both looked at her with confusion written across their faces.

'I'm talking about setting up a business. A family-run business,' Charlotte explained and smiled at Edward. 'You and me, we could be formidable together. And Johnny, of course.'

'You can fuck right off,' Johnny protested. 'There's no way I'd work for a Wilcox again. Not on your Nelly.'

'Think about it, Johnny. Think about how successful we'd be. We could be bigger and better than David Maynard ever was. Let's face it, you've been scratching around for a living for a few years now. Wouldn't you like to have pockets full of cash again?'

'Yeah, course I would, but—'

'-Then let's do it! We learnt from the best, so let's take back our part of London, rule it and get rich.'

'You're fucking mad. The pair of you, you're both fucking nut jobs.'

'Yes, that's right, Johnny. And that's why we will be successful.'

'I like the sound of that,' Edward said.

Charlotte glanced at her nephew and saw a spark in his eyes. 'What do you say, Edward? Are you ready to put the past behind you and move on to bigger and better things?'

Johnny stubbed out his cigar and pushed his chair back. He rose to his feet, stating, 'I don't want any part of this.'

'Sit down, Johnny,' Charlotte barked. 'Put Billy Wilcox

out of your mind. This isn't about him. This is about our future and I want you to be a very big part of it.'

Johnny returned to his seat and sighed deeply. 'I'll think about it, I suppose.'

'If we can learn to trust each other, we can do this. It'd be a family-run firm.'

'I ain't family.'

'You're as good as, and you'd be our top man, Johnny.'

He still looked unsure, so Charlotte turned to study Edward's face. She could see that she'd ignited something in him, but she had to prove to Johnny that her nephew could be trusted. She pushed her gun across the table towards the boy. 'I'll show you how to shoot.' She smiled.

Edward peered at the weapon on the table in front of him and then his eyes met hers. 'I'd like that, Aunty Charlotte,' he said.

'Just Charlotte, eh.'

'For fuck's sake,' Johnny moaned. 'I thought I'd got out of this game but it looks like I'm gonna be working for a woman again.'

Charlotte grinned. She'd won Johnny over and she was pretty sure that she had Edward on side too. But just in case, she took her gun back. 'Yep, you're gonna be working for a woman again. I'll never be Georgina Garrett but I'll do my best to be just like her. She taught me everything that I know and showed me that you have to be smart to get ahead. I learned from the best.'

Johnny sighed again. 'Yeah. Like I always say... the woman was a fucking legend.'

Acknowledgements

Thank you very much to Gia Notti, AKA Giascribes. Such a lovely lady and incredibly talented with words. Gia, your tagline for Siren was pure genius!

Thank you to Angie Gardiner, AKA Angie JG. Angie suggested Raven as the title for this book. I love it!

Thank you to my wonderful mum, Brenda Warren. If I had to thank you for all the things that you do for me, it would be the length of another book! As Celine Dion said, 'I am everything I am because you loved me.'

Thank you to my gorgeous hubby, Simon, who has the patience of a saint and doesn't moan too much about me being messy!

Thank you to Tracy Robinson, Beverley Ann Hopper, Sandra Blower, and Lucy Gibbons for setting up and running the Kitty Neale fan group and making me a big part of it. And a very heartfelt thank you to our dear, late friend Jay Angel Griffin. Fly high with the angels, a beautiful soul who will be sorely missed.

Thank you to all my lovely readers and for all the fab reviews! I hope you've enjoyed this book xxx

About the Author

S AM MICHAELS writes gangland sagas set in Battersea, South London, which is where she was born and bred, the council estates being her playground. After leaving school at sixteen with no qualifications, she later became an analytical scientist and then went into technical sales, where she met her husband. A few years later, they moved from Hampshire to Spain. It was then that her mother, the *Sunday Times* best-selling author, Kitty Neale, inspired Sam to put pen to paper. She now writes her novels in sunnier climates with the company of her husband, four dogs and six cats.